Tiger's Secret Desire

Nightfair Shifters

I0685898

Julye Evans

J&G Press
AUSTIN, TEXAS

Tiger's Secret Desire
Nightfair Shifters #4

Copyright © 2019 by Julye Evans

Cover Design by Melony Paradise

Editing completed by Mandy Smith with Raw Books Editing www.rawbookediting.com

Julye Evans / J&G Press
PO Box 143234
Austin, TX 78714-3232
https://Julye-Evans.com

Tiger's Secret Desire / Julye Evans - 1st ed. March, 2019

Formatted in Jutoh

ISBN-13: 978-1-7335677-2-5

Dedication

To G, you are my heart. I know you've got my back. Always.

Acknowledgments

Thank you to everyone for reading my books. Special thanks to MB for reading the books first. I wouldn't be publishing this book without you. Erin, thank you for your help and suggestions. My guildies in DL – thank you for your input. Shal, please forgive any butchering I've done with the science, any errors are all mine. Mandy, you ROCK. You are an AMAZING editor. And to my readers, I wouldn't be here without you.

Thank you!

Social Media

Like me on Facebook:
www.facebook.com/JulyeEvansAuthor

Follow me on Twitter: https://twitter.com/JulyeEvans

Sign up for my newsletter and get Tiger's Heart for free:
https://Julye-Evans.com/newsletter

Like to review books? Join my Advance Reader Team:
https://goo.gl/forms/5hkG1FCtT2M2yN9Z2

Other Works

Nightfair Shifters

Tiger's Heart

Wolf's Secret

Bear's Perfect Match

Tiger's Secret Desire

Table of Contents

Prologue..1

Chapter 1..7

Chapter 2..16

Chapter 3..29

Chapter 4..39

Chapter 5..51

Chapter 6..63

Chapter 7..76

Chapter 8..86

Chapter 9..102

Chapter 10..119

Chapter 11..129

Chapter 12..141

Chapter 13..152

Chapter 14..164

Chapter 15..176

Chapter 16..190

Chapter 17..204

Chapter 18..216

Chapter 19..231

Chapter 20..242

Chapter 21..251

Chapter 22..264

Chapter 23..280

Chapter 24..292

Chapter 25..308

Epilogue...322

A note from Julye Evans...............................330

Other Books...331

Author Bio..334

Prologue

Tamsin Carter chucked the trash in the dumpster, shivering from the cold breeze. Her mind was on the bane of her existence. The thorn in her paw.

The man who made it his mission to set off her temper as often as possible. The man who teased her until she forgot herself and fought back. Who played with her, his eyes gleaming with pleasure whenever he got a response. Any response.

He was also the man who set her on fire with one look. He was sex on a stick and moved with the unconscious grace of the tiger shifter that he was. Each movement was fluid and contained power.

Chris O'Neal. Tiger shifter, and member of the Nightfair crew.

"I need to get laid," she muttered to herself.

"I volunteer," a deep voice said from behind her.

She jumped, startled, and turned around to look into deep blue eyes. Her heel caught a patch of ice, and she slipped, wheeling her arms to catch her balance.

The trash can was right behind her, but she couldn't stop her fall.

She was going to hit her head.

She braced herself for a shock of pain when hard arms wrapped around her and pulled her into a firm, warm surface.

She drew in a surprised breath and was surrounded by the scent of sunshine and browned butter.

Chris's scent.

Her hands landed on his upper arms, and she gripped his firm muscles. The heat from his body radiated out, warming her even more, and igniting pleasure in her blood. The only blessing was that they were by the dumpster, and he shouldn't be able to pick up her scent. *She hoped.*

His arms tightened around her, and she met his gaze. His face was serious, but his eyes sparkled with amusement.

"If you wanted me to hold you, all you needed to do was ask. You don't have to fall at my feet," he said with a raised brow.

"You wish," she replied, pushing lightly on his shoulders.

"I've finally got you in my arms," he said, his eyes on her lips. "You think I'm just going to let you go?"

Her panther purred in the back of her mind, happy to have him close and two seconds away from rubbing herself all over him. Honestly, her human half was happy about it, too. Their bodies touched from chest to thigh, remarkably similar to her dream from the night before.

He shifted, and she felt his erection pushing against her. She sucked in a sharp breath; his eyes remained fixed on her mouth. She nervously licked her lips, and he seemed to see it as an invitation of sorts.

His eyes shifted from blue to gold, then back again. A low rumble vibrated his chest, a purr of sexual interest. His head slowly lowered, and she knew she should push him away, but she couldn't seem to get her body to cooperate.

Her hands gripped his shoulders tighter, and she tilted her head to the side, silently inviting him to kiss her.

His lips touched hers, and a shock of desire raced through her body. Her nerves were on fire, and all they did was gently touch lips in a mostly chaste kiss. His arms tightened slightly and his mouth opened. His tongue lightly traced her lips. The touch was electric.

She opened her mouth and his tongue swept in. The chaste kiss from moments ago was gone. This was all heat and fire. He conquered, devoured. She was just as hungry for him, and after a moment, she kissed him back just as passionately. Her body was hot. Burning. She wanted more. She wanted to feel his lips on her skin. His hands running down her body.

She wanted to taste his skin. Trace his muscles with her fingertips. Touch him and watch goosebumps ripple over his skin. She moaned deep in her throat, and he pulled back with a groan.

He touched his forehead to hers. Their breaths mingled.

"Tamsin," Chris said her name in a strangled groan.

Tamsin looked at him with passion fogged eyes.

What was Chris about to say?

"Tamsin?" she heard someone call. "Are you out here?"

Her brain was too cloudy to recognize the voice in the distance, but she clearly heard the concern. She had to try twice before she could get any words out.

"I'm fine," she said softly. She cleared her throat, and repeated, "I'm fine."

Her brain cleared, and she identified the voice as one of the waitresses from her sister's bar. *Marie.*

Marie, who needed her help tonight because two of the servers had called in sick. Working in the bar wasn't her job, but she helped her sister whenever she needed it.

And being short-staffed on Saint Paddy's Day qualified as needing help.

"You sure?" Marie said skeptically as she huddled in the back door of the bar.

Reluctantly, Tamsin pushed away from Chris. Being in his arms felt so right. So perfect. Like they belonged together.

But it couldn't be.

"Yeah, I'm good." She looked around Chris's shoulder and met Marie's concerned look. "I slipped, and Chris caught me. I'm coming back in."

Marie nodded, but stayed in the doorway, waiting for her. Chris glanced over his shoulder at the woman, then back at Tamsin.

"I have to get back inside," Tamsin said.

"Bar's closed," Chris replied.

He'd been there all evening with the rest of the Nightfair crew. As usual, she watched him whenever she got the chance. *Look, but don't touch,* she'd told herself. And up until she ran into him in the alley, she'd managed to hold to that. Then she had to go and fall into his arms.

"Clean-up's not done." She turned and grabbed the handle for the trash transport cart.

When she glanced back at him, she couldn't read his expression. Her heart sank.

She knew better than to kiss him.

"When will you be done?" he asked in a low voice.

She shivered at the promise in that simple question. One answer could change everything. The one answer she could never give. Not because he was a tiger and she was a panther. Not because she didn't want to.

4

No. It was because of her work. Her project. Right now, that was the *only* thing that was important. Her panther snarled in the back of her mind, not happy about her decision.

The same decision she'd made since he started flirting with her over a year ago. He always pushed until she responded. They'd argue and fight. Play and flirt. But that didn't change anything.

Her decision was always the same. It was the same one she made every time she was tempted to see if there could be more between them.

"I don't know," she said, trying for a cold tone. Inwardly she winced when she failed. "Thanks for the—uh—hand. That might've been a nasty fall."

"Tamsin—"

"I've gotta go." She stepped past him, hauling the cart after her.

"Tamsin," he repeated, and his hand on her arm stopped her. "Wait a minute."

She met his eyes and took a deep breath. *It's not meant to be.* Her cat snarled in disagreement in the back of her mind.

"Chris, I can't—"

His rakish smile stopped her words and he slowly shook his head. "No."

"No?" she repeated. "What do you mean, no?"

"I smelled your arousal. Felt the way you responded when you kissed me," his gaze challenged her to deny it. "We may be done tonight. But we're not done. Not by a long shot. I'm not going to let you shut us down before you even give us a chance."

He leaned in and gave her a fast kiss on the lips, then turned away, whistling as he walked away down the alley.

"Chris," Tamsin called, but he didn't turn around. "There is no *us*."

Hope warred with fear that he meant what he said. She was afraid he wanted more than just sex. But that was all she could give him. And if she gave him that, she knew they'd both want more. So, she couldn't even give him that.

He kept walking, his fine ass drawing her eyes until he turned the corner. She was about to run after him when Marie called her from the door. Tamsin hurried in to help with the clean-up, her mind on Chris. Somehow, she'd have to find a way to discourage him.

She thought about that look in his eyes and shivered.

If only it was that easy.

Chapter 1

"Hunch your shoulders, you're not supposed to look *energetic.*" Justin's voice growled through Chris's earpiece.

"I *am* hunching my shoulders." Chris pulled his shoulders forward until the muscles in his back protested.

"Well, hunch them more," Justin snapped, followed by the sounds of fingers rapidly typing on a keyboard. "If you can't look right..."

"I've got it," Chris growled, barely refraining from slamming the mop into the bucket of soapy water. This was his second week undercover at this janitorial company. Next on their rounds was the lab where all signs pointed to where Tamsin was being held captive.

His tiger paced with agitation in the back of his mind. It wanted to go charging in *now.* It didn't like waiting.

"Slow down. Remember, you've mopped miles of floors and have miles yet to go before you sleep," Justin chimed. "My God, have you never mopped a floor in your life?"

"What do you think?" Chris shot back. "I have two brothers. Like my mother was going to clean up our messes."

"You had speed mopping competitions or something?" Justin asked skeptically. "I've got a brother, too, but we never mopped that fast."

"You're wolves, that's to be expected." Chris dipped the mop back in the bucket.

"What does *that* mean?" Justin snarled.

"Quiet on the comms," Mac's voice cut in sharply. "Justin, finish that trace."

Chris managed not to glance up at the camera in the corner of the hallway. That was the way the rest of the team was watching him. Mac, Justin, and Sierra monitored the video and audio surveillance from a few blocks away in a nondescript van.

His tiger found it amusing that they watched everything through the building's own surveillance cameras. Justin had hacked into the feed, and they saw whatever the cameras picked up. Just as he'd hacked into the feed for the building where Tamsin was.

Where they *thought* Tamsin was. His tiger growled in his mind, unhappy with the uncertainty. So far, none of the cameras had caught a good shot of her. There was a woman who had the same build, and the same dark skin, but they hadn't been able to get a clear shot of her face to confirm. Today was the first time they were able to get into this particular building.

The security on the building was tighter, too. Several of the floors, and even rooms, had to be hacked individually. Justin was working away on it as he heckled Chris. The team was waiting impatiently as he hunted for the lab where Tamsin was being held.

Unfortunately, this was only one of five locations where they thought she might be. Nightfair had a very high search and rescue success rate, due in no small part to the caution they exercised on missions like these. Chris told his primal self to chill. He couldn't just go charging in.

Chris's tiger didn't care. It wanted to tear each place down until they found Tamsin.

Anything could be happening to her right now.

Her sister had asked them for help two weeks ago. A lot could happen to a person in two weeks.

"I've almost got it," Justin mumbled under his breath, tapping away at his keyword.

Chris's heart started to race with excitement.

Could this be it?

Once Justin hacked into the last feed, they'd know if she was there, or if they'd been wasting time with this undercover op.

A soft sound down the hallway made the hair on Chris's neck stand on end. His supervisor had an unusual gait, and that was what he heard. The man was human, but something about him set off Chris's instincts.

"Stubborn stain on the floor," Chris muttered the code-phrase he'd created for Ron as he scrubbed at a non-existent spot with the mop. He knew Justin could see the jerk approaching on the screens, but the other Nightfair crew member often got lost in his hacking. If he missed seeing the approaching man and said something Chris responded to, it could ruin everything.

"Aren't you done yet?" Ron's nasally voice echoed in the hallway.

Chris ignored him, plunged the mop into the bucket, then barely wrung it out. He slapped the mop on the floor, causing a ring of soapy water to spray in all directions. Ron danced away to avoid getting wet, hopping on his toes. Chris's tiger laughed in the back of his mind.

"Watch what you're doing," Ron snapped as he rubbed at his nose.

9

"Oh, I didn't see you there." Chris raised his eyebrows in surprise as he looked at the other man.

Ron flinched and then threw his shoulders back to hide his brief fearful reaction. Chris was bulky, as most tiger shifters were. He knew his body looked like a middleweight bodybuilder, a typical build for cat shifters.

Ron was human and rail thin, almost delicately so. His lanky, brown hair was cut short, and he always seemed to wear colors that made him look vaguely ill. When Chris looked at him, one word came to mind.

Puny.

His head barely came up to Chris's shoulder. Chris felt like a giant football player when he stood next to Ron. The primal part of Ron's brain recognized Chris as the predator he was, and he was tentative around Chris. Careful. Chris frightened him, and Ron resented him for it.

Chris was used to this type of reaction from humans. An unnamed fear. A curiosity and awe that was obvious to shifters. Even those who knew about shifters seemed to have that initial reaction. Did Ron know about shifters? *Unlikely.* The man was too in his own head to think about anyone else.

In reaction to this unrecognized fear, Ron used his position as Chris's supervisor to make his life difficult wherever he could. From the look in Ron's eye, he had come up with something else to plague him.

Chris suppressed a sigh as the supervisor glared at him suspiciously.

"What's taking you so long?" Ron rubbed his nose again, an action he did frequently. Then he looked at the clean hallway and frowned in confusion.

Chris was almost done, when technically he should have just started. But he hadn't really been in a mopping mood and rushed it. Justin's comment about speed mopping wasn't that far off the mark. He and his brothers always had a competition about something going on. It didn't help that when they were growing up, if you finished before Mom thought you would, you might be able to escape without further chores.

In any case, it stood to reason that Ron would come check on him. The guy was obsessed with monitoring Chris's progress, popping up at odd times to check on him.

"Just because the floor *looks* clean, doesn't mean it is. Make sure you finish mopping the entire hallway before you take your lunch break." Ron glanced at his watch and cast a malicious smile at Chris. "Which starts in five minutes."

Ron wore an expression of petty superiority. If Chris cared, he'd be pissed. But Ron simply annoyed him. Chris, both the man and his tiger, didn't find Ron worthy of the energy. The man was just pathetic.

With an arrogant smirk, Ron spun to make a grand exit. His feet slid out from under him, and he cried out in surprise as he landed flat on the floor. He had forgotten the floor was freshly mopped.

A snort of laughter through the comm matched Chris's. Ron sat up and glared at him, rubbing his nose and frowning. Chris quickly got himself under control. He couldn't afford to get fired. They didn't have enough time to establish a new cover. Plus, this was the only company that cleaned their next target location. Going in as a member of an established cleaning crew was the easiest way to slip into the building unnoticed to investigate.

Still, he couldn't stop himself from pointing to the little yellow sign with a pictogram of a stick figure falling. "Wet floor."

Ron scrambled to his feet, and carefully duck-walked past Chris down the freshly-mopped hallway.

"Don't be late getting back from lunch," Ron snapped as he reached the corner.

As soon as Ron turned the corner, Chris feverishly mopped. If he moved fast enough, he might be able to enjoy at least some of his thirty-minute lunch break. As it was, he would barely have enough time to get to the van to check out the new feed Justin was hacking into and make it back before they headed over. Plus, he also wanted to glance at the building blueprints.

He had reviewed the layout of the building so many times he felt like he'd been there before, but he wanted to look again. His instincts said Tamsin was there, even if the team didn't have visual confirmation.

What if it was just wishful thinking?

He shoved that thought back. She was there. She had to be.

Chris finished cleaning and got the bucket rinsed and stored in the custodial cart, sacrificing five minutes of his lunch break. He raced to the surveillance van, careful to spend the precious time to take an indirect route. He even hopped a fence and ran through a couple of backyards.

The only way someone could follow him would be if they were a shifter, too. He didn't have time to worry about that now.

As he reached the van, Justin's voice rang out in triumph in the earpiece. "I'm in."

"Incoming," Chris said before he opened the door. Protocol dictated you announce yourself, or you could have claws at your throat. He wasn't in the mood to play, or he might just test it again.

The van looked like an old work-van, but the door opened easily. A black bug screen hung down, keeping the tech hidden from anyone looking in. He slid through it as he closed the door behind him.

He locked the door, then turned his attention to the inside of van. The left side was lined with large monitors. A series of short, shallow shelves ran the length of the van, and keyboard trays were near the monitors. There were two floor-to-ceiling storage cabinets near the doors.

Chris slid past the chairs in front of the monitors and squeezed through the narrow aisle. He crowded into one of the seats for a status update. Things were tight with everyone sitting down, but the purpose of the van was surveillance. And you didn't watch something while pacing around.

In front of him, monitors panned down a series of hallways, one of which Chris had just mopped. The ones on the left held the team's attention.

His gaze darted from screen to screen. Then he saw it.

The lab room.

Chris's heart pounded, and his eyes grew wide at the sight.

There were heavy tables against the wall with microscopes here and there. He saw several large machines, but had no idea what they were used for. He knew Tamsin was a scientist. He'd expect to find her in a lab, yet there was no one there.

Why was everyone so focused on this room? What was he missing?

"Where—" he started to ask.

"Wait for it," Justin's voice vibrated with excitement. "This is the room I've been grousing I can't hack into. I just got in."

"Our next stop?" Chris asked, staring at the empty room.

"You bet it is," Justin's replied with vindictive satisfaction from finally getting in. "And we should know who's here. Someone left the room as I got the feed. I'm hoping they'll return shortly."

Chris's heart raced with anticipation. He knew Tamsin was there. He just *knew* it. He glanced at the clock on the wall of the van. He didn't have much time before he had to head back. There was no question that Ron would fire him if he was late.

He grabbed a protein bar and ripped open the wrapper, snapping off a bite. The ticking of the second hand on the clock reverberated through his mind. He inwardly urged whoever it was to return. He quickly finished off the food, his eyes never leaving the monitor.

Thirty seconds before he had to leave.

Chris impatiently studied the screen, about to leave to go back. Then the door in the room opened. The woman who entered glanced up at the camera like she felt them watching. Her tired eyes stared straight in the camera for a heartbeat.

His heart clenched in his chest as he scanned her beautiful face. The black and white images couldn't capture the rich brown hue of her skin, the unique topaz of her eyes. Her lab coat covered her body, sleeves rolled up, hiding her petite frame.

They'd found her.

They'd found Tamsin.

Chapter 2

Tamsin stepped into the lab and took a deep breath, relief making her shoulders sag. This was her territory. Here she answered to no one.

The feeling of eyes watching her prickled the back of her neck. She glanced up at the camera on the wall before she could stop herself. *Mostly.* She tried to ignore it, pretend it didn't exist.

Well, she *was* in charge of her research, anyway. In here there weren't looming guards prowling around or odd scents that made her panther crinkle its nose in distaste. She stepped over to the nearest counter and set down the supplies she'd obtained. Tamsin gave a thoughtful look up at the ceiling, again wondering what the labs on the other floors were researching. She'd been told they were the reason for the high security.

Industrial espionage was rampant in pharmaceuticals, she knew that. But there was something off with all this security. The hairs on the back of her neck rose in warning, as they always did when she thought about the guards. Her shifter half didn't trust this entire situation. Why would they need all those guards?

Were they doing something illegal up there?

She took a deep breath and shoved the thought out of her mind. Her time was running out, and she needed to focus on her own research. Being able to concentrate all of her attention on one project made more of a difference than she had ever dreamed. In the two weeks she'd been here, she'd made great progress with the help from her assistant.

She frowned, wondering where Amy was. A fast glance around the room confirmed Amy wasn't there. Not that Tamsin needed to look to know. Although she was a wonderful assistant, Amy was noisy. Sometimes Tamsin wondered if she was trying to rival the sound of a stampeding herd. Amy was the nosiest shifter she'd ever met.

At least she got Amy to stop wearing that nasty perfume.

Now she was just noisy, not noisy *and* smelly.

Amy loved some knock-off perfume. Tamsin had no idea how she wore the horrid stuff. It smelled like nasty chemical soup to her. The harsh chemical undertone to the scent made her want to gag. In remembered reflex, she took a deep breath and froze when she caught a faint floral scent.

What was that?

Tamsin took another breath in an effort to identify the elusive scent. She looked around the room carefully for signs that anyone had been in here. Nothing looked out of place. She stepped over to check her computer when the snick of the door made her jump.

She twisted around to see Amy walk in holding a pair of steaming travel mugs. Amy was a bit taller than Tamsin with rich, dark skin. She liked to wear gold eye shadow that brought attention to her eyes. It was bold, but worked for the cheerful woman.

Amy was a shifter, but for some reason she didn't seem to have the shifter physiology. She was always complaining about fighting extra pounds. From the way the guards watched them when they walked past, the men didn't mind her *extra pounds*. There were two new guards who watched Amy in a predatory way. Tamsin didn't say anything to Amy, but she kept an eye on them.

"Oh, you're back." Amy smiled brightly, interrupting Tamsin's dark thoughts. "I thought it'd take you a little longer."

"No." Tamsin smiled back. Amy's cheerfulness was contagious. "Whoever's in charge of the chemical supply closet keeps it organized."

"I brought you coffee," Amy said. "To keep us going this afternoon."

"Thanks." Tamsin took the cup and inhaled the rich aroma. She smelled the rich heavy cream and caramel coming from Amy's cup. "Do you want some coffee with your cream and caramel?" she teased.

"Let your hair down and live a little," Amy grinned. "You should try it. You just might like it."

A shrill ringing pierced the room before Tamsin could respond. She glanced at the phone on the wall in annoyance.

"I've got it." Amy set her drink on her desk and bounced over to the phone.

Tamsin took the opportunity to sip her coffee. She was happy to let Amy grab the phone. Maybe whoever it was had a simple question Amy could deal with.

"At least they don't have a paging system," Tamsin muttered. She was glad they didn't. The last thing she wanted was to hear her boss's admin making building-wide announcements in that overly chirpy voice of hers.

"It's for you," Amy trilled, holding the phone out to Tamsin.

She repressed a sigh. *Of course, it was. Not like she wanted to get any work done today.* For once, it would have been nice if it was someone calling to talk to Amy.

She didn't bother asking who it was. There were only a few phones that could be used to call outside the building and this was not one of them. *Security.* She was getting a little annoyed with all this security. Not for the first time, she wondered what kind of situation she'd gotten herself into.

"Hello?" Tamsin held the phone to her ear. Amy's familiar scent of rosemary and spice with a touch of shea butter lingered on the plastic.

The taller woman grinned at her before moving to her computer to sit and log in. Tamsin studied the brightly-colored metal hair cuffs in Amy's box braids. She thought about the hours she spent having her hair straightened at the salon. Maybe she should simply grow out her relaxer and go natural.

Amy's hair certainly looked no muss, no fuss. She didn't want a full, curly Afro like her twin sister, Anjanae. Natural hair could be more maintenance than most would believe. But braids... that was possible.

"Tamsin," Debbie's perky voice chirped from the phone, pulling her out of her musings. "Sorry to bother you, but Mr. Groven wants to see you."

A cold knot formed in Tamsin's stomach. Her weekly meeting with her boss had been yesterday. What was so urgent that he needed to see her right away? Had something gone wrong?

"Is everything okay?" Tamsin asked calmly.

Was her project funding about to be cut?

"As far as I know," Debbie replied, sounding as cheerful as ever.

"Okay, then," Tamsin kept her tone professional. Amy glanced at her, brows raised in curiosity, then returned to her computer when Tamsin gave her a reassuring smile. "When does he want to see me?"

"Are you available now?"

There was only one answer she could give. "Of course."

Debbie's perky confirmation didn't relieve Tamsin's tension. Moments later, Tamsin headed down the hallway and to the elevator, her folder tucked under her arm. She wanted to do something to ease her anxiety. Taking the stairs would help, but there was no way to get into the top floor from the stairwell. Instead, she had to take the elevator, and pretend to be cool and collected.

She took a deep breath to calm her nerves. Her hand was steady as she flashed her badge over the scanner and the elevator opened. When she stepped in, she caught that same odd scent from earlier.

Someone had been in her lab.

Perhaps that was what Mr. Groven wanted to discuss with her.

Unlikely.

In the back of her mind, her panther paced uneasily. It was not happy about any of this. From the moment she'd accepted this offer, it had been unhappy. Sometimes she felt like the hair on the back of her neck was constantly raised in alarm.

As a result, she'd been vigilant. Other than odd things here and there, like the extreme security, there was nothing she could put her finger on to cause alarm. Things were just *off*.

Now she was being summoned to her manager's office for unknown reasons. It would be disappointing if her funding was pulled, especially this close to live trials. It wasn't unheard of, she knew that. She tried to brace herself for the possibility.

She wasn't worried about getting another job. She had a lot of contacts and was good at what she did. But her project wasn't mainstream, and it was highly unlikely she'd find another place to continue her research.

The elevator dinged as it arrived and came to a stop.

Time to face the music.

She swiped her badge again to get the doors to open.

Debbie looked up from her computer and smiled brightly as Tamsin stepped out of the elevator. Her stomach in knots, Tamsin smiled tightly at Debbie when the other woman cheerfully waved her to go on in.

She took a calming breath and gripped the cold metal doorknob. The door swung open silently to reveal her boss sitting at his desk, typing away.

He didn't look up from his computer, and she took the opportunity to study him. His light hair was going slightly gray at the temples, and he had fine lines on his face. Shifters didn't show their age as easily as humans, and she had no idea how old he really was. The simple fact he was starting to show his age, though, told her he was probably in his sixties, at least.

His desk formed an L and the computer was on the side arm, giving her his profile. His features were too sharp to be called handsome, and she always had a slightly uneasy feeling around him. It could be because he was a wolf, but she'd worked with wolves before, and they had never bothered her.

In fact, the only shifter she'd ever been really bothered by was that pain-in-the-ass tiger, Chris. There was something about him that seemed to push every one of her buttons. He made her want to laugh and scream at the same time. All while watching her with those laughing deep blue eyes.

She could almost feel him standing next to her. The heat of his body as he leaned over and whispered in her ear. His breath brushing her skin and making her shiver. When he was that close, if she took a deep breath, she'd take in his scent of sunshine and browned butter. Underneath it was the musk of tiger, all combining to make an almost irresistible scent.

Tamsin would never admit it to him, but Chris heated up her body. She had to fight her physical reaction when he was near. She'd actually taken to wearing a light perfume just to disguise her aroused scent ever since their kiss. She quickly shoved the kiss out of her mind.

Now was not the time to be thinking of that.

But her mind stayed locked on Chris. She could see his tiger in his every move. He prowled lazily with the controlled power of an apex predator waiting to pounce on its prey. Yeah, he bothered her.

Mr. Groven cleared his throat like he was about to speak, but said nothing. His eyes were still locked on his computer, so he wasn't trying to get her attention. She stood there cooling her heels, waiting for him to acknowledge her. She forced herself not to fidget and wondered why he made her so uneasy.

She took another calming breath and slowly let it out, catching a hint of that odd floral scent. Whoever had left it in her lab had also been in this office.

Groven held up a finger to Tamsin without looking at her. "One moment. I apologize for keeping you waiting, but this is urgent."

"No problem," Tamsin replied calmly as she waited impatiently while he tapped away on his keyboard. The sleeves of his light blue dress shirt were rolled to the middle of his forearms revealing lightly tanned skin. His jacket hung on a hanger on a coat rack in the corner.

She'd noticed he liked to appear *casual* in his office, but it always made her panther pace uneasily in her mind. He seemed... insincere. She couldn't stifle the feeling he was putting on an act. It wasn't something she could put her finger on, but it was there nonetheless.

From the moment she'd arrived at this facility, Tamsin had been focused on her research. She spent almost all her time in her lab. One month of dedicated work and unlimited funding. She barely took time to sleep. Lately, however, there had been more downtime as they waited for pieces of the research to process. She'd stepped out to explore, and had started to notice odd things. Hear bits of conversation that set off her internal alarms.

She'd also realized in the past week there were different guards. The new ones didn't seem as professional as the others. Especially their leader. She'd felt safe before. Now she was always on alert.

Maybe she should just leave.

In the back of her mind, her panther roared its agreement with that idea.

But that wouldn't be rational, would it?

If she just left, she'd lose her job and all the progress on her research. It's not like she could just walk out with her research, either. Sure, she could take her notes, but any current samples would be lost. Her stomach clenched in an unhappy knot.

Groven took that moment to swivel in his desk chair and face her. He smiled brightly, but his eyes remained cold. She got the feeling the cheerful, friendly face was just a mask.

Why hadn't she noticed that before?

"Tamsin, thank you so much for coming right away. Please, sit." He gestured to the chair in front of his desk.

Swallowing unhappily, she perched on the edge of the chair, waiting.

She clenched her hands on her folder as it rested in her lap, and forced a polite smile. "Thank you. What did you need to see me about? Did we not cover everything —"

He interrupted her, chuckling, and waved a hand at her, dismissing her concerns. "We covered everything. I just wanted to make sure you were doing okay. All we talk about is business."

"What else would we talk about?" she blurted before she thought about it.

He threw his head back and laughed, and a chill went down her spine. There was something very *false* in his action.

"I want to make sure you're happy here," he smiled broadly. "We've had some staff leave, and I wanted to make sure you're not lonely. I know having no contact outside this facility might be... disturbing."

Disturbing. That was one way to put it. *Claustrophobic* would also work.

"I'm fine," Tamsin said easily. "I focus on my work."

"Are you concerned your family might be worried about you?" his brows drew down in a worried frown. "Given you've had no contact for two weeks and left so suddenly?"

Tamsin felt her hackles rise. In the back of her mind, her panther hissed in alarm at the false concern she picked up from him. She'd sent a couple of messages to her sister. She'd been told they went through. Of course, she'd thought it odd that she'd gotten no response. But none of it was his business.

"I have had contact," she said, tamping down her growing alarm.

"Really?" His eyebrows rose in surprise.

"Through the approved e-mail account on the computer in the tech room," she answered, closely watching his reaction. "Was I informed incorrectly that those messages would get sent?"

"Oh, yes." He smiled warmly, his eyes cold and calculating. "Of course. That computer. How could I forget? Certainly, they went out. Not to worry."

Her stomach churned, but she smiled back at him.

"We have a cleaning crew coming in today." He picked up a pen and started flipping it in his fingers.

"I saw the memo," she answered, forcing herself to remain calm.

"Good, good. I didn't want you to be alarmed." The gold pen went around and around in his fingers.

She got the feeling he was stalling, but why? He had no need. He was the boss here and called the shots. Her feeling was reinforced when he asked her a series of questions that seemed very random. He wanted to know if she had plenty of the chemicals she needed. Was the temperature in the facility adequate? How did she find the food in the dining hall?

None of the questions seemed connected, or had anything to do with her job after the first one. Tamsin answered them all, her mind racing. After several minutes of the bizarre conversation, a soft ding sounded from his computer and he glanced at the screen.

A satisfied smile briefly crossed his face, but his warm smiling mask was back in place when he looked at her. "I'm so glad we took this time to chat. I really like to get to know my employees."

"Thank you, sir," she answered automatically, trying to figure out what the random questions had all been about.

"However, we both have work to do." He stood and Tamsin hopped to her feet.

"Thank you for your time." She nodded and moved around to the back of the chair, clutching her folder in her arms. She was reluctant to touch him, and had only realized it a few days ago. Of course, she'd only met with him four times since coming to this facility, today being the fourth.

He looked surprised as she stepped away, then that stomach-churning false smile reappeared.

"If you need anything, don't hesitate to ask," he replied as he sat down, his calculating gaze watching her every move.

"Don't worry, I won't." She quickly walked to the door and let herself out.

Debbie's desk was empty when Tamsin rushed past it on the way to the elevator. She could feel the camera mounted in the ceiling tracking her as she moved. The damn things were everywhere.

Inside the elevator, she caught more of that unpleasant floral scent again and barely kept herself from snarling. The elevator quickly moved to the lower floor and she stepped out with a sigh of relief.

Then she realized the scent continued down the hallway in the direction of the lab. She reached the door to her lab and held her badge up to the scanner to unlock it. The odd floral scent was strong. Whoever it belonged to had stood there for more than a moment.

Perhaps using their badge to get into her lab?

Her heart pounding, she opened her door and quickly scanned the room, but no one was there. Not even Amy. Nothing looked out of place.

Tamsin took a deep breath to catch all the scents and froze, picking up something unexpected. She took another deep breath, but the scent wasn't in her lab.

It came from somewhere farther down the hallway.

Sunshine and browned butter.

She turned around and, without thinking about it, stepped into the hallway. Her lab door closed with a *snick* behind her. She turned her head to the right as she heard a footstep in the hallway intersection, along with a whispering *swoosh* noise. A moment later she saw the strands of a mop swing around the corner, then back.

Her mouth grew dry. *It couldn't be.* She watched the corner, mentally urging the person to step forward and prove her wrong.

How long does it take to mop a section of the floor?

27

The sound of a squeaking wheel followed by a splash of water. A mop bucket wheeled into view. Her eyes grew wide as they met deep blue eyes full of laughter, and she was flooded with the scent of sunshine and browned butter.

Her blood ran hot, and her breath caught.

Chris O'Neal.

Chapter 3

Chris's senses strained to catch any hint that Tamsin was there. He mechanically dipped the mop in the bucket, wrung it out, then swiped it across the floor, his body on autopilot. He took in deep breaths, sorting through the myriad scents in the building. Hoping to catch a hint of *her* scent.

He pushed past the familiar sharp sting of the disinfectant from the mop bucket. The bite of harsh bleach was faint, but not notable. This was a lab building. He expected it. He momentarily paused when he caught a whiff of the musk indicating another shifter, but it wasn't her, so he ignored it.

He kept his head down, and for the benefit of the ever-watchful cameras, acted like he was nothing more than a simple custodian.

Dip, wring, swipe.

Rinse and repeat as he made his way to the end of the hallway.

Then he scented her.

Ginger and exotic spice wrapped around him, causing his heart to race. The scent grew stronger.

Tamsin's scent.

"Status?" he demanded under his breath, fighting his tiger's desire to drop everything and go hunting.

The end of the hallway was in sight. He *knew* Tamsin was just around the corner. His tiger urged more forcefully for him to drop the mop and rush to her. Make sure she was okay. He held it back with gritted teeth.

Patient. He had to be patient.

The rest of the crew was still in the van, as they had been earlier. They were currently watching everything through the cameras. He had to wait for them to give him the all-clear. No matter how unhappy that made his tiger.

"Look, you can't rush these things," Justin snapped. "If I start the loop too early, they'll get suspicious. A guard is walking down the next hallway. I have to wait for him to… *There!* You're clear."

Chris didn't waste a moment. His heart raced as he finally, *finally,* allowed himself to look up and meet a pair of light topaz eyes full of curiosity. Always full of curiosity.

She looked so *normal*—not at all how he expected a woman in distress to look.

This woman looked like she was about to stroll into her sister's bar and start barking out orders.

Just as she always did when he saw her at the Ice House.

He was too happy to see her safe and sound to wonder why she didn't look more stressed, as most abductees did.

He couldn't stop the relieved grin from spreading across his face. He set the mop in the bucket and closed the distance between them.

"What are you…" she began.

Without thinking about it, he slid his hand along her jaw to carefully cup the back of her head. His touched startled her, stopping her question. She sucked in a surprised breath, her bright gaze meeting his.

He was overcome with relief that they actually found her, and she was unharmed. He gently ran his thumb across her skin. He wanted to touch her, feel her, know she was truly okay. Cover her mouth with his and kiss her until she was breathless.

His tiger didn't believe his eyes, but it did believe touch. The heat of her skin beneath his hand warmed him, and her hair was silky over the back of his hand.

Fire raced through his veins as his body responded to the feel of her skin. He grew painfully hard, like he always did around her. Her gaze traced over his face, and she took a deep breath, pulling in his scent.

An irritating low buzz sounded in his ear, and he growled in annoyance.

The buzz continued, and he took a breath to focus. Tamsin put her hands on his shoulders, and squeezed, then suddenly cold air rushed in where her warm body had been.

Chris blinked in surprise. Tamsin stood a couple feet away with her hands on her hips and an annoyed frown on her face.

"Fuck it, Chris," Justin growled in his ear. "Listen to me."

He realized the annoying buzz had been Justin barking orders at him.

One of Tamsin's eyebrows rose, and she tilted her head in confusion.

"I'm listening," Chris responded, taking the opportunity to really examine Tamsin.

He ran his eyes over her body, searching for signs of injury. He found himself distracted by how her dark hair flowed around her shoulders in soft waves, stark against the white of her lab coat. The ends draped and curled around the soft mounds of her breasts.

She was swathed in her lab coat and pants, her creamy mocha skin covered except for her hands and face. The lab coat concealed her figure, but he knew for a fact that she had curves for days. He had often surreptitiously checked her out when she was at her sister's bar. Those memories assailed him, sparking lust that made his dick throb.

When his gaze returned to her face, she glared at him, her eyes narrowed, nostrils flared, and lips turned down in a frown. She looked annoyed.

Very annoyed.

Focus, he told himself. He had a job to do.

Tamsin wasn't his. His tiger snarled in the back of his mind at that thought, but he ignored it. He was trying. He couldn't stop himself from bringing her little gifts. Or spending all his free time at the Ice House, hoping to catch her. Just to spend some time with her. His tiger was happiest when she was around.

So was he.

"I don't know how long we have," Justin growled. "You need to get a move on."

"Copy that," Chris replied, watching as Tamsin's eyes flicked to the earpiece. She was close enough that she could easily hear what was said to him.

"You're here on a job?" Her forehead wrinkled in confusion.

Chris nodded. Her sister owned the bar where the Nightfair crew hung out. They never hid the fact they were mercenaries, the closest thing to shifter law enforcement, or that they did a lot of undercover work, too.

Abruptly her eyes darted around in alarm.

"The cameras," she whispered, eyes wide. "They can see—"

Chris shook his head. "We've got them for now. All they see is an empty hallway. We have enough time to get you out…"

His words trailed to a halt as Tamsin shook her head in disagreement.

"I don't need to get out. What are you talking about?"

"We're here to rescue you," Chris said, perplexed.

"Rescue me?" Tamsin raised one eyebrow skeptically. "*I'm* your job? What am I, some princess in a movie? What made you think I needed rescuing?"

"Your sister got a letter from you—" Chris said, stopping when she started laughing, her shoulders shaking as she tried to stay quiet.

"This is just like some odd movie plot. So, you think I'm in some sort of trouble?" she barely managed to get her mirth under control. "What did Anjanae tell you?"

"She showed us the letter you left for her. It told her you had to go away and not to look for you," he said slowly. "She was insistent that you would never say something like that to her, and the letter was a call for help. She couldn't get a hold of you, either. Did she misunderstand?"

Tamsin's mirth faded and she took in a deep breath. Her eyes closed like she was praying for patience. "Let me guess. She got my note and ran over to you, telling you I wasn't answering my phone. So, she was convinced something bad had happened to me, and my letter was some sort of code. That about right?"

Chris nodded, his eyes narrowed in thought. "Was she wrong?"

Tamsin shook her head wearily. "I should have known better. She always overreacts. I'm on a communication blackout and my phone *is* disabled. But I've sent her several emails letting her know I'm okay. I haven't been captured. I'm doing research here. This is a *job*."

"A job?" Chris echoed, a sinking feeling in his stomach.

"Yes, a job," she snapped. "And you're here playing cloak and dagger. Unbelievable. This is just my luck. Can you please tell my sister I'm fine?"

"Chris," Justin's voice hissed in his ear, "you've got to get out of there. I just got a good look at one of the guards. I recognized him."

"What?" Chris said, still wrapping his mind around the fact that this operation had been completely unnecessary. And yet, his tiger still paced uneasily in the back of his mind. *Something was off.* "We have another team here?"

"No," Justin said, typing rapidly on his keyboard. "His name's Steven. He's with Sons of Asena."

Chris's jaw clenched. Nightfair Company wasn't the only shifter mercenary group out there. Not by a long shot. Some were decent, and others you didn't want to have anything to do with. Ever.

"What's wrong?" Tamsin asked, studying his face. "You just got really pale. Who are the Sons of Asena? Why did that name make you react?"

"They're bad news." Chris glanced up at the camera in the corner, then back at Tamsin. "They take the jobs other mercs won't."

"What do you mean?" She slid her hands in the pockets of her lab coat and glanced around with a worried frown.

"We rescue people, and go after lawbreakers," Chris said. "On the side of the angels, so to speak. But them... Rumors are they will do any job if the price is right."

"Rumors," she drew out the word. "I see."

"Chris," Justin said sharply. "Steven's headed your way. So's your boss. Your time's up. I've got to start the live feed again. They're about to enter the corridor on this camera circuit."

"Shit," Chris bit out.

"We can't take a chance he'll recognize you," Mac added. "Get out of there. *Now.*"

"Roger," Chris replied sharply.

His eyes met Tamsin's. He didn't want to leave her here. But she said she was here voluntarily. Throwing her over his shoulder and dragging her out wasn't an option. Although, he didn't miss the uneasy look in her eyes or the pinched worry in her expression.

Something was really off.

"Get in your lab, pretend like you didn't see me," he said to her as he rushed to his bucket and dunked the mop in the water.

"But—"

"*Now,*" he growled, moving along the hallway, his mind racing as he thought of various excuses he could use if she still stood there and blew his cover.

It wasn't necessary, though. She stared at him for a second with a considering expression, then turned to her lab door and held out her card to the reader. The door made a soft *click* as it unlocked. Out of the corner of his eye, he saw her glance at him once more before she disappeared into her lab, the door closing softly behind her.

Something in him relaxed. She was still in danger, he *knew* it. But at least she was out of the line of fire, for now. His primal self hissed as her scent was replaced by the stench of the mop bucket.

His attention was caught by the sound of the familiar tread of his boss. He barely stopped himself from silently snarling. In the back of his mind, his tiger didn't hesitate and gave a silent warning growl.

"ETA on Steven's arrival?" Chris asked in a low tone.

"He's in an adjacent hallway. If you move back down the entry hallway, you might miss him," Justin answered. "Keep your head down, the feed goes live in three… two… one."

"Won't they notice a glitch as things start again?" Chris moved down the hallway, swirling the mop around.

"Maybe," Justin said in a light tone. "But I'm good. So not likely."

Chris shook his head over the wolf's arrogance, but he knew Justin was right. He was good. Possibly the best. Ice still crawled up his spine as he waited for an alarm to sound. He kept his gaze locked on the floor as his mop swished and swirled down the hallway.

Tap, scrape. Tap, scrape.

Footsteps approached as his boss, who seemed incapable of lifting his feet off the floor, shuffled along the corridor. He always seemed to be dragging his feet, sometimes the right foot, sometimes the left.

Tap, scrape. Tap scrape.

Just a few feet away.

Schooling his expression, Chris judged the distance, and when Ron was only a few feet away, he stuck his mop in the bucket and gave it a hard swirl. He caught the edge of the bucket with his mop, and with a feigned startled cry, let the bucket topple over. A flood of dirty, soapy mop water raced across the floor, soaking Ron's leather shoes, and splashed on the hem of his pants.

"You idiot!" Ron screamed, hopping away from the stream of dirty water and spraying even more filth all over his pants.

Chris stood still, lips twitching with the effort to hold in his laughter as he watched Ron's panicky, dirty water dance. In his earpiece, Justin chortled with abandon.

"Are you laughing at me?" Ron scowled.

Chris swallowed hard and shook his head, Justin's laughter still ringing in his ear.

Ron glared at him suspiciously, then snarled, "Well, don't just stand there. *Do* something. Only an idiot would knock over an entire mop bucket. I can't believe we hired you. What were they thinking? That any warm body could do this job? Incompetence. Pure incompetence."

"I—" Chris began.

"No, I don't want to hear it." Ron held up his hand for silence. "This mess will put us behind schedule. Clean it up."

Chris reached for the tipped mop bucket and set it on its wheels, then slapped the soaking mop into the nearest puddle, splashing more water on Ron.

The man's eyes bulged as he watched Chris shove more water in his direction.

"What are you, stupid?" he screamed, spitting in his anger. "I said clean it up, not make it worse!"

Chris swung the mop around, narrowly missing Ron, and swiped along the wall, creating a dirty wet dripping line on the pristine wall.

"Oh, sorry," Chris muttered, sticking the mop into the wringer, then rubbing the dirty mop head on the wall, making an even bigger mess.

"That's it, that's it," Ron screeched, his face flushed red with anger. "You're done. Get out. *Now.*"

Suppressing his grin, Chris shoved his mop handle into Ron's hand, managing to drag it through the water again. He turned and headed up the dry hallway to the door.

Behind him, he heard water sloshing as Ron worked to clean up Chris's mess, muttering to himself. Then there was the sound of something heavy sliding, and Ron cried out, startled.

Chris glanced over his shoulder to see the other man had slid on the wet floor, his footwear totally inappropriate for cleaning. Chris fingered the badge Ron had neglected to confiscate when he fired him.

It would come in handy when he returned. He knew he'd be back. Tamsin was still there. Chris slid out the main door before the other man could remember to ask for the badge.

Chapter 4

Tamsin forced herself to walk calmly to her computer so no one watching would think anything was happening. Her heart beat in her ears, and her mind spun in circles. She slid into her chair and typed in her password, straining for sounds of a confrontation from the hallway.

What the hell was going on?

Had she fallen into the rabbit hole? So much had happened in the last hour. First, her truly bizarre conversation with her boss, then meeting Chris in the hallway. Chris, who was apparently there to *rescue* her?

Her panther laughed in the back of her mind over the thought and at his expression when she didn't jump into his arms in relief. She shook her head. Really, what had he expected?

She frowned at her screen, not really seeing it.

"Of course, how many people have a sister who cries wolf?" She never thought Anjanae would think Tamsin was in trouble and would go running for help.

If she really had been a hostage or captive, then things might have been different, she admitted reluctantly. But she wasn't. She was here for her job.

She stared blankly at the screen, hoping none of this would affect her job or research. *She was so close to finding answers. So close to changing… everything.*

From the time she was little, she'd had a mission. One singular goal. All her work at school focused on it. She'd researched professions and determined that a chemist was what she needed to become. While Anjanae went out with friends, Tamsin studied.

Anjanae dated and worried about Tamsin's lack of social life. Her sister wouldn't stop nagging until she went out on one. "It will be good for you."

Ha.

Tamsin went out with a few men, mostly shifters and one human. Each date turned out to be a disaster one way or another. One spilled wine all over her and used *cleaning up* as an excuse to paw her. He seemed to think that was foreplay and asked her if she wanted to get it on in the car.

Another insisted on ordering her food for her. What was she, some sort of child who didn't know what she liked to eat?

There was the human investment broker who wanted her to join a pyramid scheme. He spent the entire dinner trying to convince her how great it was and that she should invest all her money.

The final straw was the panther shifter who was ready for full-on mating before the date even started. They sat, and he started talking about house hunting. *Okay, fine.* He was looking for a new place.

Then he gave her a charming smile and commented on how cute their babies would be. The two boys and one girl they would have. It didn't matter if their panthers would accept each other. No, they just had to be biologically compatible, and he found her "attractive enough." Plus, she had good hips.

Nope. Enough.

Tamsin decided she'd been right all along and focused on her work. She had no time for frivolous pursuits. Besides, a soft voice whispered in the back of her mind, when a man found out what was wrong with her, he wouldn't be interested, anyway.

Best to spend her time on something productive. Finding the elusive answers that no one else was looking for.

Her sister became known as the outgoing one, and Tamsin heard the murmurs that she was cold. Aloof, unfriendly.

She was dedicated.

There weren't answers out there, so she'd find them herself. She'd find a way to fix herself.

No one else would.

Then Chris had walked into her sister's bar and her world went sideways. She'd been able to resist the charming smiles and the suave lines from other men. A curt response and cold look quickly sent them on their way.

But not Chris. His wicked grins and teasing comments intrigued her like none before. He laughed at her short replies and seemed to take frosty expressions as a challenge to make her smile. And somehow, he did.

She did her best to hide her amusement and laughter. No need to encourage him.

Tamsin helped out at her sister's bar after her work was done, or when she was waiting for an experiment to complete. Suddenly, she found herself making excuses to be there. Hoping he would show up.

And he did.

Then he started showing up in her dreams. At first, they'd talk and he'd tease. She knew they were only dreams. Even the ones where they didn't talk. It was all heat and fire. His body and hers. Dreams where she woke up slick, wet, and aching.

Some mornings she woke feeling relaxed and sated, her panties soaked. Those mornings she found herself taking deep breaths, but only her scent was in the room. No matter how real the dreams felt, he hadn't been in bed with her.

Her breasts swelled and her nipples pebbled as she thought about those dreams. She swallowed and took a calming breath.

"Pull it together, Tamsin," she muttered.

She heard a faint cry in the hallway, and she almost jumped to her feet to find out what happened, but forced herself to stay still. She had to pretend everything was normal. That she knew nothing.

Cameras were watching. They were always watching. She knew they were supposed to be there for security, but she often doubted it. She ignored them for the most part, but it felt like eyes were boring into the back of her head. The only place she was safe was her room.

Chris's team managed to fool the cameras.

She wished she knew how. And if they'd done something to the ones in her lab, too.

Was someone watching right now?

Tamsin sighed. A few minutes of not being watched while she worked would be wonderful. Or to have control of the cameras. A small smile curved her lips. What she would give to be able to see what the cameras did.

Or to know where the guards were.

If she wasn't watched by a camera, she had a guard's eyes on her.

No other noises came from the hallway. She tapped her hands restlessly on her desk. She really wanted to know what was happening.

Would it look odd if she got up and opened the door?

If only her lab had windows into the hallway. It would have been nice to see what was going on.

Chris could have been overwhelmed by the guards and taken down. *Hurt.*

Tamsin's mouth went dry and her heart raced at the grim picture her mind was creating.

He's a professional, she reminded herself. *He has back-up.*

Nothing was going to happen to him. He could take care of himself.

She focused on how he moved with coiled strength, his body that of a trained fighter. When he entered a room, his eyes scanned the area, and he seemed to assess everyone around him. She could almost see him putting them into categories.

Threat. Possible Threat. No Danger.

Then there was the way he looked at her. He studied her like she was an intriguing puzzle he wanted to play with. After that kiss in the alley, she often saw heat in his gaze when their eyes met.

Did he think about it as often as she did?

It didn't help that her heart started racing and her body got hot when he was around. Or that she wanted to figure him out, too.

Too bad nothing could ever come from it.

She refused to be just another notch on his bedpost, and that was all they could be. So, she could look but never touch. Not that watching him was a hardship.

Most shifters were in decent shape, but his body was an outstanding specimen. Even among the other members of the Nightfair Crew.

They had to stay in shape, though. Going undercover was dangerous work. She'd heard enough stories from the Nightfair crew over the years. Her heart raced as she thought about the guard, Steven. He was a nasty piece of work. Her panther hissed in her mind whenever she saw him. She had no doubt there'd be trouble if Steven recognized Chris.

"He's leaving," she whispered to herself, not sure if she was trying to comfort or convince herself. But she had heard someone tell Chris to get out over his earpiece.

Her panther wouldn't let her drop it, and Tamsin found herself on her feet, heading to the door, her heart hammering in her chest. She had no idea what she planned to do, or how she might be able to help. But she couldn't just sit there.

She'd only taken a step when the door in front of her *snicked* as the lock disengaged. Tamsin jerked to a stop and fixed her attention on the door, holding her breath as she watched the door handle slowly turn. She clenched her fists, ready to fight, her body tense. It could be Steven.

Or an injured Chris.

The door opened, and her mind froze when the figure in the doorway wasn't tall and broad-shouldered.

Rosemary and spice with a touch of shea butter. A hint of mint.

It was neither Chris nor Steven. The scent, combined with the hint of mint, Amy's new perfume, was unmistakable. She met the startled brown eyes of her assistant.

Tamsin knew why she wore perfume, but it struck her as odd that Amy did. Most shifters didn't like the chemical fragrances. At least Amy's was closer to a natural smell. For the first time, Tamsin wondered if Amy was hiding something, too.

She was a shifter, but her scent was off. Tamsin thought she was wolf, but the perfume made it hard to tell. She wasn't a cat, and Tamsin smelled canine, but not quite right.

Amy blinked in surprise seat seeing Tamsin there, her eyes briefly landing on her clenched fists. She grinned, looking a bit uncertain.

"Everything okay? What are you doing back so soon?" One of Amy's eyebrows rose curiously.

"Yeah, everything's fine," Tamsin replied, relaxing her fists as she craned her neck to look into the empty hallway before the door closed. "You see anything unusual?"

"Unusual?" Amy's brow wrinkled as she frowned and glanced behind her at the closing door. "When? Where?"

Tamsin mentally scolded herself. Of course, Amy hadn't seen anything out of the ordinary, or she would have mentioned it when she came in.

Why did she even ask?

"Never mind." Tamsin tore her gaze away from the door as it softly closed.

"You're acting weird." Amy studied Tamsin with narrowed eyes. "You okay?"

"Yeah, I'm fine." Tamsin forced her mind away from Chris.

"What'd he say?" Amy moved to the lab table on the other side of the room and checked the display panels on the machines.

"A bunch of crazy." Tamsin forced herself to focus on work and walked away from the door and over to the diagnostic machine, her mind on Chris. Her hands itched to open the door and look in the hallway.

How would she explain that?

"What? What kind of crazy?" Amy crossed the room and lightly touched Tamsin's shoulder. "What's wrong? Is this about my vacation? Is that what you talked about? Does he want to cancel it?"

"No." Tamsin turned to look at the worried face of her assistant. *How had she come to that conclusion?* "No, you're good to go, Amy."

"Did he say something about it?" Amy chewed her lip. "He approved it before you were even hired. Is that the problem? You said you were cool with me leaving…"

"I am. I'm fine. Actually, he didn't even mention it," Tamsin answered with a reassuring smile. In the back of her mind, her panther paced uneasily. With everything else he brought up, why didn't he mention her assistant's imminent vacation? It could be that he forgot, but something didn't feel right about that.

Tamsin had only been here for a touch over two weeks, and she and Amy were really working well together. The timing of her vacation could've been better, but she wouldn't ask Amy to cancel it.

Amy sighed in relief and went back to the other side of the lab. Tamsin turned to her own side and reached for the notebook that was kept by the incubator. She glanced around on the lab counter, but didn't see it.

"Did you move the notebook that we use for the incubator?" Tamsin looked around again, but she still didn't see the notebook.

"No, I thought you did," Amy replied with a quizzical look, then returned to her notes. "You know, it's been odd, but things keep moving around. I figured you were trying to find the most efficient location for everything."

"So, you didn't move them?" A chill ran up Tamsin's spine. The only ones who should be moving things around in the lab were her or Amy.

"Nope," Amy said, still focused on her notes. "I figured I'd leave that to you. Although it did strike me as odd that you were moving things around. I thought you liked stuff to stay in the same place so we can find things."

"I didn't move them."

"Well, if I didn't, and you didn't, then who did?" Amy tilted her head in confusion as she faced Tamsin.

"Access to the lab is limited," Tamsin replied, looking around the room for other signs of tampering. "Do you know who all has a code?"

"No." Amy shook her head, the beads on the ends of her braids tapping each other. "I think even the cleaning crew has to be let in."

Her mention of the cleaning crew made Tamsin think of Chris again, and she wondered if he got out. That thought led to Steven, and she narrowed her eyes in thought.

Security had access.

This wasn't the first time she'd left the lab and returned to find things had been moved. She hadn't worried much about it, thinking Amy had done it.

"They do," Tamsin answered, remembering her new boss had been specific about that in his briefing. He seemed so proud about the lab security, he'd gone over it quite a bit.

She frowned as she took a deep breath, trying to pull in the scents around her. She wasn't in the habit of doing that in the lab. Inhaling deeply in a lab could get you a nose-full of something nasty.

But this was her lab, and she decided to take the risk. There was a slight spicy scent in the air, like cloves. It hadn't been there earlier, and was faint, fading in the air circulation.

"Hey, there's the notebook." Amy pulled it out from behind the machine. "Maybe it got put on top and it fell off. Or was shoved behind to get it off the counter."

"I don't know," Tamsin said uneasily. They never put things on top. Had someone gone through the notebook while she'd been gone and put it in the wrong place when they finished?

"At least we found it before I left," Amy said cheerfully, clearly not as worried as Tamsin was.

"So, did you decide where you're going?" Tamsin asked to change the subject as she took the notebook from Amy and flipped through it to look for any signs of tampering. She casually inhaled, casting about for unusual scents.

Amy laughed and shook her head as she headed to her desk and unlocked her computer. "I wasn't expecting so much time, so I think I'll go home and surprise Mom. I haven't seen her in a while."

Amy inhaled sharply, and when Tamsin glanced up, she saw her eyes were wide as she slapped her hand over her mouth with a look of panic.

"What's wrong?" Tamsin asked.

"I shouldn't have said that," Amy whispered, horrified.

Amy's back was to the camera, so if they were watching, they couldn't read her lips to see what she said.

Was she getting paranoid?

Tamsin walked over to her, threw her arm around the taller woman, and steered her to the machine on the far side of the room. This put both their backs to the camera, so no one could lip-read their conversation.

Yes, she was paranoid.

"What's that saying?" Tamsin muttered. "Just because you're paranoid, doesn't mean they aren't out to get you?"

"What?" Amy glanced at her.

"Nothing. Tell me what you shouldn't have said, and what do you mean by not expecting so much time?" Tamsin pulled out the notebook and randomly flipped it open, pretending they were discussing something from it.

Amy swallowed, her skin leeched of color. "My mother."

"What about your mother?" Tamsin tapped the notebook, and Amy dutifully dropped her gaze to look at it.

"When I was hired, they asked if I had any family who would be upset about me working a lot of hours, or out of reach, that kind of thing," Amy whispered softly.

"Okay, so what's the problem?"

"Well, one question led to another, and they kind of think I don't have *any* family," Amy continued.

"I still don't see the issue. What does it matter if you do or don't have family?"

Amy shivered beside her. "Long hours create family issues, they said. I told them no one would worry about me. Which is sort-of true, no one would worry for a while. But I have a large family at home."

"It's okay." Tamsin gently bumped her shoulder. "I won't tell anyone."

Amy let out a deep sigh. "Thanks, I don't want to lose my job. They seem to hire mostly loners here, haven't you noticed? People with no connections."

She turned back to her desk, looking chipper again. Tamsin stood there, her stomach in a knot, Amy's words rolling in her head. She pictured the new guards. Big, menacing, unfriendly.

Recently the Nightfair crew had been talking about some sort of drugs used on shifters. Drugs coming from an unknown source. Drugs used specifically on loners.

People with no connections.

People who wouldn't be believed if they saw something.

People who wouldn't be missed if they disappeared.

What were they doing?

Chapter 5

"Chris, this is a bad idea," Justin's voice muttered through Chris's earpiece.

"You've already said that," Chris pointed out as he leaned against a tree, trying to look casual. He studied the windowless lab building where Tamsin was being held captive.

Even if she did think she was free to go, he knew otherwise. Holding people hostage was exactly the type of crap that asshole Steven and the Sons of Asena were involved in. Plus, the place looked more like a fortress than a research facility.

Justin was still in the van, watching through the various cameras he'd hacked into. Chris didn't know how he did it, but if there was a camera, Justin could hack it. The man had a gift. He wasn't in charge though. He could think this was a bad idea all day long, and it didn't mean shit.

Mac was the one in charge of this op. He could pull the plug in a heartbeat. However, he had left half an hour ago to meet the head of the Nightfair Co and discuss the situation in person. He wouldn't return for a while, so Chris had time. Not a lot of time, but enough.

With Mac gone, that left Chris in charge, sort of. And he came up with a plan.

"Well, it is a bad idea," Justin groused.

"Your opinion is noted," Chris replied tightly, anxious to get started. "Just tell me when it's clear."

"The window will be short," Justin repeated the same thing he'd said when Chris first broached this idea.

"Not a problem." Chris pictured the hallway in his mind. "I won't need much time."

A low growl came across the comm and Chris grinned. He wasn't worried. Justin would do what he asked.

"Okay, get ready," Justin said. "Your window is about to open. I've already got the loop of the hallways, and the pats are walking out of the picture."

"Give me a count," Chris ordered as he stood. The tree was out of the line of sight of the cameras. Two steps forward and that wouldn't be true. "You have the front covered?"

"Is the sky blue?" Justin growled. "Of course, I do. And the back camera is clear."

Chris quickly walked to the door. It was in the back of the building, but still had cameras. However, all the parking was in front, so it was used less. He stood by the door, waiting for Justin to call the all-clear for inside.

"Okay, I'm waiting for one guard to walk out of the hallway," Justin announced. "There he goes. Three, two, one, *go*!"

Chris didn't waste any time as he opened the door. He took three steps inside, studying the ceiling tiles. He turned around and faced the door, then nodded.

"I hope you know what you're doing," Justin muttered.

Me too, Chris thought. He'd confidently proposed his plan to Justin, but there were several unknown elements that could bring everything crashing down.

He'd noticed when he was here before that the ceiling tiles looked a bit odd to him. The brackets holding them in place looked much stronger than normal. He had no idea why, but it sparked this idea.

Well, looking at the ceiling won't test his theory.

He moved back by the door, crouched and jumped. He slid his fingers on the bar under the ceiling tile, pushing up the end of the tile a tiny bit. In normal buildings, these were flimsy structures and couldn't hold the weight of a person. With his dense shifter bones, Chris was a bit heavier than a human. He hung from the bar for a few seconds and it didn't budge.

He wedged his fingers under the tile, but it stayed in place. He pushed a little harder, careful to push closer to the corner. If it broke, it would be less noticeable.

Suddenly the tile lifted, and he had to fight to keep the tile from falling to the floor. His heart hammered as he swung from one arm. Justin laughed in his ear.

"Dude, what the hell are you doing? You look like you're on a jungle gym or something."

Or something.

Chris didn't bother to reply, but focused on getting the tile carefully shoved to the side and keeping his feet from hitting the wall. He didn't want to leave any trace that he used this as an entrance. After all, he'd need to get out again, too.

With a feral grin, Chris held on to the cold metal bar with his right hand and used his left to push on the ceiling tile, lifting it up. He moved the tile to make a wide enough hole to pull his body up, his muscles straining from holding his weight with one arm.

Chris dropped back to the ground and studied his small entrance hole. He had to pull himself up, basically doing a pull-up, but pulling his entire body up and over the bar. He'd never tried this before, but it couldn't be too hard.

He pulled two small pieces of cloth out of the front pocket on his cargo pants and slid them over his shoes. The booties would eliminate any possible footprints. He took another rag out of his left pocket and wiped the floor by the door. He didn't see any tracks, but it was best not to take chances.

"How we doing?" he asked Justin as he put the cloth away.

"Still clear, but get a move on."

Chris jumped, grabbed the bar, and used his momentum to pull himself all the way up until his upper body was above the ceiling to his waist. He paused to look around before pulling his legs up.

Darker than expected, but not an issue.

The light from below poured through his small opening, and he shifted his eyes so he could see better. "Holy shit," he muttered.

"What?" Justin demanded. "Turn on your cam so I can see!"

Chris pulled himself the rest of the way up and moved the tile back into its frame, crouching in place. He flipped the small eye lens down and turned it on to dark vision.

Justin made a low whistle as he looked through Chris's camera. Instead of the normal thin support beams he expected, thick metal supports crisscrossed the entire place.

What were they building for? Elephants?

"The fucking place is supported," Justin said.

Chris frowned, wondering what this meant, and why they'd go to this expense. Did the owners of this building use the ceilings as Chris was about to? If so, this wasn't as secure a route as he had thought. He took a deep breath, but didn't pull in any notable scents.

The area around him was a giant catwalk with rigid beams for ceiling supports. There were beams that ran along the length of the building from wall to wall. It looked to him like this was half the building, completely open. He hoped his destination was on this side of the center support wall, or he'd have to drop back down.

There wasn't a lot of height, and he'd have to move in a crawl or crouch, but he'd been prepared for that. He had on thin knee pads under his cargo pants.

With the booties on his feet, his shoes would glide along. He just had to be careful not to touch the flimsy ceiling tiles.

"Starting the live feed," Justin reported, letting him know he was stopping his loop to avoid suspicion from a feed that only showed an empty corridor.

Chris took Justin's announcement as an admonishment to get moving. He gripped the support beam he perched on and silently crawled forward.

"Directions," he kept his voice soft. There may not be any guards around right now, but he didn't want to get sloppy.

"Go straight," Justin ordered. "I'll tell you when you need to move to the next beam."

"Copy that," Chris replied, anxiety a knot in his stomach that he ignored.

It was odd, moving through a building with no walls. He saw small points of light coming up through the ceiling tiles. Not enough to illuminate the area, but enough to tell him which rooms were occupied. He might need that information if things went south.

"At the wall, you need to move to your left and cross four beams," Justin instructed.

Justin was using Chris's feed and combining it with what his cameras told him, to give Chris directions. Chris silently followed his instructions. His foot slipped on the third beam, tapping the ceiling tile, and Chris's heart raced.

He froze, looking at the dark tiles, waiting for someone to sound an alarm. It took him a moment to process that the tiles were dark. That meant no one was in the room below.

Chris let out a silent breath of relief and continued to the fourth beam.

"Shit," Justin snarled.

"What?" Chris halted, waiting to find out what the problem was.

"There are no cameras in the rooms," Justin replied. "Just the hallways."

"What the fuck?" Chris hissed softly. "Why didn't you say something earlier?"

"I didn't realize it earlier," Justin snapped. "I thought I just hadn't found the hack for those feeds. But there are no cameras. I can't see what you're going into."

Chris swallowed and thought about aborting. His tiger growled lowly in the back of his mind.

He had to get to Tamsin.

"Is the tracker still stationary?" Chris asked.

When he'd seen Tamsin earlier, he'd managed to attach a tracker to her lab coat, taking the chance that she'd keep it on. Sure enough, it had been moving up until half an hour ago.

"Yep," Justin answered. "No change in location."

"Then let's continue. We'll just have to take the chance that she's alone."

A sigh sounded through his earpiece. "Move forward about twelve yards. I can only see the hallways, but think that will put you in a room. Not sure it'll be the right one, though."

Heart pounding, Chris followed Justin's instructions. He took a deep breath but wasn't able to pull up any scents. A sneeze tickled his nose, and that was the end of his scenting for now. Not unless he wanted to have a sneezing fit and give himself away.

He cautiously moved forward to what he thought was the wall for the hallway. He couldn't tell where the walls were for the individual rooms.

What to do?

Chris laid down on the beam, stretching his legs and hooking them on the sides to support his body. He carefully reached to the tile on his right, leaned over, and put his ear to it. These tiles were supposed to provide sound reduction, so he wasn't sure if he would be able to pick up anything.

Silence.

It could mean no one was in the room. Or it could also indicate that the room was occupied and he just couldn't hear anything.

Chris carefully sat up on the beam, reached to his small belt pouch, and flipped the hook. He pulled out a small scope camera. It was as thin as a pencil with a lens on the end and a long USB cord. He pulled his phone out of a pocket in his tactical vest and plugged the USB end into it.

The scope was light, and he set it on the tile to his right. The tiles were made to be lifted from below, not the top, and there were no handles for him to pull it up.

"Your tracker says you're close to the hallway," Justin's worried voice broke into his thoughts, his tone worried.

Chris glanced at the wall beam a couple feet behind him.

"I am," he replied softly, concerned about Justin's comment.

"Steven is patrolling that hallway." Justin spoke softly, like he was afraid of being overheard.

"Location?" Chris dropped his voice to a whisper.

"He's headed in your direction."

"Copy that." Chris looked at the tiles above the hallway. Not that he could see anything.

Chris went silent, watching the hallway, listening for any signs of the other shifter. In the back of his mind, his tiger growled in warning. It didn't like Steven at all. Chris felt a growl rumbling in his chest, and he took a deep breath to shove it back down again. Growling would definitely give him away.

"He's stopped, a few feet from your location," Justin told him. "And he's looking around."

"He caught my scent?" Adrenaline surged through Chris as he whispered back.

"Unknown," Justin's replied tensely. "I'm getting the loop in place, just in case."

Chris grew icy calm. If Steven found him, it would be difficult to escape, even with Justin taking over the cameras and putting in a loop of an empty hallway. He'd have to immediately incapacitate the man without any bloodshed. The scent of blood would be unmistakable, and all shifters would know there was trouble.

The seconds ticked by and Chris's body grew tense. He didn't dare move because he might make a slight noise that would attract attention. Justin didn't say anything, and Chris wondered if the communication feed had disconnected.

A soft sigh came through the earpiece, startling Chris. "He's turned around. You're in the clear. Do what you came here for and get the fuck out."

A wry grin crossed Chris's face. "Copy that."

He turned his attention back to the ceiling tile, pulled out his multi-tool, and flipped out the nail file with the small hook on the end. He dug the hook into the side near the corner, and carefully pulled up the tile. This one lifted easily, and he slid the camera scope under the corner.

He put his multi-tool back in its pocket and picked up his phone, twisting the camera to get a better look at the room. It was a small, utilitarian bedroom with a bed, nightstand, lamp, and a small dresser. There were three doors.

Based on the location, he guessed which one led to the hallway. One of the others likely led to a closet and the third a bathroom. The room was empty, although the light was on.

"Can you pinpoint which room she's in?" he said softly, irritation running through him. In his planning, he never figured he'd be stonewalled by an empty room.

"Negative. Your tracking dot and hers are close, but the equipment isn't precise enough for me to get closer than within a few feet," Justin answered.

Chris clenched his jaw and watched the empty room. Then he pulled the camera out and pushed the tile back down, but not all the way in case he needed to get it back up. He turned his attention to the other room and repeated pulling up the tile and slipping the camera in.

He was looking at another bedroom, a mirror of the first. Also completely empty. Chris snarled. "You sure I'm in the right place?"

"As sure as I can be," Justin snapped. "Don't snarl at me because the rooms are empty."

Chris opened his mouth to reply when the doorknob turned. He pulled the scope up so it was barely in the room, his attention fixed on the door.

A moment later, Tamsin entered the room. She paused and glanced around, her brow furrowed in confusion. She looked around again, then shook her head.

Chris waited until she closed the door and flipped the lock before he pulled up the scope. He quickly packed it away and slid his phone into his pocket. He made sure his supplies were all collected, then carefully lifted the edge of the tile.

He looked in the room, but Tamsin wasn't in sight.

It didn't matter, this was the right room.

He moved the tile to the side to create an opening. He dropped into the room, landing silently on the floor.

A moment later, one of the side doors jerked open and Tamsin stood there. A look of relief flashed across her face, to quickly be replaced by an angry glare.

"I *knew* I scented you. Where the hell did you come from?" Her gaze shot to the ceiling, and her eyes grew wide, then narrowed.

His tiger purred in pleasure. *She recognized his scent.*
"I—"

"No." She waved her hand in the air, cutting him off. "You know what, I don't care. You go back where you came from."

"Look," Chris spoke quickly, "I know you think you can leave at any time, but... "

"I can," she replied, her eyes flashing. "And I don't need your help. If anything, you being here may just get me in trouble. This is a *secure* facility. You know what that means, right?"

"Chris," Justin hissed softly in his ear.

"Not right now," Chris replied.

"Not right now? *Not right now?* Oh, I don't think so," Tamsin snapped as she folded her arms over her chest.

Damn, she was adorable when she was pissed.

Her eyes flashed with her anger. She looked like a ferocious kitten. One he wanted to kiss until her anger melted away and she was pliant in his arms. He mentally scolded himself for that thought.

Now was not the time.

"There's a guard—" Justin said quickly, followed by a loud pounding on the bedroom door.

Tamsin's eyes widened in surprise and she glanced at the door, then back at him.

"Everything okay in there?" a male voice called.

"Yes, just a moment, please," Tamsin called out.

She turned to Chris and pointed to the room she had stepped out of. "Get in the bathroom," she told him through clenched teeth.

Chris crossed his arms, not wanting to move. She stomped over to him, turned him bodily, and pushed him toward the bathroom. He allowed her to manhandle him and stepped into the small room. He closed the door most of the way and turned off the light in case his body made a shadow. Silently he yanked the scope out of his pocket and quickly hooked it into his phone.

Through his camera screen, he watched Tamsin glare at the bathroom door, then stick her tongue out at it. His tiger huffed in laughter, and he didn't hide his grin.

She took a deep breath and unlocked her bedroom door. She turned the knob and swung the door open wide. Chris got a good look at the guard.

"Oh shit," Justin muttered in Chris's ear.

Steven stood in the doorway.

And Chris had left the ceiling tile off.

If the guard looked up, he'd see where Chris had entered the room.

Chapter 6

Tamsin fought her anger and desire to scream. She couldn't *believe* Chris had returned, and through the ceiling no less. What was he thinking? She'd told him she didn't need his help. She watched him go into the bathroom.

Someone that bossy shouldn't have such a fine ass.

She made a face at the bathroom before she turned to face the door.

At least he didn't know about her dreams.

She forced herself to focus on the task at hand. She took a deep breath and forced her shoulders to relax as she opened the door wide, so Chris could see who it was from his hiding place. As soon as she did, she regretted it. She met Steven's cold gaze and forced a smile on her face.

"Can I help you?" she asked in a formally polite tone. In the back of her mind, her panther snarled in unheard warning at the guard.

"I heard yelling," he said, his cold eyes running over her body, then flickering into the room.

Suddenly Tamsin remembered how Chris had entered the room. There currently was a hole in her ceiling. Something someone like Steven the Creep would notice unless she distracted him.

"I can't yell in my own room?" Tamsin spoke coldly, causing his eyes to snap to hers in surprise.

She raised one eyebrow as she looked at him.

"Security is my business," Steven narrowed his eyes as he looked at her.

"It may be," Tamsin replied, "but did I push the emergency button?"

A slow flush crawled up his neck, and he shook his head.

She stepped to the side, closing the door as she went. "I do not need your assistance. I'll let you know if I do."

Before he could say anything else, she closed the door in his face, sagging against it as she flipped the lock.

Chris appeared in her tiny room seconds later, his scent invading her senses. It was a good thing Steven hadn't picked up on the foreign scent.

"See, you're a prisoner." Chris picked up their argument as if it had not been interrupted.

Immediately, her anger reappeared, and she clenched her jaw.

He was not in charge of her.

Tamsin let out a frustrated sigh and gestured to the door. "Just because Mr. Steroids has a hard-on for security, doesn't mean I can't leave."

"Prove it." His eyes met hers, and he raised his chin in challenge.

She raised one eyebrow, meeting his gaze. "If I do, will you leave me alone?"

Chris gave a curt nod. "I'll leave. And I won't return unless you call for help."

A bark of surprised laughter burst out of her. *Right.* He'd probably be back tomorrow. "Fine. Whatever."

"What does that mean?" he said with a wary look.

She didn't want him coming back tomorrow, or the next day. But she had to give him an answer.

"Well, it'll be hard to call for help if my phone doesn't work, and cell phones don't work in this building."

A devastating smile curved his mouth, and she forced herself not to react. The man was too fine for his own good.

He reached to one of his pockets on his vest and pulled out a small cell phone. "Here, you can call me on this."

"How?" She studied the phone in his hand warily and didn't reach out to take it. "I told you, phones don't work in this building."

"This one will," he said confidently, waving the phone back and forth in front of her.

Tamsin sighed and decided the argument wasn't worth pursuing. She plucked the phone from his hand. "Fine. I'll prove to you I can leave whenever I want."

His cocky smile was full of doubt as he gestured to the door with a wave, inviting her to leave. "Be my guest. I'd love to see it."

Tamsin glanced at the door, then back at Chris. Her eyes locked on his entrance location. "Before I do, can you fix the hole in my ceiling? You know we lucked out that he didn't notice it."

Chris followed her gaze and started to walk to the location directly under the tile.

"Better yet," she said before he jumped up. "You can just haul yourself out and save us both the trouble."

"Funny," Chris said as he jumped up and grabbed the rail the ceiling tile had previously rested on. With his other hand, he lifted the off-kilter tile and scooted it into place.

"I had no idea those rails were so sturdy," she muttered, her eyes locked on his muscles as he easily held himself in place with one hand and moved the tile with the other.

She had no idea he was that strong.

He effortlessly hung there by one hand.

"Normally, they aren't." He finished putting the tile in place and lightly dropped to the ground. "There's something odd about these."

He studied the tile thoughtfully, and her heart hammered in her chest. There was just something about this man that pushed every one of her buttons. She wanted to run her hands through his hair, trace his chin and feel the slight stubble, and hold her body close to his hot, muscular one.

Chris turned his gaze to her and gave her a cocky smile. "I'm ready if you are."

Her mind froze, and she had a horrifying idea that he could read her thoughts.

"Ready?" It came out as a hoarse croak. She swallowed and had to do it again. "Ready? For?"

"Your demonstration that you can just waltz out of here at any time. What else?"

"Right." She cleared her throat. "Well, back in the bathroom with you."

Chris smiled tightly and returned to his hiding place. She couldn't stop her eyes from running over his backside as went.

He really had such a fine ass.

He closed the bathroom door, as he had before, and she shook herself. *Behave.* Chris was off-limits. Okay, so maybe she couldn't touch, but why couldn't she look?

With a slight shake of her head, she slid on her shoes and went to the door. A quick glance at the bathroom to make sure Chris was out of sight, and she unlocked her bedroom door.

Tamsin suppressed a chill as she stepped into the silent hallway. There was something creepy about this building at night, but she couldn't put her finger on it. This section was where the bedrooms were. There wasn't a lot of socialization that went on, and she didn't really know many people here.

She moved past the empty rec room and the equally silent gym. She felt unsettled and didn't like it. She'd been completely focused on her work while she'd been here, it hadn't bothered her that she didn't see anyone else.

Did the other floors have bedrooms, too?

She glanced up, but only saw the ceiling tiles. And the camera staring at her from the corner.

This place did feel like a prison.

Well, it may feel like a prison, but she could leave. She turned the corner and stumbled to a stop. Steven stood at the end of the hall with two other guards she didn't recognize.

Were they new?

"Are you lost?" asked one of the guards she didn't recognize.

"No," Tamsin replied.

"There's nothing down this hallway," the other guard added.

She took a breath and realized they were all wolves. That explained why they were standing like a unit. Well, that and the fact they were all guards who worked together.

"Actually, the door is behind you," she said archly as she continued walking.

"It leads out of the building," Steven responded in a condescending tone.

"Yeah, I wanted to go outside." Tamsin stopped in front of the three men. They were all big and broad-shouldered. They were also completely blocking the way. She would have to shove through them to get past. Her panther recoiled in her mind at the thought of touching them.

"We'll be happy to escort you on your walk," Steven offered.

"I don't require an escort, thank you," Tamsin replied coldly. "Could you please move?"

"We're waiting for someone," the guard on the left said.

As soon as the words left his mouth, the other guard punched him in the arm. He flinched and glared at his attacker.

"This late?" Tamsin asked, surprised. "Who?"

"Never you mind," the guard who threw the punch snarled.

"We're guards," Steven explained. "We're always waiting for someone."

"Really?" Tamsin studied them. "Well, in that case, please let me pass, and you can continue your guarding."

"Your safety is our primary concern," Steven bared his teeth in what he probably called a smile. "So, we can't let you out there alone."

Her stomach turned and a shiver of fear went up her spine. She kept her emotions hidden and replied, "Oh? I didn't realize this was such a dangerous area."

"There are dangers everywhere," Steven replied, his tone menacing. "You'd be better off, heading back to the safety of your room."

His eyes bored into hers, and he tried a dominance stare-down. Tamsin was a cat, and he wasn't in her pride, let alone her hierarchy. Plus, cats didn't do dominance stares. She continued to meet his gaze. His lip curled. A low growl rumbled through his chest.

She decided she was done messing with this creep. Plus, her cat wanted to either get away from him or attack. In this case, retreat seemed the better option.

"You ought to go to the infirmary and get that cough checked out," she raised one brow. "I think I'll take your advice and return to my room."

She tilted her head in a slight nod and turned around, her spine itching as she felt their gazes on her.

She half expected them to attack her from behind, but managed to calmly walk down the hallway. She got to her room and slid her ID in the lock. It clicked with a *snick* and her hand shook slightly as she turned the knob.

She stepped into the room with a feeling of relief and closed the door behind her.

"What did they say?" Chris immediately came out of her bathroom.

"What?" Tamsin asked. "Who?"

"The guards," Chris clarified.

"How did you...oh, the cameras," she said.

"We had video, but no audio," Chris replied. "But your face shut down, like it does when you're pissed. What did they say?"

Her face shut down when she was angry?

She had no idea he paid that much attention to her expressions.

"It doesn't matter." She slashed the air with her hand. "But they did say something of note. They're waiting for someone."

His eyes narrowed. "They are?"

She nodded and chewed on her lip as she thought. "They were at the front door. Is that how you came in? Could they be waiting for you?"

"Unlikely, but possible. I came in through the rear." Chris looked off to the side, and she heard a voice through his earpiece warning him the guards were headed in this direction.

Worry ran through her. *Were they coming to check on her again?* She didn't like the guards, and she was uneasy with all the attention they were giving her.

"You need to leave," Tamsin said urgently, seriously worried about him. "I'll be fine. And I have your phone if I need help. I have to finish my research here, then I'll go."

"Really?" Chris looked at her doubtfully.

"Really. Just… let my sister know I'm okay?"

A small smile crossed Chris's mouth, and he nodded. He reached out and briefly ran his thumb over her cheek, the gentle touch sending a shock of desire through her body.

His eyes held hers for a heartbeat, then he moved to the spot he had dropped down from, and jumped, easily pushing the tile out of the way. He effortlessly pulled himself up, making her mouth go dry with his feat of strength. A few seconds later, he disappeared into the ceiling.

Tamsin watched as the tile dropped back into place, and she listened closely. She didn't hear any sounds of movement. She narrowed her eyes, wondering what it was like up there. Chris was taller than her and easily jumped to grab that bar. She was a cat, and could jump pretty high, but wasn't sure she could jump that high.

The soft noise at her door of someone using their key card to unlock it grabbed her attention. She watched in horror as the handle slowly turned.

She'd forgotten to turn the deadbolt. The door was unlocked.

Her heart raced in her chest and a chill ran up her spine as she rushed to the door. She flipped the interior deadbolt lock. It was the only way to keep someone who had a card keyed to the room from opening it.

Why were the guards trying to get into her room?

The handle stopped turning, and her heart hammered as she watched the door. The handle slowly moved back into the normal position and she let out a silent sigh of relief. After a few seconds of silence, she stepped to the door and put her ear near the hinge. She started to relax when she didn't hear anything.

She flinched when she heard voices.

"Think she's in there?" a man said outside her room. The voice was slightly muffled, but she was pretty sure it was one of the guards she'd encountered.

"Yeah, her scent is strong on the doorknob, and door's locked." Steven's voice came through clearly. There was a pause, then, "She was afraid."

The last was said with satisfaction and sent a cold chill up her spine.

"Think she'll try to take a walk again?"

"Nah," Steven said, his voice starting to grow faint, like he was moving away from her door. "She'll be in there all night. C'mon. Let's get this test subject processed."

Test subject? What test subject? As far as she knew, there were no live trials conducted here.

What were they talking about?

Her throat thick, Tamsin pushed her ear harder against the door, but didn't hear anything else. She nervously chewed her lip. She had to know what was going on. She took the phone Chris had given her and pushed it under her mattress. She didn't want anyone finding it.

Before she could talk herself out of it, she went to the door and slowly turned the top lock, the one she'd just latched. With a deep breath for courage, she threw back her shoulders and opened the door.

When things were quiet at the Ice House, Chris often talked her into sitting with him. He'd tell her tales about his ops and things he'd seen. Places he'd broken into. He always added humor to the stories, but she got the feeling they hadn't been so amusing at the time.

For one op, he'd had to rescue a kidnapped child held in a busy warehouse.

He had simply strolled in and snatched the child out from under their noses.

"How?" Tamsin had asked, enthralled. "Why didn't anyone stop you?"

Chris grinned, his eyes dancing. "The best way to blend in is to act like you have every right to be there. Act hesitant, and you draw suspicion. Act like you belong, and very few will question you."

She kept those words at the front of her mind as she stepped into the hallway, quickly glancing around. It was empty. A deep breath told her she'd been right. Steven and the other two guards had been outside her door. She sniffed her door handle and picked up Steven's scent. He was the one who had turned it to see if it was locked. *Figured.*

She wasn't sure which way they'd gone. She took a chance and went to the right, the direction of the back door. Earlier, she'd tried to go out the front door. The scent was still strong halfway down the hallway, so she continued to follow it.

The hallway T-d off and she took a couple steps to the right and didn't catch any scents. She picked up Steven's scent going down the next hallway, but not the other two. They must have split up.

She spent the next thirty minutes following Steven's scent around the building, worried the cameras would see her and someone would alert him. But she was more determined to figure out what was going on than she was afraid of being caught.

Suddenly, she heard a commotion near the end of the hallway. She tried the handle on the nearest door, but it was locked. Her heart pounded in her chest, and her mouth grew dry. She had no idea what they'd do if they caught her. She tried the next door, and the one after that.

The commotion grew louder, with one man yelling to be let go, and feet stomping on the ground. There were several grunts. The yelling abruptly stopped with a cry of pain, then started up again.

Had they hit him?

Even if they had, she couldn't help this unknown stranger. Her hand scrambled at the nearest knob and she caught her own scent. She froze, panicked, not recognizing the area. Her panther pushed at the back of her mind insistently, and she realized it was telling her this was the supply closet.

She fumbled with her ID and managed to get it unlocked, cursing at herself for not trying her ID before. She wrenched open the door and slipped inside, quickly pulling the door closed behind her. She kept it open a crack so she could hear what was going on.

The noises grew closer, and the steps louder. From the other end of the hallway, she heard a low growl.

"What the fuck? Why haven't you tranqued him?" Steven growled.

Her mouth grew dry. He was the one most likely to catch her scent and find her.

"Can't get him... to... hold... still," one of the guards said, his words interspersed with agitated grunts.

"Do I have to fucking do everything?" Steven growled, then there was a startled cry accompanied by a fist striking flesh. The sounds of struggle stopped.

"He's got fight, that's good," Steven said with satisfaction. "He'll be a perfect test subject for the *Rejen* experiment."

They moved off. Tamsin opened the door, her stomach churning. She saw Steven's back as he led two guards dragging a man down the hallway.

Rejen was the name of her project. She didn't want to believe it, but her gut said they were testing her drug on live subjects without her permission.

The drug was still unstable. All of the scenarios she'd run indicated it would send a shifter into an uncontrollable rage. If they were testing it on people, they might kill someone.

The *test subject* hadn't sounded willing, either. If he had been, they wouldn't have needed to knock him out. She remembered the Nightfair crew talking about loners being abducted off the street. Her hand shook and she balled it in a fist to gain some control. Were the Sons of Asena responsible for that? If they were taking people off the street, what else were they doing?

And what did they have planned for her when her research was complete?

Chapter 7

Tamsin's body was in a cold sweat by the time she got back to her room. Whatever they were up to was much bigger than she thought.

How had she missed this?

She'd followed them for a while and discovered her key card got her in many more places than she'd been told. There was a lot of activity in the hallways, and she'd had to use the card to slip into more unfamiliar rooms to hide. She'd gone into a wing of the building she'd never entered before, one she'd had no reason to go to.

At least two more people were brought in. One silently fought, and the other was already unconscious when they passed her, a bruise on his cheek from being roughed up.

There were so many guards on the move that they didn't catch her scent at all. They were focused and didn't even look around as they headed to their various destinations in groups of three or four. She had no idea there were this many guards here. She felt like she was in a prison.

She'd been terrified she'd be caught, but couldn't figure out what they were up to. She finally headed to her room, her mind racing in circles. She secured the top lock on her door and leaned against the wall, her heart hammering. Her gaze fell to her bed.

Chris's phone.

She took a step toward the bed but stopped. *No.* She wasn't going to leave her research to be misused.

Now she regretted her intense focus on her project. She should have paid more attention to what was going on. Could the moved and misplaced items in her lab be related? Had they been looking for something?

Years ago, she'd developed the habit of keeping her research in different coded files, always keeping a critical piece separate. There was no way they could have developed her formula from her notes.

They must have stolen a recent sample.

That was the only way they could have gotten a dose of her serum to test.

What if they were replicating it?

She hadn't made an antidote. It was supposed to be a cure. Help shifters whose animals were trapped inside them. Not make them go violently bloody, like she feared it would if used incorrectly. Such as in the case of giving it to a shifter who was normal.

Tamsin spun around and flipped the lock, intent on going to her lab to get her notes and alter the data. She yanked open the door and immediately caught Steven's scent. She froze in her tracks and looked to her left, in the direction the smell was strongest.

He stood there facing her with two other guards, ones she didn't recognize.

"Pretty late to be going somewhere, isn't it?" he asked in a curious tone, yet his gaze was predatory and his stance alert.

"I... had a thought about my project. Wanted to try something," she blurted out quickly. Mentally, she winced.

That was the best she could come up with?

"It's late." Steven took a step closer to her and her cat silently hissed in her mind. "You should go back to bed. Don't want to make any mistakes, do you?"

She swallowed hard at the menace in his tone and shook her head. "No, I don't."

The two guards followed him, standing slightly behind him on either side. Her mouth grew dry, and she forced a smile as they watched her with expressions so neutral they were practically glaring. Clearly, they didn't want her roaming the hallways right now.

"Well," she said as she stepped back into her room, "you're right. I'll just make a note and take care of it in the morning. Good night. I hope this is the most exciting thing that happened for you tonight."

She watched them as she closed her door. They silently stood there, gazing at her with cold eyes. With shaking hands, she flipped the lock and let out a gust of breath. She pushed her ear against the door, but couldn't hear a thing. She didn't know if they were still there, or if they'd left.

It didn't matter.

Come morning, she was out of there.

***

Tamsin quickly walked down the hallway, her scalp creeping with the feeling of being watched. Last night she hadn't even thought about the cameras and woke after an uneasy rest with a terrifying idea.

What if someone had been watching her the entire night?

Could all the hiding that she'd done last night been for nothing?

No. If they had been watching her, someone would've intercepted her.

Her mouth was dry as she hurried to her lab.

She had to get out of there.

She had no idea if they recorded what the camera saw or not. But she knew in her gut that if someone realized she'd been wandering the hallways last night, had seen them bringing those test subjects, it wouldn't go well. She didn't know if she would become another subject, or if they'd use that information to coerce her. In any case, she was getting out.

She took deep breaths as she moved, pulling in the scents. The guards had been in this area, but not recently. She picked up Amy's scent, too. It was fresh. She paused as she reached her lab door and deliberately fumbled with her ID.

Tamsin used the time to take in the smells, trying to see who had recently touched her door. Amy's scent was very strong. Underneath that was the odd floral scent she'd caught before. Her brow wrinkled and she considered that. It occurred to her that someone could be hiding their scent. Using the floral smell to disguise themselves. Like spraying air freshener in the room. Still, the scent wasn't fresh.

She used her ID to open her door. As the lock clicked and the door swung open, she quickly glanced around her lab. Amy was sitting at her computer rapidly typing something. The other woman glanced over her shoulder with a surprised look.

"Hey," Amy said as she stood. "I didn't expect to see you so early."

Tamsin glanced at the clock and realized it was just after five in the morning. It was really early for her. Although she spent a lot of time at the lab, she preferred to work late, not early. Many shifters were more night creatures, especially the cats.

"I couldn't really sleep," Tamsin replied with a shrug. "So, I figured I'd get here early. Do you always get here this early?"

Amy grinned and shook her head. "No. Honestly, I usually only beat you to the lab by a few minutes each morning."

"So why are you here at this ungodly time?"

"My bus leaves in about an hour." Amy waved her hand to the door. Tamsin glanced over and saw a bag she hadn't noticed. "I wanted to finish up these notes since this is the last time I'm going to be working on the project here."

"Last time?" Tamsin asked, the knot in her stomach starting to roll.

Did Amy suspect something?

"Yeah, I'm gonna be gone for two weeks. Didn't you tell me that's when your contract is supposed to be over?"

Two weeks?

"I didn't realize you were going to be gone for that long. For some reason, I thought it was only a week," Tamsin replied, her mind racing.

Why would they have her assistant be gone for the last two weeks of her contract?

"We talked about it yesterday. Didn't they tell you I was getting two weeks?" Amy tilted her head to the side curiously.

"No. You mentioned getting more time than you thought, but didn't say how much time. Come to think of it, I was never told how much vacation time you were actually taking," Tamsin said uneasily. She'd been preoccupied with Chris's arrival and the missing items in her lab. Normally, she didn't let details like that slip by her.

"Oh," Amy said, her eyes wide. "I'm sorry, I thought you knew. I got an email yesterday telling me that I was to take a full two weeks paid vacation. When I returned, I'm to report to a different lab facility. I kinda figured they'd move me where you were going, too."

After everything she saw last night, this only made Tamsin more on edge. She didn't know if they were trying to get rid of Amy, or if they were planning to get rid of her. In any case, at least Amy wouldn't deal with any of the fallout from her leaving.

"It probably just slipped their minds," Tamsin replied calmly, seeing how worried Amy looked. "I'm not sure what will happen when my contract is over."

Amy's face fell, and she frowned in disappointment. "I really liked working with you. Maybe they'll assign me to your lab?"

"That would be great," Tamsin answered honestly. She'd really liked working with Amy. Although, with the way things were going, she wasn't sure she wanted to go back to her first place of employment. She might just be looking for a new job now. She forced a smile. "Maybe

I'll steal you if they don't. Let's trade numbers and we can keep in touch."

Amy's eyes lit up. "That'd be great." She dug her phone out of her pocket.

"It'll be easier if we just put in each other's numbers." Tamsin pulled out her phone and held it out to Amy.

She pulled up the contacts screen and hit *add* then hesitated. She had no idea what was going to happen. They knew her phone number. They knew where she lived. She chewed her lip, thinking. She had no idea what she was going to do next. Or where she was going to go.

Chris could help her.

Nightfair had all sorts of contacts. They could help her hide if she needed to. Which might mean losing her number. Her contact information wasn't safe.

Without actually thinking about it, her fingers flew over the keys inputting a number. She typed her name and scanned it before she hit save. The number she put in was familiar, but not her own. However, if Amy needed help, she'd get it.

Tamsin returned Amy's phone to her, forcing a smile. "I hope you enjoy your vacation."

"Thanks." Amy handed Tamsin her phone. "I haven't had paid time off in… forever. My family will be so surprised."

"Don't worry about anything here." Tamsin tucked her phone into her pocket. "Just relax and enjoy."

And stay safe.

Amy shouldn't be in danger. Tamsin had all the information. She would be their target, not her assistant.

"You're the best." Amy turned back to her computer to finish up her notes.

Tamsin moved to her own computer and logged in. As Amy typed away near her, she opened up her main research file where she kept all her notes. There were a couple changes she could make in her notes that would render the formula inert if someone was stealing it. Turn it into nothing more than a boost to the immune system.

Her heart hammered in her chest with what she had planned. If they figured it out, it would make her a giant target. But she couldn't let them misuse her work.

Tamsin was so focused that when a bell chime sounded in the room, she jumped. She jerked her head up and saw Amy messing with her phone.

"That's my alarm." Amy gave her a bright smile. "Time for me to go."

Tamsin forced a smile on her face and stood to give Amy a hug. She was going to miss her. Amy was the best lab assistant Tamsin had ever worked with. Amy's arms wrapped around her, holding her tight, and she knew the other woman felt the same.

They stepped apart and a moment later there was a knock on her lab door.

"Steven said he'd give me a ride." Amy hurried over to the door. "He's so polite. Always knocks and never bursts into the lab."

"Steven's giving you a ride?" Tamsin repeated. She had no idea why the guard didn't make Amy as uneasy as he made her. For some reason, Amy seemed to really like him.

"Well, one of the guards will take me." She waved her hand toward the door as she grabbed her bag. "I'm sure he doesn't have the time to waste schlepping me around."

Amy opened the door to reveal Steven standing there. His cold gaze met Tamsin's as his face creased in a charming smile.

"Ready to go?" he asked Amy.

Tamsin suppressed the chill his tone sent up her spine. His eyes remained locked on her as he stepped back, holding the door open for Amy to step out.

"Sure am," Amy cheerfully replied.

Tamsin wanted to sit at her desk, but couldn't bring herself to turn her back on Steven. Her cat hissed at the thought and gave a warning growl.

"Travel safe," Tamsin managed to get out, pleased her voice sounded calm.

Amy gave her a happy grin and nodded. "I'll keep in touch."

Steven kept his reptile gaze on her as the door closed, and before it shut him out of her sight, a cold smile curved his lips.

Tamsin stood there staring at the door, her mouth dry. She lived with people who could shift into animals that could tear a person's throat out. Yet nothing scared her as much as that man. In the scheme of things, wolves were not as powerful as panthers.

But wolves traveled in packs, and that was where their power came from. And she never saw Steven alone. Cats may be ambush hunters, but something told her Steven would have no problem with taking someone unaware.

Her lab suddenly felt like a prison. Tamsin hurried to her computer to copy her files and alter the ones that were left. She covertly pulled out a thumb drive and moved so the camera couldn't see her inserting it into the computer. She quickly highlighted all the files she wanted copied and started the process.

Her heart hammered in her chest, and she did her best to keep her expression from showing her fear. The hair on the back of her neck crawled with the knowledge that they were watching. Even more than before, she had the feeling of being observed.

The last file finished and she removed the drive, keeping it hidden. She tucked it into her sock by her ankle in case anyone searched her. It wasn't likely, but right now she wouldn't put anything past them.

For the next hour she made minor alterations in her notes. She had to be subtle. As she worked, she became more certain than before that someone was taking her work and trying to replicate it.

Well, not anymore.

A cold sweat broke out on her body as she saved the last file. *Done.*

Now to get out of there.

Chapter 8

Chris moved quickly through the dark streets, a sense of urgency riding him. In one hand he had a bag with breakfast burritos, and the other held a cup-holder with three cups of coffee he'd picked up from the corner store.

He'd barely slept the previous night and was up much earlier than usual. Before the sun, even. The clock had said five when he jumped in the shower.

He was a cat, and night was his prime time. He was not on good terms with the sunrise. However, his mind was locked on Tamsin, and he couldn't stop worrying about Steven's presence at that building.

Something was wrong.

Mac was supposed to get back to them late yesterday, but an incident in Oakdale had tied up Nightfair. All they were told was that it was top priority, but they had it under control. For now, Chris's team was on their own.

He wanted to check out the surveillance footage from last night. Now that they had eyes on the building, he needed to see what they were doing. Especially when everyone was supposed to be asleep. He also found it odd that there were cameras in Tamsin's lab, but none in the labs on the fourth floor and up, only in the hallways. They'd figured that out late yesterday.

What were they up to?

After his shower, he sent a text to his other team members and had been surprised when he got immediate replies. They were up, too, and just as anxious as he was to see what had happened last night. None of them had any question in their minds that *something* was going on.

Justin was a wolf, and they were often up with the dawn, so his response wasn't too odd. Sierra, on the other hand, was a bear. She hated getting up before seven in the morning, although she wasn't nocturnal like Chris was. The fact that she was up told him her instincts were on alert, too. In a normal stake-out situation where they watched 24/7, Chris would take the night shift, and Justin would take early morning until afternoon with Sierra in the middle.

But this wasn't a normal situation. They didn't need to watch all day and night, so they'd retreated to their various rooms for the night. Same as they had every night since this mission started, changing motels every few days.

They were each in different motels, and the van was parked in a nearby *Wal-Mart*. The sun was still not up when Chris reached the van and used his key to unlock it. He'd only managed to make it inside and set down the food when Justin and Sierra both showed up.

"Coffee, gimme." Sierra closed the door behind her. Her bear nose must have picked up the scent because she hadn't even looked inside to see the cups.

Justin immediately went to his beloved computers and started booting everything up, grabbing the cup Chris handed him as he went.

After breathing in the steaming beverage, Sierra grabbed a burrito and moved to the driver's seat. She latched open the partition door before she buckled up and started the van. Chris and Justin slid into seats, each grabbing their own burrito as the screens flickered to life.

"Can we see what's happening now?" Chris asked as he took a bite of his burrito.

"Yeah, just a sec," Justin replied, his fingers flying over the keyboard.

Sierra put the van in gear and pulled out of the parking lot. "I'll drive around a bit, then find a place to pull over and go over the footage with you."

"Great," Chris replied with a glance to the front. The street was empty like they were the only ones awake. *Smart people.* But he couldn't sleep any longer, anyway.

"Top left." Justin paused long enough to bite into his burrito. His coffee cup was in a holder to his right, leaving his hands mostly free.

Chris turned his attention to the screen and saw it flicker white before twelve small square boxes appeared. Most of them were empty hallways. A movement in one caught his attention as Chris saw someone walking down the hallway.

"Can you put three-alpha up on its own monitor?" he asked, using their reference code for that square.

Justin nodded and his fingers tapped the keys. A moment later, the image was on its own screen, and Chris cursed under his breath. All the hallways looked the same, but Chris knew which area that camera was tuned to, and it was close to Tamsin's lab.

"What are they up to so early?" he muttered as he grabbed another burrito from the bag.

He glanced over and saw Justin had finished his, so he put one in front of the wolf. He slid out of his seat and took another burrito forward to Sierra, too.

"What'd you see?" she asked with a grateful nod for the food.

"Steven and two others in the hallway near Tamsin's lab," he replied.

"Early, isn't it?" She stopped at a red light and picked up her burrito, quickly exposing one end.

"I think so, but we don't know their routine yet." He returned to his seat in time to see the guards standing outside Tamsin's lab, and Steven knock on the door.

"They knock?" Justin said, his brow furrowed. "That strike you as odd? Why don't they just go in?"

"Maybe their key cards don't give them access?" Chris guessed.

"They're security. If a contracted janitorial company gets access, wouldn't security?" Sierra asked from the front.

"Point," Chris replied as he saw Tamsin's lab door open and Amy appear with a suitcase.

"What's going on?" Justin asked.

"No idea." Chris wished they'd had time to install bugs and get audio, too.

"Does Tamsin look... worried to you?" Justin asked as they watched her turn around on the screen and face her computer, and coincidentally, the camera in her lab.

She did. Really worried.

What had happened?

"Can you blow up the cameras in the hallway?" Chris turned his attention to watch Steven as he left the building.

The three guards escorted Amy out with her chattering animatedly. Steven smiled and responded, but the two other guards frowned and didn't comment at all. Amy looked back at them once, and then avoided doing so again.

They left the building, and Justin switched to the exterior cameras. Steven reached out and touched Amy on the bare skin where her neck met her shoulder. She gave him a startled look, then slowly shook her head. When they reached the car, she glanced back at the building and blinked, like she was confused. She frowned and shook her head again.

One of the guards said something, and she turned back to the car. She staggered as she took the few steps to get in the black Buick. The other guard opened the trunk and swung her bag inside.

"She was fine a few moments ago," Justin's tone was worried.

"What'd he give her?" Chris was certain the guard had drugged Amy.

The car pulled out, giving the team a perfect view of the license plate. In the back seat, Amy held her phone up and her fingers fumbled across the screen as she rested her head against the door. The guard in the back seat with her had his attention out the window and didn't seem to notice.

"Where are they going?" Justin muttered as the car pulled out of view. His fingers danced across the keyboard, and he muttered a curse. "No other cameras around. I can't follow them."

Chris turned his attention back to his view of Tamsin, but she was furiously working on her computer, her expression almost serene. That sent a spike of fear up his spine. Tamsin was never serene, not like that. She was hiding her expression.

She was doing something that would get her in trouble.

"What happened last night?" Chris asked impatiently before he took a sip of his lukewarm coffee. Maybe the recording would give some answers to what was going on now.

"Already ahead of you," Justin reported. With a few taps, a feed of twelve blocks popped up, all of the hallway cameras on one screen.

"Is this playing?" Chris asked. "Or paused?" All of the hallways were empty.

"It's playing," Justin grumbled. "Nothing's happening."

"I've driven around long enough, I'm pulling over," Sierra announced. Moments later she parked the van and joined them staring at the unexciting screens.

"Can you speed it up?" Chris asked.

"Yeah, one sec." Justin tapped on the keyboard. There was a little wave at the top of the screens as the recording picked up speed.

"Stop," Chris ordered when he saw a flicker of movement.

Justin tapped the keys, and they watched as Tamsin stepped out of her room and encountered Steven. The video was now at double speed, Tamsin and Steven jerking about like marionettes on a string as they moved. In another situation, Chris might have found it amusing. When Tamsin went back in her room, Chris's shoulders relaxed.

Hopefully the rest of the night was uneventful.

Steven went down the hallway, his cronies following. Chris clenched his jaw when Tamsin's door opened and she slipped out to follow the guard.

Justin switched the feeds so the hallway Tamsin was in stayed on the main screen. When Chris saw the guards dragging in the struggling man, he couldn't stay in his seat anymore and jumped to his feet. His claws pushed at his fingertips, and his cat growled in the back of his mind as he watched her try door after door, unable to get in and hide.

He hissed a relieved breath when she managed to get in a room barely seconds before a group of guards came around the corner. He knew she eventually got back to her room safely, but seeing her in danger, even recorded danger, put him on edge.

One of the guards paused by the door she had entered, and Chris caught his breath again. The other guards kept moving. After a brief hesitation, the straggling guard rushed forward to keep up with the others.

"If she'd been any slower, they would've caught her," Sierra's quiet voice broke the silence.

They watched the events of the night on double speed, with most of the feeds from the hallways. Justin put up the hallways with the guards and captives on another large screen and studied it carefully.

"Where are they taking them?" Justin asked, his eyes glued to the clearly unwilling people the guards brought in. "And why don't any of my hacks go past that door?"

The groups of guards with captives went to a large door down another hallway. They paused, swiped their key, then disappeared inside.

"Thirty minutes. The guards come back out after thirty minutes. We need to figure out what they're doing in there," Sierra muttered.

Chris agreed, but that wasn't this mission. "No, we don't. Our mission is to extract Tamsin."

"But—" Sierra protested.

"We don't have the resources," Chris said firmly, glancing at the real-time feed of Tamsin in her lab. She stood from her computer and stretched, then sat again. "We're a small strike team. In and out with a specific mission."

"I don't like this," Sierra muttered.

"I know, and I don't either," Chris replied. "But we'll tell Damien, and he'll find out what's going on and get us in there. Besides, the three of us can't take on that type of firepower to rescue an unknown number of people."

With a soft, unhappy growl, Sierra settled in her chair.

"We don't even know why they are there," Justin added. "It could actually be legit."

Chris inclined his head, but he didn't agree. Something about all of this set his instincts screaming. Of course, when Nightfair hauled in a stray rogue, they didn't come quietly, either. The rogues fought wildly, especially the ones apprehended more recently.

Since that drug hit the scene.

His tiger stirred uneasily in the back of his mind. All they knew was that someone was using an unknown drug to make shifters go rogue. They had identified the wolf in charge, and he was caught.

Or was he?

Something about the entire situation seemed too easy. Like that wolf was set up to be the fall guy.

The activity in the halls continued until four in the morning, then everything went quiet until Tamsin came out of her room and headed to her lab, a determined look on her face. Chris turned his attention to the real-time feed and saw her still diligently working on her computer. She impatiently pushed back a lock of her beautiful hair but didn't pause whatever she was doing.

Her shoulders were slumped, and he wanted to ask Justin to zoom in on her face so he could see if she looked tired. He kept his mouth shut and silently watched the feed. Chris had thought about slipping in to get her out last night and now was glad he didn't. With all the activity, they would have been caught.

Tonight. He'd get her out tonight, no matter what. She'd seen something was going on and had to cooperate. There was no way she'd want to stay there. Especially with her assistant gone.

Justin started over the recording from the evening activity, and Chris noted the time that the guards started hauling people in. If that activity was the norm, then they'd have to extract her before then. This time, he'd bring Sierra with him. Between the two of them, they should be able to convince Tamsin to leave. Hopefully.

"What the fuck?" Justin cried.

Chris glanced over at him, then followed his gaze to the screen of real-time, not the recording. A man staggered out the back door of the building. He shook his head and stumbled around. His clothes were ripped, his face was bruised and bloody, and he moved like he hurt.

"Wait a minute," Sierra snarled. "He's the first guy they brought in last night."

Chris frowned and studied the man's face. "You sure?"

"Look below the bruising." She pointed at the screen. "It's him."

Justin put the feed from the back camera on a large monitor, and Chris suppressed a low growl. "You're right."

"What do we do?" Justin asked.

"Put up a loop, fast," Chris ordered. "Don't let them see him there at the back door."

Justin's fingers flew across the keys. "Done. But if they were watching…"

"Then we're screwed," Chris finished. "Sierra, let's go pick him up."

A feral smile crossed her face, making her look more cat than bear, and she jumped to her feet. "On it."

As she drove, Chris watched the man from the camera feed. He cautiously crossed the parking lot, his right arm over his stomach and his face twisted, clearly in pain. He reached the trees behind the building and stumbled forward. Chris watched him move through the trees until he disappeared out of sight.

"He's not moving fast, that's in our favor," Chris muttered.

"Where is he?" Sierra asked as she slowed for a stop light.

"Not sure," Chris replied. "We lost the camera feed."

"I'll track him." Justin stood and started stripping. Seconds later, a large gray wolf stood on the floor.

Chris took one of the surveillance harnesses out of the storage cabinet bolted to the van wall. This one was specially modified to fit a wolf shifter. Justin dropped his head and flattened his ears so Chris could slide it on. They quickly had it in place. It looked like a modified muzzle and slid over the head and ears, but it left the jaw open and free in case Justin needed to defend himself.

With a flick of a button, Chris turned on the camera and audio device. It would allow them to see what Justin did, as well as talk to him. In his wolf form, he'd be limited in his replies, but if it was critical, he could always shift to answer them. Chris glanced over at the wall of screens and saw the feed come up.

"Don't forget the collar," Sierra said from the front. "Mac'll have your hide if he gets nabbed by animal control, and we have to break him out."

Chris glanced to the front then back at Justin with a thoughtful look. Justin gave a wolfish grin, followed by an impatient yip when Chris didn't move to grab the collar.

He grinned and relented. Not like he would leave it off. If Justin was caught, the collar would make the human animal control more comfortable. For some unknown reason, a simple collar seemed to turn a wolf into a family pet in their eyes.

Too bad that didn't work for cats.

Of course, Chris and Sierra would be monitoring everything, so in the unlikely event he was caught, they'd intercept animal control before he could be brought in.

Justin flicked his ears a couple times and yawned, checking the fit and feel.

"Good?" Chris asked.

The wolf lifted his ears and sneezed, indicating it was acceptable.

"ETA?" Chris asked Sierra.

"Almost there. I'm going to pull over a few blocks away. Justin will have a bit of a run, but better than getting our van caught on their cameras," she replied.

Chris pushed the button on the microphone and leaned in close. "Radio check," he whispered to avoid getting feedback in the van, then released the button.

Justin sneezed again.

"Great," Chris replied. They were ready.

Sierra pulled over, and Chris opened the back door. Justin leaped out and immediately took off, quickly moving out of sight in the bushes. Chris closed the door and hurried to the screens.

Sierra had already pulled up the feed from Justin's camera, and they could see what he saw. The camera jerked back and forth as he ran, the trees and bushes racing past. Chris glanced at the feed from Tamsin's lab. She was still working at her computer, her shoulders tense.

"He's there," Sierra announced.

He briefly saw the lab building through the trees, then they had a great view of the ground as Justin cast about, tracking by scent. Chris looked at the screen with the visual from the back of the building and saw a shadow in the trees. If he didn't know it was Justin, he would have thought it was just a dog.

Justin spun about and faded into the shadows. Chris looked back at the wolf's camera feed to see him weaving through the trees. Sniffing noises loudly came through the comm and Chris bit back a sigh.

"We should have sent you," he muttered to Sierra.

"Why?" She glanced at him with a grin.

"Bears can track by scent just as well, and aren't so obnoxiously loud about it."

She laughed and shook her head. "Yeah, but we can't blend in as well."

On the screen, Justin jumped over bushes and continued to move away from the lab building.

"Where's he going?" Chris muttered.

Sierra jumped from her seat and went to the front of the van. "Don't know, but we'll go find him."

Chris pulled out his phone and opened the GPS tracker app. He typed in the code for the tracker on Justin's harness. A map appeared, and after a moment it zoomed in.

"Where to?" Sierra started up the van and pulled onto the street.

He zoomed out so he could see the streets and their dot. This app was one that a Nightfair tech had developed. It showed the user's location and the tracker dot as the destination. Even though Chris wasn't really familiar with this city, he was able to immediately tell they were going in the wrong direction.

"Turn around," he began and had to grab a hold of the counter as Sierra cranked the steering wheel, doing a turn that would make a stunt driver proud. "Shit, Sierra!"

"Directions," she snapped, unrepentant.

With a grumble under his breath about her driving, he looked at the phone. Based on the direction Justin was headed, he told her where to turn. Chris looked at the screen with Justin's camera feed, only to see bushes and trees moving past at a fast pace.

"His query must have started to feel better," Chris told Sierra. "He's running."

"That can't be good," she replied, and the engine revved as she picked up speed.

"Don't get a speeding ticket," Chris ordered.

"I won't," she snapped, but she slowed a bit.

He looked back at the screen to check on Tamsin and saw her still sitting at her desk. The next screen had the visual of the back door. As he watched it, the door burst open and a man raced out. He moved quickly but didn't turn to face the camera. In fact, it almost seemed he ducked so his face avoided it.

He moved easily, so his injuries either weren't too severe, or they didn't bother him. He didn't hesitate as he raced into the trees, running like his life depended upon it. He headed in the opposite direction as the captive they were tracking.

Chris narrowed his eyes, trying to figure out a way they could pick him up, too. If they got this first man, then circled around... He looked at the map, tracing the roads with his eyes as he plotted a course.

It would take time, but was doable.

The back door to the building opened again on the screen and several guards piled out. They paused and examined the area, a couple raising their noses and breathing deeply as wolves do when they're scenting. Then they split up with three heading in the direction of the man who'd escaped, and three going the same way Justin had gone.

"Crap," Chris snarled.

"What?" Sierra demanded.

"Justin's about to have company."

Chris studied the map then pushed the button to activate the microphone. "Are you hot on his trail?"

Justin gave a bark and kept running.

"Is the trail fresh?" Chris asked him.

Justin barked again.

Chris looked at the screen. "We're going to try to get ahead of you. Watch your six, you might get company soon."

Justin yipped in acknowledgment and kept running.

Chris released the button and gave Sierra directions. With their speed, they'd get ahead of the other guy and hopefully trap him. They had no idea what the man's frame of mind was, and he would likely think they were part of the team hunting him, those who had captured him.

Chris went to the cabinet and took out the holster for a tranquilizer gun. If they encountered any guards, he'd rather knock them out and slip away than fight. The tranq guns Nightfair used had been created specifically for shifter enforcement use. They looked like normal guns, and the tranq darts fired in a manner very similar to a bullet. Except they were darts with tranquilizers in them.

If a human saw the gun, they'd think it was a normal handgun, unless they examined it closely.

He selected a gun and loaded it with several darts. Then he went back to the map. They were just about there.

"Turn down the next street and pull over," Chris said. "We're going to box him in."

"Human? Or should I shift?" Sierra said as she pulled over and turned off the van.

"Human," Chris said. "We'll be less likely to startle him."

They jumped out of the van and closed the door. Chris looked at the tracker and saw Justin's dot closing in.

"This way," he said, plotting an intercept course to the dot.

Sierra matched his pace, rushing alongside him.

They reached the edge of the trees, and he paused to look at the phone again. Justin's dot hurried in their direction.

"Chris," Sierra said urgently.

He glanced up at her to see she was watching something in the trees. He followed her gaze and saw a pair of eyes gleaming a few feet in the woods. They were up high, human height, but glowed as only a shifter's would.

They'd either found the escaped captive, or the guards had just found them. Either way, things were about to get interesting.

Chapter 9

Tamsin hurried down the hallway, intent on going to her room and getting the hell out of there. She reached the hallway that led to the Animal Care Facility and paused.

She had several test subjects in that room. Ones who were recently given a dose of her serum. She couldn't leave without checking on them. Even if it increased the odds of her getting caught. Plus, she had to remove any doses of her serum that were there. Make sure there were no notes. No traces.

A cold knot in her stomach, she turned down the hallway. Something pushed in the back of her mind as she went. Her cat paced in her thoughts, trying to share something with her. Finally, she understood what it was trying to tell her. None of the guards had gone down here last night. At least, not when she was following them.

They must not be interested in this wing. Did that mean this area was safe?

She realized she'd never seen any guards down this hallway at all, although she'd caught their scents frequently, but never Steven's.

With the Animal Care Facility down here, she thought this would be a prime area for protection. But why had she never seen them? *Whatever.* It wasn't a puzzle she could solve now. She had one thing she had to do. *Get out.*

She hurried down the hallway, trying to move quickly but not look like she was rushing.

Hurry, but don't look *like you're hurrying.*

It was still very early, and she didn't encounter anyone. The door to the Animal Care Facility was plain, with a small label that simply said *ACF*.

Tamsin took a deep breath and used her ID to open the door. Immediately, she was overwhelmed by the musk of the test animals. The predominant scent was of rodents and the shredded paper used for the bedding. Based on the smells, Faith, the lab tech who took care of the animals, hadn't arrived yet.

That was good. Fewer people to ask questions.

She first went to the locked fridge where the samples were kept. All of the lead scientists had keys to open the padlock. ID cards didn't work here. It was just an old-fashioned lock.

The fridge was kept very tidy, with the various samples in locked metal bins with labels on the ends. Her mouth went dry when she pulled out her bin.

The lock was missing.

Her hands shook slightly as she opened the lid. Four samples sat in plastic holders.

There should have been eight.

She'd visited the ACF the day before yesterday. Yesterday had been Amy's turn. Her assistant hadn't said anything about missing samples. Her stomach churned. She trusted Amy.

Had she been stealing the serum? Or had she not realized some were missing?

Tamsin took a deep breath and decided it didn't matter. She'd take the remaining samples and get them out. She needed something to safely carry the vials in. They couldn't just be loose in her lab coat. She sat the box on the counter and looked around the lab. Her gaze landed on a pile of newspaper next to the shredder, and a slow smile curved her lips.

Tamsin quickly wrapped the vials and tucked them out of sight. She closed the sample box and slid it back into place in the fridge, just as she heard the tell-tale click of the door lock. She jerked and almost pulled the box back out. She shoved it back in place and slammed the fridge door. Her heart in her throat, she slid the lock on the fridge and locked it with a *click*. She schooled her expression before she looked at the door.

Had one of the guards come this way?

When Tamsin saw the door open to reveal the lab tech, she briefly closed her eyes in relief. She opened them and met Faith's surprised brown eyes.

"What are you doing here so early?" Faith asked curiously as she quickly averted her eyes and carefully shut the door behind her.

She was a bit taller than Tamsin, and her brown hair was tightly pulled back in a braid. Tamsin had never seen her hair in any other style. Her lab coat was clearly pressed, and she had on her usual khaki pants and sneakers. Faith scanned the room, visually checking on all her charges.

In the back of Tamsin's mind, her cat purred. It liked Faith.

"Oh, I know," Faith continued in her typical flat tone. "You want to check on your mice."

"Right, I wanted to see how they were doing," Tamsin replied, glad she had gotten the vials out of sight.

Faith went around the room turning on the full-spectrum lights above the cages. "Time to wake up," she repeated to each cage as she turned on the lights.

The animals reacted to her voice and the lights, and shortly, the room was full of scratching and squeaking from the various rodents.

"The notes on the test subjects are right here." Faith nodded to a notebook stored on a shelf above the rodent cage for Tamsin's subjects. "Amy checked on them yesterday. I've been keeping a close eye on your subject Alpha."

Tamsin moved to the cage and looked at the mouse in question. Hers were all deer mice with dark brown fur. The rodent looked back at her and twitched its nose. *That was new.* The first time she got near this mouse, it ran and hid. It was now showing interest in her, which was a much less timid behavior.

Due to the nature of her research, she had specifically requested the most timid mice. She'd even developed a test to determine their personalities. Subject Alpha was the first one she'd tested here and happened to be incredibly timid. The mouse was literally afraid of his own shadow. Well, it had been.

"Oh?" Tamsin said, not hiding her interest, and wanting more details.

Faith continued turning on the lights. She next went to a large plastic bin against the wall and opened the airtight lid. She reached in and pulled out a scoop of the animal food, not answering Tamsin.

Tamsin watched, curbing her impatience, as Faith methodically went from cage to cage, refilling the food. The food dispensers were made to hold several days' worth of food, so it could have waited. However, Faith had an order to how she did things. That order couldn't be interrupted, or she became upset and simply stopped.

Tamsin had also learned that it did no good to try to help. That also disrupted the other woman's routine.

As Faith began cleaning the bedding for the cages, Tamsin looked back at her not-so-timid mouse. The rodents could smell her predator and were often afraid of her until they got used to her. She made it a point to visit them often to get them used to her. She handled treats and put them in the cage.

Now, most of her mice were used to her, and although they wouldn't come forward, they didn't try to hide and escape. Except for subject Alpha. He was actually at the side of the cage, sniffing at her direction.

She couldn't leave him behind. She couldn't leave any of them behind.

Not only had they been injected with various levels of her serum, but they were also starting to show reactions. Perhaps she simply needed to give the doses over time. Like a vaccine.

Faith finally finished her routine and approached Tamsin.

"Yes, look." Faith carefully opened the cage and reached in to scoop up the subject mouse. All of the mice watched her, their little noses twitching curiously. Faith was human and had an affinity for animals. Tamsin had never seen one afraid of her. When she'd commented on it once, Faith had shrugged and said she understood them.

Subject Alpha sat calmly in Faith's hand and looked at them. Tamsin reached over to the container full of treats and took one out. The mouse ran to the edge of Faith's hand and quivered with excitement. It practically grabbed the treat out of Tamsin's hand.

In the cage, the other mice started squeaking, their noses and whiskers twitching.

"They want treats, too," Faith said. "It's only fair."

"They're acting much less timid," Tamsin commented as she pulled out more treats. She carefully opened the cage and held them in the flat of her hand. The mice hesitated, then one by one raced forward, grabbed a treat, then ran away from her hand to munch on it.

She closed the cage lid, then looked back at subject Alpha. The mouse calmly ate its treat while sitting on Faith's hand. Tamsin lifted her hand and held it in front of the mouse, prepared for it to jump off in panic.

It paused and looked up at her, then continued to munch on the treat, twitching whiskers the only sign of its wariness. Faith watched the mouse impassively, but Tamsin knew she cared for the animals. If Tamsin just took them, Faith could get in trouble. Possibly even fired. The woman lived for these animals.

"I need to take my subjects," Tamsin stated, deciding to get directly to the point. Faith would appreciate that more than any dancing around the subject.

"Okay," Faith replied. "For how long?"

Tamsin's took a deep breath. She didn't want to lie to Faith. The woman seemed to have a sense for when someone was dishonest with her. Faith didn't seem to fully understand most interactions, but Tamsin had been there when someone had lied to her, and she'd reacted. It had only been a slight widening of her eyes, but she did it every time.

"I'm leaving the lab. Not coming back." Tamsin studied Faith for her reaction to the news.

Faith kept her gaze on subject Alpha and didn't look up to meet Tamsin's eyes.

She put the mouse back in the cage and closed the top. "No one said anything to me."

"No one knows. But you," Tamsin replied softly.

Faith's surprised gaze darted up to meet Tamsin's, then returned to lock onto the mice.

"I can pack up some food. You need to change their water every day," Faith answered, not addressing Tamsin's comment.

"I have to sneak out," Tamsin admitted, deciding to trust Faith. "Travel light. I'm going home to Oakdale."

A wistful look crossed Faith's face. "I've never been to Oakdale. It sounds like it would be a nice place to call home."

That took Tamsin aback. She'd always lived in Oakdale. She couldn't imagine living anywhere else.

"When you finish here," Tamsin told her, "you can have a home in Oakdale."

She had a lot of contacts and knew she could find Faith a job. The woman was amazing with her charges. Tamsin might even be able to convince her Alpha to make Faith a member of the pride. Then she'd never be alone. There was also the Nightfair Co. They might be a mercenary group, but they had support people and might have a place for her.

Faith moved to the food bin and paused, not otherwise reacting to Tamsin's statement. She stood still for several heartbeats, then scooped out some food. She moved to a cabinet and retrieved a bag for the food.

Tamsin frowned. That seemed like a lot of food. She'd said she had to travel light. She couldn't take that much. Faith grabbed another bag and went back to the food bin, pouring another scoop into the second bag.

"I need to—" Tamsin began.

"You have to have enough food in the container for three days," Faith interrupted, speaking quickly. "Three days. Each bag holds enough for three days. This is six days of food. Six days, then you will be out of food."

"I don't know—"

"On this bag is the label for our food supplier. Call them when you have almost finished the first bag. They will get you more food in two days. They are fast. But you want to be prepared for something to go wrong."

"Go wrong?" Tamsin glanced at the label. It had a company's name, phone number, and the brand of food.

"I kept a few of these bags in case we needed the information. In case someone forgot where to get the food," Faith explained in response to Tamsin's glance.

Tamsin nodded. "But what could go wrong?"

"Travel delays. Shipment delays. Other issues. It is important you feed these mice the same food. You don't want something to make them sick." Faith looked sternly at Tamsin's ear, her version of strong eye contact.

"Right, I don't want them sick," Tamsin responded to Faith.

Faith gave a sharp nod and set the bags of food on the counter. "In three days, you have to get more food. That way you can still have three days of food in the feed container." Faith looked at Tamsin's ear again. "Three days. You have to get the food in three days."

"Okay, I'll order food in three days," Tamsin agreed.

Faith moved to a storage closet that Tamsin had never looked in. "My business is the mice. I take care of them.

Now you have to take care of them. Promise me you will. You will take good care of them. Promise."

Sometimes Tamsin found it odd that Faith was so worried about these lab animals. They were test subjects. Experimented upon. Faith knew that. She was there when they were injected, or when their blood was drawn.

In fact, Faith insisted on being there when anything was done to them. Tamsin suddenly understood. Faith was always there to make sure the animals were treated as well as they could be. Treated as gently as possible. She knew this was their role in life, but she wanted to make it as good as she could.

"I'll take good care of them," Tamsin promised.

She thought about trying to take Faith with her, but her cat sent a sharp stab of denial in her mind. *Right.* There was no way Faith would voluntarily leave her animals.

"Do you have anything I can use to take them with me?" Tamsin asked.

Faith stepped out of the closet with a small cage in her hand and held it up. "This."

Tamsin frowned. The small metal cage was not what she expected. It had a plastic bottom, white wire sides with a water bottle sticking on the side, and some sort of tube on the other side and other tubes in the center. It had a wheel and a small house, too. It looked like some sort of mouse play gym.

"I don't think—"

"It breaks down, like this." Faith disassembled the contraption and soon had it laying in small pieces. "I saw it online and thought it would be a good retirement home. You take it. Have them live in it."

Faith's voice lacked emotion, as it always did, but she gently ran her hand over the cage.

"I will," Tamsin pledged, frantically trying to figure out a way to get all of this out without anyone noticing. "I'll make sure they're happy."

Faith nodded briskly and went back to the closet. This time she emerged with a small brown box that had little holes near the top and a folded bag. "This is good for travel only. They will eat through it if left in there too long. Don't keep them in here for longer than four hours."

"Okay." Tamsin watched Faith put some of the shredded paper in the bottom of the box.

She added a block that looked like a solid granola bar along with some chopped up carrots. "These are treats, but will keep them occupied and not hungry."

"What about water?" Tamsin studied the small box. "Will they be okay without water for a few hours?"

Faith nodded. "They'll get fluid from the treats. But it will only be good for four hours."

She scooped out the four mice and put them in the box. Faith closed the lid with a soft command to the mice. "Be safe. Goodbye."

Faith set the box on the counter, then put some of the clean shredded bedding in a plastic bag. She took the folded bag and opened it. It was a large messenger bag, the type you'd see at trade shows. It had the logo of a feed store on it. Faith put the broken-down wire cage in first, then added the bags with the bedding and food. She carefully slid the water bottle in next to everything else.

Tamsin studied the bag dubiously. She had to get out with her duffel and the mice. She'd have to change her plans if she added that bag, too. But there was no way she would leave it behind.

"You take them. Keep them warm," Faith ordered. "I'll get this outside. Put it by the trees where you like to walk. Hide it. You get it when you go."

Relief flooded Tamsin's body. She had no idea how Faith knew what she was worried about, but she was glad the other woman had a solution.

"They let you go outside alone?" Tamsin asked. She'd taken a few walks with Faith, and the guards had always been with them. She'd thought it had been for both of them, but perhaps it was just for her.

Faith nodded. "The guards don't like me. They say I'm weird. They don't bother me."

Tamsin felt giddy. Not only would Faith be safe, but she could help her get the supplies outside.

"Thank you," Tamsin said simply.

Faith picked up the box with the mice and handed it to Tamsin. "You will treat them right. You always do. I know you won't hurt them."

"Do you want to come with me?" Tamsin asked, even though she knew the answer.

Faith shook her head and looked around the room. "They need me. The others aren't so nice. I have to protect them."

Tamsin swallowed at the hard note in the woman's voice. Faith would stand up for the animals. Hopefully, it wouldn't get her in trouble.

"When you are finished here, find me in Oakdale," Tamsin said again.

"How?" Faith looked at Tamsin's ear, then her gaze darted to a spot on the wall.

"I'll give you my number," Tamsin answered. "And you can give me your number, too."

Faith stared at the wall for a few seconds, then nodded and pulled out her phone. Tamsin set down the box with the mice and pulled out her phone. They exchanged phones.

Faith looked at Tamsin's phone and hesitated. "Your phone is almost dead. You need to charge it. You should always keep it charged."

"Thank you," Tamsin replied. "I'll do that as soon as I get someplace safe."

Quickly, Tamsin put in her number, then added Chris's, just like she'd done with Amy. If she knew Damien's number, she'd put it in instead, but she didn't. The head of Nightfair would be a better contact for Faith, but it wasn't an option.

"I'm giving you two numbers." Tamsin typed in both contacts. "Mine, and Chris O'Neal's."

"Who is Chris O'Neal?"

"He's a… friend. He's part of Nightfair. If you need help and can't reach me, call him." She returned Faith's phone and took hers back.

"Why would I need help?" Faith asked, a tilt to her head.

"I don't know if you will," Tamsin lied. Faith's eyes widened slightly, showing she caught it, too. "Okay, so there's something wrong about this place. That's why I'm leaving. But they won't let me just walk out. So, I have to sneak out."

Faith took a deep breath and nodded. "Is Chris O'Neal in Oakdale, too?"

Tamsin picked up the box with the mice. "He lives there, too."

Faith studied the cages around her. "I'll call if I need help."

"I have to go." Tamsin hesitated, then asked, "can I hug you?"

Faith looked at her, briefly meeting her eyes before glancing away. She considered it, then answered with a jerky nod. Tamsin stepped in and wrapped her arms around the woman, careful not to jostle the box with the mice in it.

Faith held still with her arms at her sides, her shoulders stiff. Faith didn't like to be touched or hugged.

Tamsin considered Faith a friend, and never touched her without asking first. Not even a touch on the shoulder or hand. The fact that Faith let her give her a hug was monumental for the woman. It also told Tamsin that Faith considered her a friend, too.

"Be safe," Faith whispered as Tamsin stepped back.

"You too."

Tamsin buttoned her lab coat and slipped the box of mice underneath.

"You can tell there is a box there," Faith stated.

"Yes, in person," Tamsin replied, glancing at the sharp outlines in her coat. "But the cameras won't know what it is."

Cameras. Her gaze snapped to the camera in the corner.

Had she just shown everything to them?

"They don't watch me." Faith followed her gaze to the camera.

"They don't? How do you know?"

"There is no red light," Faith explained.

Tamsin looked back at the camera and realized the other woman was right. "Why not?"

Faith shrugged. "I don't know. But I have my own eyes. I make sure no one messes with my charges."

Tamsin followed Faith's gaze to a small shelf holding a plant. The pot was oddly decorated, and filigreed. She studied it, and realized there was a camera in there. It was positioned to keep an eye on all the animal cages. Not the door, nor the fridge, only what Faith considered important.

It was odd that the animals weren't monitored, but it wasn't something she needed to worry about right now.

One of the cages rattled, and Faith glanced over at it. She moved in that direction. "Snack-time."

Tamsin slipped out of the lab and hurried down the hallway. She took deep breaths through her mouth and nose, checking for tell-tale scents of the guards.

Just as she reached the door to her room, she smelled Steven. Her heart in her throat, she swiped her badge and the door unlocked. She stepped into the room just as he came around the corner.

"Tamsin," he called.

She grabbed the mouse box from under her coat and quickly set in on the floor behind the door. She moved back to the door and held it mostly closed as she looked into the hallway.

Steven approached with two guards behind him.

"Why aren't you at your lab?" he asked.

Was he her keeper now?

What business of his was it where she was?

"Why do you care?" she snapped.

"Something happen? Or are you missing your assistant already?" he smirked, setting her teeth on edge.

"I'm not feeling well, if you must know." She replied with a sniff. "I may be coming down with something."

He took a deep breath, then a fast step back. "You smell like rodents."

"I'm a research scientist," she said dryly. "What am I *supposed* to smell like? Roses?"

He took another step back with a curl of his lip.

Was he afraid of rodents?

"Disease-filled creatures," he snarled.

"You're afraid of mice," Tamsin stated.

She took a step forward, and he took another fast step back, the two guards behind him backing up as well to stay out of his way. She managed to suppress her smile.

"You're probably not feeling well because you stink of rodents," he growled, ignoring her comment.

She glanced behind him and widened her eyes. "Oh, was that a mouse I just saw?"

He whirled around, his head twisting as he searched for the tiny threat. "Where? *Where*?"

"I must have been mistaken," she said sweetly. "Oh, was there something you needed?"

He didn't stop looking for the non-existent mouse on the ground. "No, you go about your business."

She stepped back into her room and closed the door. He didn't even glance in her direction, but continued to scan the floor for the minuscule threat.

"Let's get out of here," he muttered to the other two guards.

The three turned and headed back the way they came. If she wasn't planning on escaping right then, she would have found it amusing, and might have even followed them.

The power of the mouse.

It also explained why she didn't see many guards in the hallway for the ACF. Maybe Faith *would* be safe.

She stepped back into her room and locked the door. She pulled her packed duffel from under the bed and unzipped it. She quickly moved the rolled clothing around, making a hole for the mouse box. She slid the box in and zipped the bag, leaving it slightly open above the mice. She picked up the bag and let out a breath when the clothes didn't move.

The box was secure.

Tamsin quickly pulled her hair back in a braid and secured it with the hair tie she'd left on the nightstand next to the bed. She didn't want it getting in her way. She moved a chair beneath the spot where Chris had dropped down. She was a cat, but she was still on the short side in her human form. She *might* have been able to jump up and grab it like he did, but she didn't want to take that chance.

Tamsin still had to give a small jump to reach the tile. Her hand hit it, and it bounced up. She jumped again, this time grabbing the beam. She used her other hand to push the ceiling tile to the side. Once it was out of the way, she dropped back down to the chair again.

Before she could move her bag up, she had to see what she was dealing with.

Was there even a place for her to put her bag?

She chewed her lip and considered calling Chris. He could take over the cameras and she could just walk out the front door.

No. She'd get out on her own. At least, she'd try this, and she could call him if it didn't work.

With a deep breath, Tamsin jumped and grabbed the beam with both hands. She used her momentum to pull herself up. It was harder than it looked, and her arms protested. She glanced around, shifting her eyes to her cat so she could see in the dark. Ahead of her was a place where she could put her bag.

The rest of the area was mostly open. There were no wall markers or anything. It was like a big open room.

Where was the front door?

She dropped down and landed on the chair. She stared at her duffel bag containing Chris's phone.

Did she try it on her own, or call for help?

She took a deep breath, stepped off the chair, and reached for her bag.

Chapter 10

Chris slid his phone in his pocket and widened his stance, ready to attack or defend. He shifted his eyes to his tiger's so he could see through the shadows, and everything burst into sharp relief.

He still couldn't clearly see more than the eyes in the trees. They had hidden themselves in deep shadow, watching them.

Sierra took a few steps away from him and assumed a similar posture. They were both as prepared as they could be. He had no idea where Justin was, or how soon he would arrive, so he couldn't be counted to help. But it didn't matter. For all intents and purposes, right now they were on their own.

Whoever was in the tree line had frozen. The other shifter studied them, then rushed forward with heavy steps. Chris didn't move his hand to the tranq gun. He wasn't sure if this was going to be a fight, and he was sure there were others coming. Soon.

The escaped captive burst through the foliage. He was the same one they'd seen on the camera.

He staggered a few steps, his hand reached out imploring. "Help me," he rasped.

Sierra darted forward and slid her shoulder under his arm, supporting him. Chris stayed where he was, eyes searching the trees behind the man. He gave his senses over to his primal half, allowing his tiger to come forward. He drew in a deep breath and even opened his mouth to deeply pull in all the scents around him.

The foliage the man had crushed in his uneven movement flooded his senses. The sharp scent mixed with the stench of fear pouring off the man.

No, wolf. He was a wolf shifter.

Chris pushed past that to pick up any other scents. Pine sap along with the scent of oak trees melded with dirt and the light musk of squirrels and other small animals.

He didn't pick up the scents of any other shifters. Either the guards were somehow masking their scents, or they were nowhere nearby. He didn't relax, though. Just because he didn't pick up anything else, didn't mean they were safe.

The man Sierra supported stumbled alongside her, drawing Chris's attention. He looked like he could barely manage to take another step. He seemed to be leaning all his weight on her. Chris didn't step in to help. If this was a trap, he needed to be free to defend them.

That was also why he didn't pull out the tranq gun, now, too. Judging by the size of the man, plus the way Sierra moved, the man was heavy. She was a shifter, stronger than a normal human, but shifters were also heavier than humans, too. If he knocked the guy out, it would take both of them to move him. Better for him to move on his own, for now.

Chris wanted to race back through the trees and see if Tasman had slipped out, too. His tiger growled lightly in the back of his mind. It didn't like this. Not at all. He reminded himself that no matter what, he was going to get her out that night. It had looked like there might be a window of inactivity before the guards started messing with captives. That was when he would make his move.

"Chris, I need your help," Sierra cried.

He looked over and saw the man collapsing, slowly folding to the ground. She was going down with him, unable to bear his weight on her own.

"Let him go," Chris ordered.

Sierra gave him a narrow-eyed glance and finished lowering the man to the ground.

Chris pulled out the tranq gun and handed it to her. Her eyes widened in surprise, but she took it from his hand.

"What—"

"I'm going to carry him on my shoulders," Chris explained. "One of us needs to be free to defend us. If he gets aggressive, tranq him."

She nodded sharply and checked the gun. She flipped the safety off. If she needed to fire it, she could.

"Ranger roll," she stated with a nod, and her eyes went the golden brown of her bear before she turned her attention to the area around them.

Chris bent down to the man and positioned him so he was on his back. This was a technique Damien had them practice frequently. With a roll-like movement, Chris had the man up on his shoulders and he was on his knees.

The entire maneuver only took him seconds, and in the next breath, he was standing with the unconscious man over his shoulders. He wrapped his left arm around the man's leg, and grabbed the man's arm, leaving his right hand free.

Chris knew from experience he could carry a man heavier than this wolf using this method. Not far, but that didn't matter now. The man was heavy, but not heavier than Chris, and the van was close.

Sierra's eyes met his when he got to his feet. She didn't give him the tranq gun, even though his hand was free. If they needed to knock someone out, it would most likely be the man over Chris's shoulders.

He knew if they had to fight, she'd give him the gun and shift to bear form. For now, though, the goal was to get the man out and to safety.

He took the lead heading to the van, letting his tiger's senses lead the way. His mouth open, he deeply drew in surrounding scents, his eyes shifted to better see in the trees.

"Where's Justin?" Sierra muttered from behind him.

He was worried about that, too. Justin should have joined them by now.

"Wonder if he ran into the guards," Chris suggested.

"We'll know when we get back to the van," she answered, her voice holding the growl of her bear.

Chris couldn't glance back at her without turning his entire body, thanks to the man over his shoulders. He hoped the growl was only in her voice, and she hadn't started to shift. Although no one was around them right now, it didn't mean someone couldn't stumble upon them. The last thing they needed was to explain this situation.

One unconscious man over his shoulder with a bear trailing behind him. Yeah, he could just see trying to explain that. Although the situation was serious, his tiger huffed with amusement in the back of his mind and urged him to have Sierra shift. Plus, she could carry the man on *her* back. As a bear, she'd have no issues with the weight.

His tiger wasn't wrong, he thought. *But, no.* It was a bad idea.

"Keep it together," he ordered.

"I am," she said. Her voice sounded more human, but still held a touch of a growl.

Something caught his tiger's attention. Chris looked into the trees to his right.

"Something's coming," Sierra said in warning.

He stopped walking and turned his body to see her staring in the same direction that had caught his tiger's attention. Sierra lifted her head to the air and slightly parted her lips. He did the same, but wasn't able to pick up what was approaching.

Sierra's shoulders relaxed. "It's Justin."

"You sure?" he asked.

She nodded and tapped her nose. "No mistaking it. Not just wolf, but definitely him. Bear's never wrong."

Many people thought a wolf's sense of smell was the best among the animals. They were wrong. Nothing topped a bear. Chris grinned at her smug tone and continued the trek to the van. The man on his shoulders was completely limp, telling him he was still unconscious. Chris was under no illusion that he would stay that way.

"Good. We'll need his help," he replied, trying to move quickly.

"He's still out?" she asked, moving up next to him, but still scanning the surrounding area.

"So far," was his simple reply.

He listened closely to the man's heartbeat. If it changed, he'd have to drop him to the ground immediately. He'd known of injured shifters whose

123

primal sides woke before the human sides. Sensing danger, they'd shift and attack.

Sierra nodded, knowing what he meant.

"No sign of the guards," she reported, sounding uneasy.

He echoed her feelings. When they'd watched the guards on the camera earlier, they'd been moving fast. He expected them to arrive soon. There were too many of them for the small Nightfair crew to fight. Their best course of action was to escape. The last thing they wanted was to become additions to whatever plans they had for the captives.

If he was a captive, though, would it be easier to get Tamsin out?

He quickly dismissed the thought. With Justin's hacking, it would be better to take over the cameras and slip in. He wanted to know how this man escaped. Had they grown lax in security, or had something happened and he took the opportunity?

And then there was the second person who escaped.

Maybe that's what has the guards occupied. They didn't realize they lost two subjects.

"Justin's here," Sierra announced.

Seconds later the bushes next to her rustled, and the wolf appeared. He took in Chris's burden and immediately dashed into the trees behind him.

"What's he doing?" Sierra asked, stopping in her tracks.

"Probably going to cover our tracks. Maybe flush some critters in the trail," Chris answered, seeing the opening in the trees. The van was just ahead.

"Should we wait for him?"

"No. Keep going. We need to get this guy in the van. Justin won't go far."

He paused in the tree line, in view of the van. Sierra stepped forward and inhaled deeply. "We're upwind," she muttered.

She moved to the side, and Chris impatiently waited for her to check the area. They had to make sure no one had messed with the van. Sierra would pick up any stray scents.

He watched her move in a wide circle around the van, then gradually move in closer. Finally, she was next to the van and dropped down to a crouch, taking a deep breath.

She moved to the back and did the same. Justin burst from the bushes behind him and gave a sharp bark.

"Time's up, we gotta go." Chris hurried to the van.

Sierra unlocked it and got inside. Justin jumped in next to her and shifted to his human form. The harness slid off his head. He caught it and put it on the chair. The two of them moved forward and took the unconscious man off Chris's shoulders and put him on the floor of the van.

Chris felt like he was floating without the man's weight on him. He jumped into the van and closed the door. Sierra moved to the front of the van to start it up. Justin grabbed a pair of pants and quickly put them on. Shifters were casual about nudity, but it was still considered polite to get dressed after you shifted.

"What happened?" Justin asked as Sierra put the van in gear and pulled onto the road.

Chris quickly filled him in on the man's arrival and subsequent collapse as he pulled out a tranquilizer injection and an alcohol swab.

"Why the tranq?" Justin asked, watching Chris's movements.

"We need to get him someplace safe," Chris replied. "I don't want him waking up and panicking in the van."

"How about our motel?" Sierra asked. "My room's on the ground floor, and the door faces the back fence."

"Not as secure as I like, but our options are limited," Chris replied. "I'd prefer to take him back to HQ, but we can't go back to Oakdale without Tamsin, and need to make sure he's stable. Any other suggestions?"

He met Justin's gaze and the other man shook his head. "Nope."

"Then do it."

Chris and Justin watched the unconscious man on the drive back to the motel. His breathing was shallow, and he had a light sheen of sweat on his skin.

"He doesn't look too good," Justin commented. "What did they give him?"

"Don't know," Chris answered, agreeing with Justin's assessment.

Overall, shifters were tough and didn't require much in terms of medical care. Each pack or pride had their own medical team, and they didn't involve the human health care system. If they were in Oakdale, they'd take him to their medic. But they weren't.

"Is there a local pack we could go to?" Sierra asked from the front.

Chris ran over the briefing information Mac had given him. This was one of those odd places with few shifter groups. Probably why the lab was set up here. But that also meant any shifter captives they brought in, like the man in front of them, were taken from farther away. That would make tracking them even more difficult.

"No, we're on our own," Chris replied. "Until we get Tamsin and head back to Oakdale."

"What about the other person who escaped?" Sierra asked.

"What's that?" Justin looked up sharply.

Before Chris could explain, they pulled into the motel parking lot, and Sierra backed the van in front of her room and parked it. Justin opened the back door.

Chris grabbed the man's upper body and Justin lifted his legs. Sierra raced ahead and opened the door. They took him into Sierra's room and put him on the bed.

Sierra took the man's vitals and Justin went back out to the van.

Chris pulled out his phone to text Mac about the events and saw the screen was blank. He pushed the start button and it didn't light up.

"Crap, my phone's dead."

Justin raced back into the room. "We have a situation."

Chris raised one eyebrow and gave Justin a half smile. "You think?"

"No." He shook his head. "A new one. The fire alarm's going off at the lab."

Cold dread crawled up Chris's spine and he raced back to the van. Justin jumped ahead of him and they wasted precious seconds as the surveillance system booted up.

"How do you know about the alarm?" Chris asked as he stared at the black screens.

"I have my phone linked to the emergency systems in the building," Justin answered.

"Did it just go off?" Chris asked.

Justin looked at his phone, and when his expression met Chris's, his stomach churned.

"No. It went off ten minutes ago. Shortly after we got him in the van."

Ten minutes. The words echoed in his mind. A lot could happen in ten minutes.

Just then the screens came to life and Justin pulled up the building feeds. People were hurrying up and down the hallways, but there was no sign of a fire. The camera feed in front of the building showed a fire truck with several firefighters milling around.

"There's no sense of urgency," Chris commented.

"False alarm?" Justin asked.

Chris didn't answer, his eyes searching through the crowd for Tamsin's familiar features. He didn't see her with the others outside. He snapped his attention to the small squares of the hallways and her lab on the video screens.

"Where's Tamsin?" he muttered.

Justin scanned the screens, too, and shook his head. "She's not there."

Dread crawled up Chris's spine. "Where is she?"

Did the guards take her, too?

Chapter 11

It took everything Tamsin had to not run to the tree line. She'd never thought walking calmly would be so hard. Her duffel bag hung over her shoulder, and the fire alarm screamed from the building behind her.

She tried to move like a casual visitor. It helped that her lab coat was tucked in her bag, and the bag looked like something someone would take to a gym.

The phone Chris had given her was in her pocket, and she clenched her hand to keep from reaching in and pulling it out. *Again.* She'd already sent him a couple texts with no reply.

Did that stupid phone even work?

She'd sent the first text before she began her nightmare journey through the ceiling.

Her mouth grew dry, and she forced her thoughts away from that. That was one memory that would no doubt return to haunt her in her sleep. The only blessing was the mice had remained quiet. Were still quiet.

She hoped they were okay. And hadn't chewed through the box.

In her mind, she could just see them happily chewing a hole in the box, then escaping into the bag to gnaw through her clothes. That would be just grand. Her panther snapped its teeth in her mind in mock threat.

Well, she couldn't check on them yet. She had to get to the bag Faith left her and keep going. A cold knot sat in her stomach. If Chris didn't get her message, she was on her own. She had never been permitted to leave the facility, so had no knowledge about this town.

She didn't know how big it was, or even if the lab was close to anything. They'd picked her up from the airport and drove about an hour to get here. When she'd taken her walks, all she saw was road and trees.

She could be in the middle of no-where for all she knew.

She was feeling like an idiot for trusting them. But it had been a job. A dream job.

You know the old saying, if it looked too good to be true, it probably was.

A sense of urgency rode her. She could move faster if she stashed her bag. Then she could roam around and get a good feel for the area. But she didn't want to leave her bag, or the mice. She'd promised Faith she'd take care of them, and she planned to. But she had to be someplace safe to do so.

She glanced back at the building to see people pouring out with irritated frowns on their faces. It was a sea of white with all the lab coats. Her heart raced in her chest.

Where were all the guards?

There should be a bunch of people dressed in the black of guard uniforms, but they were conspicuous in their absence. She kept walking, chilled with the thought that someone would recognize her and call out to her. Her mouth was dry and her hands icy with fear by the time she made it to the tree line at the street corner. She turned and let out a small sigh of relief when the trees blocked her from view.

She left the sidewalk and stepped into the trees. She crouched down and looked back at the building. People were milling and talking in small groups. No one looked in her direction. No one had seemed to notice that she was walking away. And there were still no guards in the groups.

The high-pitched sound of emergency vehicle sirens in the distance pierced the air, and she realized why she saw no guards. *The captives.* They were probably trying to secure them somewhere, in case emergency personnel entered the building.

At least they weren't looking for her.

Tamsin needed to get going, but she had to find that bag with the mouse food. She bit her lip, looking around.

Where would Faith put it?

She tried to think like a human, but had no idea how far into the woods Faith would go. She closed her eyes, irritated with herself. She should have known better and clarified *exactly* where it would be.

Tamsin took in a deep breath to calm herself and froze as she picked up Faith's scent.

Where was her brain?

Faith would have hidden the bag in a place that she found logical, but Tamsin didn't have to hunt it down. She only had to track Faith.

She followed the scent of shredded paper and rodents. Underneath was Faith's scent of lemons and pine trees. She had moved in a straight path through the trees, then stopped. Her scent was very strong on one of the trees. Tamsin's brows drew together.

"Did she *mark* the tree?" she whispered.

Faith didn't know Tamsin was a shifter. Yet her scent was very strong on the tree. The only way she'd get it that strong was if she rubbed her body on it. Marked it like a bear. In fact, along this entire path, there had been a clear scent trail.

Had Faith rubbed her hands along the trees as she passed?

What would make her think to do so?

As with so many other things, that was a mystery for another day. Tamsin looked around on the ground, but didn't see the bag. A strong sense of urgency rode her as the sirens grew louder. Once they made sure the building was safe, she feared her absence would be noted and they might look for her. She had to be far away by then.

Her eyes went back to where the scent was the strongest, and she realized it continued *up* the tree. Tamsin blinked in surprise when she saw the bag carefully hanging from a branch above her. Way too high to jump and reach. She set her duffel on the ground and her nails pushed out of the tips of her fingers.

She quickly scaled the tree, her claws digging in and giving her easy purchase. She was grateful that the partial shift came easy to her. As she moved up the tree, she marveled at the bag's location. It was high enough that it would be difficult for most people to reach. It also would escape casual notice.

"How did Faith do that?" That woman was full of surprises.

Given its position in the tree, it must have taken Faith a while to get it in place.

She must have left right after Tamsin did.

There was one other way she'd get it in place and return to the lab. Of course, maybe she hadn't returned to the lab. Tamsin didn't recall seeing her in the group of people in front of the building.

"She could have gone out the back, too," Tamsin muttered.

As could the guards. But she didn't think they would have left the front of the building unattended. Not unless they were busily occupied with something else.

She reached the branch the bag was hanging from and slid her arm through its handle. She had to dig her claws into the branch to stay stable while she untied it. Shortly it was swinging from her hand, and she jumped out of the tree, easily absorbing the impact of the landing. She pulled in her claws before she damaged the bag's handles.

Tamsin looked back where the bag had hung and shook her head again. It had to have been challenging for Faith to get it up there. Hopefully, she'd see her again and could ask about it.

The sirens suddenly cut off and Tamsin froze. The emergency crew must have arrived.

She slid the strap to her duffel back over her shoulder and put the bag with the mouse food and cage on top. She looked in the direction of the road she'd left. It would be more likely Chris could find her there, if she followed the road.

It would also be more likely the guards would find her, too.

She headed in the other direction. When she'd taken one of her walks, she'd headed in this direction and found another street. It wasn't too far. But the clock was ticking. Faith had said not to leave the mice in the box for more than four hours.

Was that how long it would take them to chew through it?

Tamsin *really* didn't want mice in her clothes.

She'd better move faster.

She kept her senses on alert as she hurried through the trees. Her mouth was parted and she breathed in deeply, pulling more scents than normal by using both her mouth and nose. Alarm shot through her when she caught the sharp tang of fear.

Whoever had passed by here had been terrified.

She could tell it was a male. She also picked up blood. *An injured male.*

She paused and moved back down the trail, but didn't pick up any other scents. He hadn't been followed. *Not yet.* She wasn't sure which direction he had traveled. A chill ran down her spine. If he came from one way, he had left the lab. If he came from the other, he was heading *to* the lab.

She took a step in the direction of the lab when she heard a small squeak from her bag. *The mice.* She didn't have time to follow him. Besides, if he had headed to the lab, he was already likely there.

So were the paramedics.

Perhaps he stumbled in that direction for help.

Conflicted, she turned and headed in the direction she'd been traveling. Although she couldn't see it, she knew the road was directly ahead. Her tiger caught the faint scent of vehicle exhaust. A small bit of tension left her shoulders. Once there, she could try to reach Chris on the cell again.

What if she couldn't reach him?

She shoved the thought away. She'd figure something out. The faint squeaking in her bag continued, and this time she heard a gnawing sound. Hopefully they were munching on the treats Faith had given them. If they'd already finished them, though, then that might just be their box they were working on.

She reached the road and paused. Sweat trickled down her back from her hike, and she wished there was a slight breeze to cool her off. Even by the road, without the trees to block the air, there was no wind. The empty expanse stretched off in both directions with no lights, no street signs, nothing. If it hadn't been paved, she would have thought it a maintenance road.

Tamsin dug in her pocket and pulled out Chris's phone, wiping her arm across her brow to remove the beads of sweat. Her phone was tucked deep in her bag and turned off. She'd shut it off when she packed it away. She had no idea what it would do once it got reception. She'd had a mental image of it chirping and chiming as it got messages and leading the guards directly to her.

So, Chris's phone it was. Plus, she had contacted him before she left the lab. Hopefully, he'd text her back. She'd put it on silent before she left lab, in case he decided to call her.

The cell was an inexpensive flip phone, and she flipped the top to expose the number pad. The screen lit up and it vibrated, startling her. She jerked and it jumped from her hand. She bounced it from hand to hand before she managed to keep a hold of it. Her heart raced in her chest, and she drew in a deep breath as she caught it. The screen read *Chris* and she quickly pushed the answer button.

"Tamsin?" Chris sounded slightly hollow, like he was on speaker phone. There was also some road noise in the background.

"Yeah, it's me," she replied with a soft sigh of relief. "Are you in a car?"

"I'm in the van. I have you on speaker, but it's just me."

She didn't really care if anyone else was in the vehicle. She needed a lift, plain and simple. "Did you get my message?"

He briefly hesitated, then answered, "Ah, my phone died. But I'm on my way. Stay there."

Her brow wrinkled as she thought about his statement. If his phone died, how did he know she needed him to come get her?

"I'm not at the lab," she told him. Her cat felt too exposed, and she moved back in the trees. She still had a clear view of the road, but the vehicles going past wouldn't be able to see her. Not that there were any on the road at the moment.

"I know," Chris replied confidently.

She frowned. *How did he know where she was?*

"What do you mean?" she asked suspiciously.

"I know where you are," he replied, his tone factual, like he was telling her he knew it was a sunny day. "Stay put. I'll be there in about ten minutes."

"Chris—" she said, but the phone chirped. She looked at the screen.

He'd hung up.

About ten minutes. That's what he said. She looked at her watch, then slid the phone in her pocket. He wouldn't call again unless something delayed him. Another trickle of sweat ran down her back.

She was tempted to stand by the road to wait. It wasn't like anyone was driving on it, although there was no more air there than in the trees. Her panther sent a shaft of warning through her. She tried to figure out what had it upset, but all she got was a sense of danger.

Fine, then.

Tamsin heaved a sigh and crouched down, setting the bags on the ground. The squeaking in her duffel had stopped, but the gnawing continued. She looked at the bag wryly.

"Are you eating your snacks or chewing through your box?" she asked softly. The gnawing paused, then picked up again.

She studied the bag with narrowed eyes and considered opening it to see what the little creatures might be up to. Visions of mice jumping out and making a break for freedom stilled her hand. If they got out of their box, it would be better for them to be loose in her duffel. At least that way she could find them. If they got out in the trees, it would take her *hours* to track them down. If she even could.

How would she tell the scent of one mouse from another, anyway? Not like she'd stuck her nose in their fur to pull in their individual scents. If she ever put them near her face, they'd probably run in fear, convinced she planned to eat them. They barely tolerated her holding them and usually froze in place until she put them down. They knew she was a predator, even if they had never seen her in cat form.

It suddenly struck her as odd that Faith had never commented on their behavior in her presence. It wasn't in her to hold her tongue to be polite. If Faith had a thought, she shared it.

The low rumble of a vehicle came from the road and distracted her from her musings. Tamsin stood, but stayed in the cover of the trees.

It hadn't been ten minutes yet.

Chris may tease and joke, but he was reliable. If he said ten minutes, he meant it.

She looked at her watch, just to double check.

Nope, not ten minutes.

A black Buick came down the road, and Tamsin dropped to a squat, hiding behind a bush. Steven was in the passenger seat. The only reason he hadn't seen her was he was looking at the other side of the road.

Her heart pounded madly as the vehicle drove by. She kept her head down, and her body low. She couldn't stop herself from looking again. In her brief glimpse, she saw another guard in the back seat.

The vehicle slowed and she scrunched lower. She dared to raise her head again to peer through the bushes. If they had spotted her, she had no choice but to run. It would be awkward with the bags, but she wasn't leaving them behind. Not only because of her promise, but they had Faith's scent all over them. There was no way she was leaving evidence that Faith had helped her.

The Buick pulled over across the road and the back door opened. The guard got out and scanned the area.

Had he paused when he looked over here?

She had no idea if she could be seen or not. She thought she was in shadow, but she could be wrong.

He stepped away from the car and took a few steps into the trees on the other side of the road. The front door opened, and Steven got out. He raised his head and took a deep breath, sampling the scents in the air.

She'd never been so thankful for no breeze in her life. The sweat chilled on her body, and she didn't dare move.

"Hurry up," Steven snapped.

She looked over at the guard who had gotten out. His back was to her, but his hands were around the front of his body. They were too far away for her to hear anything, but she was pretty sure he was taking a pit stop.

Why not just wait until they get back to the lab?

Maybe they weren't going back to the lab.

Could they be looking for her?

"I'm coming," the guard muttered and headed back to the car.

Steven looked around once more before getting back in the car. The guard climbed in and closed his door. The car sat there with the engine running.

"What are you waiting for?" Tamsin whispered.

She looked at her watch. Chris would be there in a few more minutes. She needed the guards to leave. *Now.*

Another black Buick came down the road and slowed down. Steven's vehicle pulled out. The other vehicle sped up to match the speed of the first, and they continued on down the road.

As soon as they were out of sight, Tamsin picked up her bags and started walking the opposite direction the vehicles had gone.

"If Chris says he knows where I am, then he can find me," she muttered.

Tamsin walked faster through the trees, afraid another set of guards might come down the road. She was so close to freedom, she couldn't get caught now. Plus, she had the USB with all her research notes on it, and the remaining vials of her serum.

If she got caught now, there would be no way for her to explain what she was doing with all of that. And the mice, too.

She kept glancing at the road, straining to hear the sound of a vehicle. Inside her bag, the gnawing sounds continued. She understood their need for freedom. It rode her, too. She realized she'd been trapped in a box, just as they were. But for her, it wasn't as simple as just gnawing on the wall to get out.

"Hurry up, Chris," she said as she moved through the forest, trying to get as far as possible from the lab before someone else found her.

Chapter 12

Chris glanced at the speedometer and eased his foot off the gas. The last thing he needed was to get a ticket. A cop would take one look in the back of the van, see all the surveillance equipment, and it would be a trip to the police station. Especially in a podunk town like this.

Damien would straighten it out, but Chris would lose precious time he didn't have. He'd also be late picking up Tamsin. That wasn't an acceptable situation.

His other option would be to not cooperate, but Damien frowned on that. The human police were just doing their job, same as Nightfair. They only dealt with mundane crimes, people under the influence, and other similar situations. They had to worry about getting shot or stabbed, not about having their throats ripped out by an enraged predator. No, that was Nightfair's task.

He gripped the steering wheel tighter.

Best not to get pulled over.

He glanced at the GPS unit with the tracker dot from Tamsin's phone. He was following it instead of the tracker on the lab coat, although when he first looked both dots were on top of each other.

There was no one on the road, which could have been a bit on the creepy side, except this was a rural town. It was late morning, a time when most people were at work.

Out of habit, he glanced in his rear-view mirror and saw a black Buick coming up behind him. Fast.

Must not be worried about cops.

He didn't recognize any of the men in the vehicle, but glanced again.

They all wore black shirts and had the look of security. If a vehicle was full of the Nightfair crew, they'd pretty much look like that. Before Chris could pull to the side, they pulled into the left lane and rushed past him.

The vehicle looked just like the one Steven had used that morning to transport Amy.

Were they part of the same team?

He didn't recognize any of them from his brief glance.

He was tempted to follow them, but he needed to pick up Tamsin. That was his priority. He memorized the license plate number. He could have Justin look it up, later. Plus, tailing someone was always better when you had a team. On a two-lane road like this, it would be obvious he was following them.

Even if the others were with him, they'd need multiple vehicles, which they didn't have. The van was the only one they had here.

He glanced at the GPS screen again and saw her dot, which had been stationary, had moved. It wasn't moving fast, so she must be walking. Irritation shot through him. He'd told her to stay put. He had the training in search and rescue, not her.

His eyes narrowed in thought. She was smart and knew he was coming to get her. If she was moving, then there had to be a reason. Something had her worried. He put his foot on the gas, cops be damned. If they pulled him over, he'd deal with it.

The tracker showed him getting closer and closer to Tamsin. He scanned the surrounding wooded area, looking for her. All he saw was dense trees and bushes.

Where was Tamsin?

The tracker was accurate to within about twenty-five feet.

About the length of a hallway in a house.

With all the trees, it might as well have been a mile. She'd probably stay close to the road to watch for him, but all she knew was he was in a van.

He should have given her a description of the van.

He was messing this one up with each turn. He wasn't a rookie.

What was wrong with him?

His cat pushed in the back of his mind, forcing himself to be honest.

Tamsin was what was wrong with him.

She had him all twisted up in knots. Had for a long time. But he couldn't walk way. Didn't want to walk away.

Maybe this situation would finally allow them to sit and talk. He knew she wanted him. He saw it in her eyes. In how her scent changed around him. His cat found her use of perfume amusing, but he wasn't going to tell her it didn't work.

She went to all that trouble to try to disguise her scent. It worked for everyone else, but Chris was attuned to her. His cat picked up the slightest changes in her scent, like her spicy anger. But the scent he enjoyed the most was the sweet scent of her arousal. Even if it left him walking around with a painful hard-on.

He felt his body respond to just the *thought* of her arousal, and he forced himself back to the task at hand. He had to find her. Get her to safety. His eyes scanned the trees as he drove, hoping to catch a glimpse of her.

Frustration was riding him as he drove for half a mile more, then realized he'd passed her dot. He quickly turned around on the empty road.

"Driving around randomly isn't working," he muttered to himself.

Chris pulled over and picked up his phone. He quickly dialed the cell he gave her.

"Hello?" she answered quietly after only one ring.

Alarm shot through him.

Was she hiding from someone?

"Tamsin, where are you?" he asked, wincing at his curt tone.

"I'm getting my nails done," she snapped. "I'm hiding in the trees. Where do you *think* I am?"

His alarm eased. She wouldn't give him a sarcastic answer if she was in danger.

"Look, I know you're around here, but not exactly where," he replied, frustrated.

"Are you here already?" she asked. He heard the sound of branches brushing past her. "It hasn't been ten minutes yet."

She was still moving.

"I'm close to you, but not sure of your exact location," he admitted, hoping she was moving toward him, and not away.

"What do you mean?"

"My tracker isn't that precise," he answered. "I know your general location."

"Tracker?" Her tone sounded odd, but he couldn't place the emotion. "In the phone. Right?"

Mentioning the additional tracker in her lab coat probably wouldn't be a good idea right then.

"Yes, the phone has a tracker," he replied cautiously, his eyes scanning the trees for any sign of her. "It has around a twenty-five-foot accuracy."

"That's helpful," she said dryly.

"I'm parked by the road, white van." He picked up the phone, turned off the van and got out, closing the door. "You're north of my position."

She was silent. He could hear her passage through the brush over the phone, but nothing nearby.

"Honk the horn," she ordered.

"What?" He had to have misunderstood.

"Honk the damn car horn," she snapped. "So I can get a reference for your location."

The phone chimed and went dead. He blinked, surprised she'd been so angry. He figured north of his position was enough reference. Obviously not. Maybe she didn't know where north was like he did. When they were kids, he and his brothers would blindfold each other and spin around, trying to see how disoriented they could get each other. It never worked on him. He'd point north every time he stopped spinning.

He slipped the phone back in his pocket and returned to the van. He opened the door and tapped the horn. One sharp blast had to be enough. Any more and they might draw unwanted attention. He softly shut the door and returned to the front of the van, listening and watching.

The birds chirped in the trees, and some bugs were buzzing nearby, but he didn't hear anything else. No tell-tale sounds of branches breaking, sticks being crushed, or leaves crackling. No signs something large, like a person, was moving through the trees.

Where was she?

Chris pulled the phone out and was about to call her when he saw a movement in the trees ahead. He stilled. Something looked off. He took a cautious step forward. In the distance ahead he heard the faint rumble of a vehicle's engine.

Someone was coming.

He needed to find Tamsin, and fast. The hairs on the back of his neck rose in primal warning.

"Tamsin?" he called softly, staring at the location of the movement in the trees.

"What?" she answered from behind him.

He jumped and twisted, stumbling back as he met her amused gaze. She was a few feet behind him, two bags over her shoulder with twigs caught in her braided hair.

"If you're here," he replied, "what's in the trees?"

"Where?" she asked, her brow wrinkled.

Chris looked back at the dark place in the trees just as two squirrels raced forward on a branch. They chased each other, circled the tree, and jumped from one branch to another. A moment later, they disappeared back into the shadows.

"Never mind," he muttered.

"Did you think that was me? A pair of squirrels?" She looked at him with a slight smile on her face.

"Glad you find this amusing," he groused. "Get in the van."

"Were you frightened by a pair of *rodents*?" She rocked back on her heels, her slight smile now a full grin.

"I was not." He narrowed his eyes in warning. He hadn't been *scared*. Concerned, but not scared. He was a tiger shifter. Squirrels didn't scare them. They were snacks.

"Umhm," she said, her eyes dancing with amusement.

He loved seeing her eyes light up with laughter. Tamsin needed more laughter in her life. She took things too seriously.

"Do you want to stand here all day discussing this," he waved his hand in the direction of the stupid rodents, "or get the hell out of here before that vehicle arrives?"

The smile immediately left her face, and he felt the loss like a punch to the gut.

She glanced at the still empty road. "What vehicle?"

He tapped his ear. "Listen."

She shook her head and moved to the van. "I believe you. Let's get out of here. I saw some of the guards drive down the road earlier."

That explained her caution and why she was hiding in the trees, and not by the road. *Smart.*

"We can put your bags in the back." He moved around to open the back door.

"Only this one," she told him as she followed him.

Her scent washed over him as she stepped up next to him, and he couldn't stop himself from inhaling deeply.

She held out the messenger bag with a half-smile and one brow raised, and he realized he'd been sniffing like a wolf.

He reached for the bag and frowned when he saw the wire bars. "What—"

"Don't worry about it," she cut him off. As soon as he took the bag from her hand, she headed to the front of the van. "Let's get out of here."

147

He put the messenger bag in the van with a frown. He couldn't help but wonder why she had something that looked like a flattened cage with her. With one more glance at the bag, he closed the back door.

Tamsin had already gotten in the van and had herself situated in the passenger seat. She had unbraided her hair, and was pulling the twigs out. Her duffel was on the floor at her feet. It struck him as odd that she wanted to keep the bag with her. He closed his door behind him and stuck the key in the ignition. Just before the engine turned on, he thought he heard the sound of... gnawing?

"Tamsin, what's in the bag?" he asked as he pulled onto the road.

"My stuff," she replied shortly as she rapidly re-braided her hair.

He glanced over at her with a raised eyebrow. "And your stuff chews on things?"

"That's a bizarre question to ask," she replied with an offended look.

"I noticed you didn't answer it." His tiger chuffed with amusement in his mind.

She huffed and looked out the window at the side mirror. "Could you tell which direction the other vehicle was coming from?"

His tiger purred.

He liked her.

Puzzles. Tamsin was full of puzzles. Ones he wanted to solve.

Fine, keep your secrets.

He'd find out soon enough what was in the bag.

"No. The trees distorted the sound," he finally replied.

She nodded, keeping her eyes trained to the mirror. He kept glancing in his mirrors, looking for other vehicles. The road was hilly, and he couldn't see what was ahead.

They reached the top of a hill, and he saw a black vehicle ahead.

"Tamsin," he warned.

"I see it," she replied tensely. "That's the type of car the guards drive. You think it's them?"

"Don't know. Duck."

She immediately bent over, putting her head to her knees, her head turned to face him. There was nothing he could do to disguise himself. If it was the other mercenary group, the Sons of Asena, he'd be screwed.

Only if he saw someone who knew him.

The other vehicle grew closer, and Chris tightly gripped the steering wheel. He clenched his jaw, his mind frantically considering his options.

As the other vehicle grew close enough that they could clearly see each other's faces, Chris turned his head to the side, like he was talking to Tamsin and someone in the back. It only took a moment, but that was long enough for the vehicles to pass each other.

She watched him with wide eyes.

"You okay over there?"

Chris glanced in the mirror at the retreating vehicle. All the occupants were in black, like the guards. No one had turned to look back at him, so his ruse must have worked.

Of course, he didn't get a good look at them, either. So maybe there had not been anyone in the vehicle that would have recognized him.

"Yeah," he told her with another glance back at the other vehicle. "You can sit up now."

She sat up, her eyes on her own mirror. "Was it them?"

"I think so," Chris answered solemnly.

"What are they doing?" She watched the mirror like she was waiting for them to come up behind them like in a car chase from the movies.

"I don't know." He didn't like this. His instincts told him they were up to something. His cat grumbled in the back of his mind, unhappy as well.

He wished he knew what they were up to.

The gnawing noise in her bag picked up again. He hadn't realized it had stopped. Chris glanced down at it with a frown.

What was that?

It wasn't a cell phone. It didn't have that electric type of buzz.

"So, where to?" Tamsin pulled her duffel off the floor and put it on her lap. She gently tapped the top, but the noise didn't stop.

"You sure you don't want to tell me what's in the bag?"

"I told you. My stuff. Don't worry about it." She looked at him with a raised brow. "Now, where are we going?"

He made a non-committal hum, intensely curious about whatever-it-was in her bag. If she wasn't going to tell him, he'd have to find out on his own.

"I've got a room at a motel in town," he replied, letting her think he'd accepted her answer. "We'll head back there, rendezvous with the team."

Her brow wrinkled as she thought about his answer. "Why aren't they with you? Don't you usually travel together?"

Surprised, he glanced over at her. He didn't realize she'd paid that much attention to the workings of the team.

"We usually do, yeah. But Justin and Sierra stayed back at the motel," he answered.

He left out that they were monitoring the injured shifter because he didn't want to worry her. She'd find out soon enough. Not that Chris was going to expose her to the injured wolf.

No, he was going to keep Tamsin safe.

He turned onto the road to the motel. It suddenly struck him that he was going to be taking her to a room. With one bed.

His mind flashed to the kiss they'd shared months ago. His body, which he'd managed to get mostly under control, roared to life and his dick hardened. His tiger eagerly purred in the back of his mind at the thought of being alone with her. Really alone with her.

He glanced at Tamsin's profile as she watched the road. The sun caressed her beautiful bronze skin. The tips of his fingers itched to stroke her skin. He wanted to feel her body against his.

He forced himself to focus on the road.

He'd keep her safe, even from himself.

Chapter 13

Tamsin stared unseeing out the van's front window. All her focus was on the man in the seat next to her.

They were going to a motel. Together.

In her mind, all she could see was a bed. A giant bed. The sheets pulled back, ready for them. Together. Her body heated. She licked her lips as she grew wet between her thighs and her nipples pebbled in her bra. Her body liked the idea of sleeping with him. Her panther purred in her mind, all on board with that.

She imagined him lying on the bed, his clothes off. She'd run her hands over every inch of his muscled body. She grew wetter, and her body started to throb.

Not good, Tamsin. Not good.

This wasn't a booty call. She didn't do booty calls. She squeezed her legs together, glad she'd put on her usual scent-camouflaging perfume that morning.

She tried to get herself under control, but couldn't stop herself from watching him out of the corner of her eye. His hands lightly gripped the steering wheel, and she could so easily see the long fingers, blunt tipped and a little calloused, trailing over her body. Touching her. Teasing her.

Focus.

His team members were going to be there. It wasn't just going to be the two of them. The thought was like a dash of cold water. It brought relief and disappointment twining together.

Tamsin tried to pay attention to the road and the unfamiliar town around her. He turned right, then turned right again. She recognized that convenience store. They'd just passed it.

He was circling the block.

He pulled into the parking lot of a motel that he had already passed once before.

"Did you miss your turn?" she teased.

He glanced over to her and grinned. "Looked that way, huh?"

"Well, yeah."

"Nope," he answered with a smile that made her heart stop. "Just making sure we weren't followed."

Tamsin blinked, startled. She hadn't even thought of that. At least one of them had their mind on the task at hand. She'd been so lost in her fantasizing anyone could have followed them, and she wouldn't have known.

He drove to the back side of the motel, and she wondered if he was going to circle it, too.

Maybe this wasn't their real destination.

When she glanced at him, she noticed his eyes carefully scanned the area.

Looking for threats. Or followers?

She looked around, but didn't see anyone who might cause problems. She didn't see anyone, period. There were a couple vehicles parked on this side, but that was it. Of course, it was late morning on a weekday. She didn't really know when motels were busy, but she figured it'd be at night.

A tall cinder-block wall circled the back of the parking lot. It could probably be scaled, especially by someone like Chris. However, other vehicles wouldn't be getting back here except by entering from the front street. She wasn't sure if that made it more, or less, secure.

He pulled forward and backed the van into a parking space.

"We're here," he said as he put the vehicle in park and turned it off.

He didn't wait for a response as he opened his door and jumped out of the van. She reached for her own door with a glance down at her bag. Under her hand, the mice were quiet. She really hoped all that gnawing was on the treats and not the box. Otherwise, the silence might mean they were done gnawing through the box and had started on her bag. Or her clothes.

"You behave," she whispered to them, and herself.

Chris opened the back door to the van, and she glanced back to see him pick up her other bag. "You coming?" he asked, meeting her gaze.

"Yeah," she muttered, unhooking her seat-belt and opening her door, a bit embarrassed at her reaction to him. She was an adult. She could control herself.

She slid out of the tall vehicle as he closed the back doors. By the time she shut her door, he was next to her.

"I don't have a spare key to the room," he told her. "But we won't be here long."

Chris held up a key fob and pointed it at the van. It chirped as he locked it.

"That's okay," she replied. "Not like I'm going anywhere without you."

"It's a safe place, for now." He pulled a key card out of his pocket and walked to the nearest door. She noticed gauzy curtains hung in the window. They were the type that let in the light, but made it difficult to see into the room.

He slid his key card into the lock and it made a *snick* sound.

She hurried after him.

Tamsin stumbled to a halt in the doorway. There was no one in the room other than Chris. A large queen-size bed took up the majority of the floor. The rest of the room held standard cheap motel furniture. A dresser with a television perched on it, a small desk with a lamp and a task chair, and nightstands on either side of the bed, both with lamps. The one farthest from the door also had an alarm clock with a digital display indicating ten o'clock.

There was a closet on the far side of the room and a door for the bathroom. She took a deep breath, but the only scents in the room were hers and Chris's. There was a chemical scent overlay from the cleaning products that deadened her nose to anything else. But it didn't smell of urine or worse, which was a plus.

"Where are the others?" she asked, nervous butterflies taking off in her stomach.

She'd been counting on his team members to serve as a buffer. To keep her from climbing him like a tree. To make sure cooler heads prevailed when her mind drifted to hot and sweaty thoughts of her and Chris together.

"At a different hotel," he said, setting her bag on the floor by the wall. "Why? Did you expect to find them here?"

She swallowed what felt like a dry lump in her throat and nodded, forcing a smile on her face. "Yeah, I guess I kind of figured we'd be meeting up with them."

He pulled out his phone. "Right now, it's best that we're not together. But I can touch base with them."

The rest of the team wasn't going to be joining them. It was *just* the two of them. Her eyes went to the bed again, her body growing warm.

Chris didn't seem to notice her reaction and pushed a button on his phone. It rang once, then the same voice she'd heard talk to him over his earpiece answered.

"You back?"

"Yeah," Chris answered, glancing from her to the door. "How's the guest?"

Tamsin stepped inside the room and closed the door behind her. The room was well lit from the window, she didn't bother turning on the lights.

"Still out cold, but stable. Sierra's monitoring him."

That didn't sound good. She met Chris's eyes and raised her eyebrows in question.

He gave a slight shake to his head, and she frowned. Did that mean he didn't want to tell her now, or he didn't plan to let her know what was going on?

"Any word from Mac?" Chris asked.

"Nothing new. Same as before. Stay put. He'll check in for a briefing in a couple hours."

"Copy that," Chris replied, staring at the wall.

The other voice didn't sound worried, so maybe this wasn't an issue. But it sounded like trouble to her.

"Tamsin okay?"

"Yeah, she's fine." Chris glanced at her with a smile.

She set her duffel on the floor by her other bag. She wasn't sure what that look meant, or what was going on.

"You staying there or heading this way?"

"We'll bunk down here until we hear from Mac," Chris said. "Best we aren't all in the same place."

Stay here? She thought with the guards all over the place, they'd book it out of town right away. Chris had said they wouldn't be there long. She'd thought that meant a few minutes. But *bunk down* implied longer.

Why did they have to wait?

"Ten-four. Sierra thinks our guest will be out a while more. I'm going to catch some shut-eye. She'll stay on watch."

Tamsin had been about to unzip her duffel to check on the suspiciously quiet mice, but her hand stilled as she listened to the conversation.

"Good idea. We'll probably do the same. Rest while you can. No idea when things'll blow up," Chris ordered. "Let me know if there's any change in the situation."

"Will do."

Without another word, Chris ended the call.

He took a deep breath, then looked at her. "Looks like we're going to be here for a while."

"When will we leave?" She stood, her heart picking up speed.

And what will she do to keep from jumping him?

"Not for several hours at least, unless we hear from Mac. Most likely tonight." His eyes scanned her body, like he was checking to make sure she was all in one piece.

She nodded. "So, what do we do until then?"

He stepped closer to her, and his hand cupped her jaw. "I was worried about you."

She closed her eyes, the gentle touch setting her nerves on fire. She took a deep breath, pulling in his scent of sunshine and browned butter.

Tamsin looked at Chris, and his eyes flashed from blue to topaz as his tiger returned her gaze. She saw the near panic in his eyes, and it struck her how much control he'd had to hide it. It was only when looking into the eyes of his primal side that it was revealed.

Her panther pushed at the back of her mind, and she admitted how much danger she'd been in. But she was safe now. With Chris. And the bed.

"I—I got out." She licked her lips. She wanted to kiss him. Touch him. Prove to herself they were both safe.

His eyes shifted back to his human blue.

"How?" He sounded curious. His eyes dropped to her mouth, and his hand traced down to her throat, drawing a line of heat.

"I followed you," she said as she leaned toward him in invitation.

His eyes lit with heat, and when his mouth covered hers, it was all fire. She opened her lips, and he swept in and devoured. Desire raced through her veins, and she moaned low in her throat as she grew wet between her thighs. She grabbed his shoulders, trying to hold onto reality as sensation overwhelmed her. She tried to remember why sleeping with him wasn't a good idea, but her mind went blank.

Chris wrapped his arms around her and pulled her in tight to his body. Their clothes did nothing to diminish the heat between them. But she wanted more. She wanted to feel his flesh against hers.

Friction. She needed friction.

His erection, confined by his jeans, pushed against her, and she rubbed her body against him. He groaned, and she felt his hand against her skin under her shirt sliding up to cup her breast. A shock of pleasure shot through her when his thumb brushed her nipple through her bra.

He broke off the kiss to give her little bites and nips along her jaw. His skin on hers... the raspy stubble on his jaw... it felt so good. She tilted her head to the side to give him better access. His hand continued to play with her breast, but the clothing was irritating. She wanted—needed—it gone.

Tamsin pulled back and yanked her shirt over her head, tossing it to the side. Her fingers fumbled as she unhooked her bra and removed it, too.

Chris watched her with dark, passion-filled eyes. He gave a low growl of approval when he looked at her breasts.

"You're beautiful," he groaned. He cupped her left breast with his hand and brushed his thumb over her nipple, making her shiver.

Then he dropped his head and pulled her breast in to his mouth. He swirled his tongue around her nipple, and pleasure skittered over her skin and shot directly to her core. With his hand and mouth, he worshiped her breasts, and she dropped her head back as pleasure overwhelmed her.

"Chris," she moaned, arching her back toward him.

His other hand slid down her body and to her pants. He cupped the globe of her ass, then moved his hand to slide his long fingers under the waistband and down into her panties. She caught her breath as his hand moved closer and closer.

And damn, he found her center, parted her folds carefully, invading her wet heat with calloused fingers. He rubbed her clit, and the pleasure built.

He pulled his hand out.

No! her mind screamed.

But then he was back, undoing her pants all the way. Exposing her. Touching her in all the right places.

He put more pressure on her clit and rubbed faster. She slid her hands under his shirt, wanting, needing, to touch his skin. The pleasure was building, and she couldn't stop herself from pumping her hips against his hand.

He slid rough fingers inside her. He pumped his fingers and then—

Stars. Stars exploded behind her eyelids. Her body stiffened and shuddered. She cried out as she came.

"You smell so good," he whispered against the sensitive skin of her throat, and she shivered.

She drew in a deep breath and could smell the change in his scent, too. The smell of his arousal hung thick in the air, mixing with hers. He slowly pulled his hand out of her body, and she trembled with aftershocks of pleasure.

She palmed the erection straining at the crotch of his jeans. He pushed against her hand with a low moan.

With a wicked smile, she slid her hand into his pants, touching the silk-covered steel. He sucked in a sharp breath as she pumped her hand up and down his shaft. He shuddered, and she bit her lip. It felt so good to touch him. But she wanted more.

She pulled her hand out and quickly undid his jeans. She shoved them down, and his dick sprang free, thick and hard. Ready to fuck.

A drop of pre-cum leaked out, and she bent to lick it off.

"Tamsin." His voice was a guttural groan.

She wanted to lick and suck on him, but her panther wouldn't let her. It wanted him inside her. *Now.*

Her pants were still around her thighs, but she quickly finished stripping. She climbed on the bed and knelt, presenting her ass to him. She looked over her shoulder at him and saw his nostrils flare as he looked at her dripping entrance.

"Chris," she demanded, rocking back.

Chris sucked in a breath, but a heartbeat later his hands were on her hips. The tip of his cock teased her entrance, and she pushed back, trying to get him to slide in. His hands tightened, then he gave her what she wanted and slammed into her.

They both moaned as he filled her completely. It felt so good, but she couldn't hold still. She moved her hips, needing him to move with her.

Her muscles squeezed around him, and he pulled out, then shoved back in again. He did it again, pulling out more, then shoving back in. He leaned over her body, his front to her back, and fondled her breast. Shocks of sensation shot straight to her core. He pumped his hips, moving in and out, faster and faster.

She moved her hips in rhythm with his, and her body grew even wetter. He was so deep, so thick. His hand moved from her breast to slide a finger in her wet folds.

He pumped his hips and rubbed her swollen clit. She moaned, and he moved faster. The sound of his body slapping into hers combined with their harsh breathing and moans of pleasure.

The pressure built, and her body exploded in ecstasy as he shouted out with his own release. He continued to pump into her as she came down from her orgasm.

His heavy breath fanned the back of her neck, then he slowly pulled out, sending another wave of delicious sensation through her. In the back of her mind, her primal self curled up, fully sated.

He moved away from her, and she frowned in confusion as he got off the bed. She met his gaze and saw with surprise that his eyes were dark with passion.

She looked down at his cock and blinked in amazement. He was at half-mast again.

"I'm not done with you," his voice was a low rumble.

Before she could ask what he meant, he picked her up with his arms around her back and under her knees. He moved to lay her fully on the bed.

He looked at her, then licked his lips. He crawled on the bed and leaned over her, bracing one arm on the bed next to her. Before she could figure out what he planned, he licked her nipple, then gently blew on it. The heat followed by cool made it immediately pebble, and her body heated up again.

He proceeded to worship her body with gentle kisses while fondling her breasts. He kissed a path from her neck down her shoulder, causing her to shiver. He managed to find a place near the base of her neck that she had no idea was sensitive. Not until he lightly nipped at it.

He soon had her squirming as her body grew wet again. She was swollen again, and it started to border on painful. She needed him. Again.

"Chris, I need you." She arched her hips.

He stopped suckling her breast to meet her gaze. His hand trailed down her body and slipped into her folds, avoiding her clit and circling her entrance.

She groaned in protest and tried to arch her hips to get him to touch her where it hurt.

"You want this?" he said in a hoarse growl.

"Yes," she said shamelessly, grabbing his wrist and trying to get him to touch her in the right place. Now that she knew how good his touch felt, she didn't want to wait.

He removed his hand and moved down her body to replace it with his mouth. His tongue lapped at her clit, and fire shot through her.

"Chris," she cried out.

He continued to lick her, and with each motion her pleasure shot higher. Then he latched onto her clit and sucked, shoving a finger inside her. Her orgasm crashed around her. It was so strong she arched her back as she cried out. He continued to suck, causing the pleasure to sky-rocket again and again.

She shuddered as waves of satisfaction continued to run through her body until he stopped. He moved to curl around her, and she couldn't keep her eyes open, little aftershocks of pleasure still rocking her.

Chapter 14

Chris held Tamsin against his body and studied her sleeping face. An unnamed emotion filled him, and he dropped a kiss on her forehead. He'd dreamed of touching her for so long. The dreams paled next to the reality.

The little noises she made told him how she liked to be touched and where. They were music to his ears, and his goal was to give her more pleasure than she'd ever had before. Given how she passed out, he'd have to say he was successful.

His jaw cracked in a yawn. She was safe, and he could finally relax. While she'd been missing, his cat had been on edge. Now it curled up in the back of his mind.

He'd rest for a bit. When she woke, he'd check in with the team again. Nothing was going to happen right now, anyway. He carefully slid his body away from hers, and she grumbled in her sleep.

He grinned at the adorable sound and pushed the covers back. He picked her up and put her on the sheets, then slid in beside her, pulling the covers over both of them. She snuggled into his body, and his cat purred in his mind.

He closed his eyes, not intending to really sleep. A small noise disturbed him, and he opened his eyes wondering what it was. He glanced at the clock next to the bed and frowned. It read twelve o'clock.

That couldn't be right.

He looked at his watch.

He'd slept for two hours.

Tamsin was curled in his arms, her back to his front. He inhaled, pulling in her scent. Just the feel of her next to him made his body spring to life, not that his hard-on had really gone away. It never went away around her.

She'd pulled his arm over her body like a blanket, and her hand was twined with his. He ran his thumb over her knuckles and smiled. She made a small happy sound and moved against him. He wanted to wake her and explore her body, feast on her as he had before they fell asleep.

Then he heard a soft crunching noise in the room.

What was that?

It hadn't come from either of them. He froze and heard it again. He got out of bed, careful not to disturb Tamsin. He slid on his briefs and pants, then stood silently, listening.

The noise was near the door. He padded in the direction of the sound, soundless in the way of tiger shifters. The soft noise continued. He tracked it to Tamsin's duffel bag.

A grin crossed his face. He'd wanted to explore that mystery, anyway.

How did he forget that he'd heard some sort of gnawing noise from it earlier?

Well, he had been a bit distracted by a gorgeous woman, but she was asleep, and the mystery was right in front of him. Ready to be solved.

He bent and studied the bag as the faint noise continued. The zipper was open a tiny bit, but he couldn't see inside. He tugged the zipper. It made a soft noise as it opened, almost a gravelly purr.

"What are you doing?" Tamsin asked in a sleepy voice.

Chris froze and looked over his shoulder. She was sitting up in the bed with one eyebrow up in inquiry. He was disappointed to note she had the sheets pulled up over her chest. She had a spectacular body, and he'd not complain if she wanted to wander around naked. His body started to grow hard at the thought, and he quickly stood and adjusted himself before he got pinched.

Of course, he'd get nothing done if she walked around naked. And he'd be in even more of a perpetual hard-on than he currently was.

"Uh, what do you think I'm doing?" he replied. He knew he couldn't lie to her. Shifters could tell when someone lied to them. But growing up, he'd learned how to deflect with the best of them, and knew to never fess up first.

"Chris, are you digging in my bag?" Tamsin looked irritated, but her eyes sparkled with amusement.

"Nope," he replied honestly. He hadn't gotten it open enough to fully investigate.

The gnawing paused, and he glanced down at the bag.

She made a non-committal hum and looked around the room. Her eyebrows rose slightly when they landed on her shirt and bra. "Can you please hand me my shirt?"

He grinned and shook his head. She rolled her eyes and started to push the sheets back when his phone rang.

His smile died as he turned to grab the device off the dresser. He glanced at the screen as he picked it up and saw *Justin.*

"Everything okay?" Chris asked.

He could hear the rustle of sheets as Tamsin got out of bed. She lightly touched his shoulder as she passed him.

"We have a development," Justin replied.

Tamsin gave him a worried glance as she grabbed her clothes and went to the bathroom. He forced himself not to watch her as she walked across the room. He had to focus on the conversation, not on how fine her ass was. The door shut softly behind her.

"What kind of development? Is it related to our guest?" Chris moved to his shoes and slid them on his feet. Justin wouldn't have called him if he didn't have details.

"In part. He briefly woke up, but is out again," Justin answered.

"Was there trouble?" Chris paused, worried his team had an incident and he wasn't there to assist.

"No, it was nothing to worry about," Sierra's voice was clear, but faint, as Justin's phone picked her up. "No aggressive behavior, just the need to sleep due to injuries."

"But when he woke up," Justin said, "he gave us a communication earpiece."

"An earpiece?" Chris's body tensed.

"He obtained it from one of the guards," Justin said, sounding pleased. "When they captured him, he managed to nab it and hide it. It made it with him during his escape."

"A plant?" Chris asked, uneasy. He paced in front of the dresser.

"I don't think so," Justin replied. "I think it's legit."

Chris stopped walking and smiled slowly. "Are you in?"

"Yes," Justin replied, sounding smug. "They are a very chatty group. I've been monitoring it for about thirty minutes now."

"Recording?"

"Of course," Justin sounded offended.

"You need me over there?" Chris grabbed his shirt and set it on the bed as Tamsin opened the bathroom door. She stepped out fully dressed.

"Not yet. I'll let you know if I hear anything of note."

"Copy that." Chris ended the call.

"What's going on?" Tamsin crossed her arms and leaned against the wall.

"What do you want to know?" Chris studied her wary face.

Did she think he was hiding something from her?

A small frown wrinkled her brow as she thought about her answer. He wanted to smooth it out with his thumb, but forced himself to stay in place.

"Let's start with who was that?" She glanced at the phone, then back to his face.

"Justin. One of my team members." He picked up his shirt and slid it on.

"Okay. Earlier he said Sierra was monitoring a guest. Who is Sierra, and who is this *guest* she's monitoring?" Her curious gaze met his, and something in him relaxed. She didn't look like she didn't trust him, but more like she just wanted to know.

"Sierra's another team member. As for the guest... that's complicated."

"Then explain it," she replied calmly, one brow raised.

Chris's jaw clenched, then he nodded.

"We watched the feed from the lab last night." He watched her closely.

Her eyes narrowed, and she tilted her head to the side, a look of confusion on her face. Then her eyes grew wide and she said, "You saw the captives? Did you rescue one?"

"Yeah, we saw," he said, fighting his reaction to the memory of seeing her following the guards. "This morning one escaped. A wolf shifter. We picked him up before the guards could."

"That explains it," she muttered.

"Explains what?" he said, his tiger suddenly on alert.

"I caught a scent in the trees before I saw you. I wonder… could that have been the escaped captive?" She caught her breath. "What happened to him?"

"He was injured," Chris said darkly. It took a lot to put a shifter out for the count like that. "He asked us for help before he passed out. We had just got him back to the motel when the fire alarm went off at the lab building."

"And you came to get me," she finished. "Can any of the local packs—"

He shook his head, cutting off her question. He figured she was going to ask if any of the local packs could provide medical assistance.

"We don't know who we can trust around here."

"What do you mean?" She frowned and moved to sit on the bed and watch him.

"There's something going on with the lab. We don't know if the local packs are involved. If they are…" he trailed off, his tiger growling in the back of his mind at the thought.

"You'd be delivering him right back to his captors," she finished, looking as unhappy about it as he was.

"Our best option right now is to take care of him ourselves." He picked up his phone and turned it around in his hands. "Sierra's a medic. If things turn, she'll let us know."

"Why are we staying? Why don't we take him back to Oakdale, or somewhere where he can get help?" She studied his face.

"We need to make sure he's stable before we leave." Chris took a step closer to her, his brow furrowed as he took in her expression. "The van isn't set up for patient transport. Right now, he's better off in a bed."

"If he's that hurt—" she trailed off, looking alarmed.

"Human medical facilities won't be able to help," Chris replied with a sigh. "He's not injured severely. There's a lot of bruising, but nothing broken."

Most humans thought shifters were some sort of myth. If they took him to the hospital, not only would they not know how to treat his fast-healing body, but if he shifted, they'd panic and probably shoot him.

"So, how isn't he stable?" Tamsin leaned forward. "What's wrong?"

"We don't know," Chris admitted. "He passed out. So, we're keeping an eye on him. We don't know what they gave him, or if he's going to get worse."

"And if it triggers him, the last thing you need is to be in a van with him when it happens," she finished with a slow nod.

"At least with a hotel room there is more space to maneuver," he agreed.

"What about the call just now?" She again glanced at the phone in his hand.

Chris grinned, happy to be able to share good news, and told her about the earpiece.

"Why does that make you so happy?" she asked with a curious half-smile.

"We can monitor their communication. See what they're up to."

By her confused look, he knew she didn't quite understand how great it was to have an in with the enemy camp. He knew nothing may come of it, but on the other hand... maybe they'd get some decent intel into what was going on around here.

He opened his mouth to explain when he caught movement out of the corner of his eye. Chris set his phone on the dresser and focused his attention on where he'd seen the movement, trying to figure out what it was. It had been small, dark, and fast, but he wasn't sure about anything else.

"What?" Tamsin asked, following his gaze to the floor. "Did you see something?"

Chris debated what to tell her. *It could have been a cockroach.* Some people over-reacted to the creatures. He'd seen people jump to their feet, screaming and dancing around madly when one landed on them. He'd also seen them run away in terror, which he just didn't understand.

"Chris," Tamsin demanded sharply.

"Yeah," he reluctantly replied. "I saw something. But it was small. I don't know—"

Her eyes grew wide, and she jumped to her feet. Her gaze dropped to her leg, and she took a step forward, twisting and holding her leg out to look at the back side of her pants.

He scanned her body and then he saw it. A small mouse was scaling her like she was a fucking ladder.

With a low growl, he stepped forward and swiped at the creature, his claws out. He'd catch the intruder who clearly had upset her.

"*No!*" she cried. "Chris, wait."

He pulled up short as she grabbed the creature and held it carefully in her hands.

"Why?"

Her alarmed gaze met his. "It's mine."

His mind ground to a halt. "Say that again."

She took a deep breath. "The mouse. It's mine."

"You have a mouse?" he asked slowly.

"No. Yes." she chewed on her lip. "Kind-of."

Kind-of? What the hell did that mean?

Was this a pet? A snack?

"What do you mean, *kind-of?*" He watched the mouse as it calmly sat on her hand.

"It's complicated," she huffed. "Did you hurt it?"

He almost smiled as she used the same word he'd said to describe the injured shifter.

Did he hurt it? That was typically not the type of question one expected in relation to mice in a living space. They normally wanted them out, no matter what.

There were plenty of rodent repellents and traps on the market to attest to that.

"No, it's uninjured," he replied. "I didn't even touch it."

"Well," she said with a nervous laugh, "guess it got out of the box. I'd better see if the others did, too."

Out of the box?

He turned and glanced at her bag.

Others.

She had *more* mice?

What for?

Well, at least the puzzle of the sound was solved. But... now there were mice. Here.

"Let me get this straight." He was still processing the fact she had a mouse, no, *mice,* with her. "You ran for your life and brought *mice* with you?"

The way she acted, they were clearly some sort of pet, and not a snack. His cat grumbled in the back of his mind. He personally didn't like to eat rodents. When he hunted in cat form, he wanted larger prey. Mice were just too much effort for not enough reward. Plus, they were *mice.* With little beady eyes, twitching noses, and those whiskers. Now, a juicy rabbit, on the other hand...

She disappeared into the bathroom. He heard her moving around, but he dropped his gaze to her bag. *The others.* There were more mice in there.

And they might have gotten out.

"I told you," she grumbled as she returned to the room and grabbed the other bag. Not the duffel with the mice in it. "It's complicated."

She pulled out the wire bits he'd felt and started assembling something on the bed. He stepped closer.

"Is that a mouse cage?" he asked, astonished.

"Well, where else will the mice live?" she asked as she locked the pieces together.

"I don't know, wherever they came from?"

She laughed like she thought he was joking.

"How many mice are we talking about?" He looked at her duffel. It was pretty large. There could be an army of mice in there. Little squeaking, whisker twitching, beady-eye watching mice.

"Not many." She snapped a plastic bottom to the wire bars. She reached into the messenger bag and pulled out a plastic bag full of shredded paper.

Chris peered into the bag. He saw another bag of the shredded paper, and something that looked like pellets. *Mouse food?*

"How many is not many?"

She put some of the paper in the bottom of the cage and paused to look at him. Her eyes lit up with amusement. "Are you *afraid* of mice?"

"I'm not afraid," he immediately said. "I just don't like them, okay?"

"Looks like afraid to me." She laughed and put pellet food in a dish in the container before she headed to the bathroom.

She immediately returned, her hands cupping that mouse again. She put it in the cage and closed the door.

She grabbed a bottle with a screw top and a protruding piece of metal and went back to the bathroom. He heard water running and then she returned. She hooked the contraption to the cage, and he realized it was some sort of water bottle for the mice. The cage was big enough for several mice.

"Seriously, Tamsin, how many mice are we talking about?"

"Well," Tamsin replied as she knelt by her duffel and unzipped it, "four total."

He watched as she revealed a brown box from her duffel, surrounded by rolled clothes, forming a safe square of protection.

She opened the box. There were two mice in the box and a chewed-out corner.

"Shit," she muttered, meeting his gaze. "There *were* four."

He looked around the motel room as she scooped up the other two and put them in the cage. She pulled the box out of her bag and zipped it shut.

"We need to find the missing mouse." Her worried gaze darted around the motel room.

Pets. Most definitely pets. That meant they had to catch it. Unharmed.

A variety of thoughts raced through Chris's mind. He clenched his jaw, holding them all back. He searched the room for beady eyes. Only the ones in the cage looked back.

Great, just great.

He thought he saw movement by the bed and took a step in that direction when his phone rang. He grabbed it off the dresser and looked at the display. *Justin.*

He swiped it to answer, and Justin spoke before he could say a word.

"You need to leave. Now."

Chapter 15

Tamsin frantically looked around the hotel room. It had seemed like such a tiny space, and all bed. However, in terms of mouse hiding places, it was a palace.

She didn't even bother taking in a deep scenting breath. There was no way she'd be able to track a mouse by smell in this room. The cleaning chemicals they used didn't *stink*, but they dominated all other smells in the room. The mouse would have to make a noise to let her know where it was.

It wasn't like she could just say *Oh well* and walk away. All of the mice had been injected with her serum, but the one missing had been subject Alpha. She had to have him back.

The other three were exploring their new abode and didn't seem to realize they were missing one. "Fat lot of help you are," she muttered to the mice.

Chris's attention was fixed on the far side of the bed. She opened her mouth to ask him what he saw when his phone rang. He grabbed it off the dresser and swiped it to answer. He didn't even get it to his ear when Justin spoke.

"You need to leave. Now."

His tone was so calm; it took her a second to register the words. Alarm shot through her.

What had happened?

"Danger?" Chris asked calmly.

Her heart raced in her chest, and they were no more excited than if discussing what to have for lunch. They'd probably be even *more* excited to discuss lunch plans.

"Trouble," Justin replied. "They've found the other escaped captive."

Chris briefly closed his eyes, a look of sorrow on his face. Then his eyes opened, and the look was gone, like it had never been.

"We can't do a rescue mission," Chris responded. "We've already discussed this."

"We can if we get to him first," Justin countered.

"What do you mean?" Tamsin asked, her alarm fading into confusion.

"They're hunting him, hardcore," Justin growled. "We can't let them get him. Not if they want him this badly."

"If they're out in numbers—" Chris began.

"They're hunting him," Justin interrupted. "But they only have a general idea of his location. They're spread out and don't know where he is, *exactly*."

"How do they not know where he is *exactly?*" Tamsin asked.

"I may have helped a little," Justin replied, sounding smug.

"You have his coordinates?" Chris asked.

"Yes, and he's close. If you go now, you can get to him first."

Chris looked her over, his gaze stopping at her feet. She grabbed her socks and quickly slid them on, followed by her shoes, glad she'd fixed her hair when she got dressed.

"We're heading out," Chris said. "You need us to pick you up?"

"No," Justin replied. "I've got my laptop and everything is set up here. Besides, I don't want to leave Sierra without back-up."

"Copy that," Chris acknowledged. "And I'm good. I've got back-up."

Tamsin jerked her head up and looked at him. His eyes were on her.

She was his back-up?

She glanced around the room, hiding her pleased smile. This was starting to feel like she was living in some sort of action movie.

As Chris got more information from Justin, she hunted for some sign of subject Alpha, but the mouse remained elusive. She grabbed the small transport box and dropped some food inside before placing it on the floor. Hopefully the easy access to food would keep her in the room.

Ready to go, she looked back at Chris. He glanced at the box and raised one brow. She tilted her head innocently and smiled. She'd probably need to tell him how important those mice were, but that could be another time. When things weren't so exciting.

His eyes laughed at her as he grinned and tilted his head to the door.

Tamsin nodded and hurried after him, her heart racing in her chest. She grabbed the *Do not disturb* sign and hung it on the door as she closed it. She didn't want any maids going in and hurting her mice while they were gone.

Nerves warred with excitement inside her. Chris looked cool and calm as he started up the van and drove it through the parking lot.

Like it was nothing unusual.

That thought made her pause. She glanced to the back of the van at all the equipment. This really *was* his office. Nightfair had been showing up at her sister's bar for a couple years now. She'd caught bits and pieces here and there.

She thought she *knew* what they did. Now she was going to get to really see.

And what was this other escaped captive thing? He hadn't mentioned it before.

"Who are we going after?" Tamsin asked.

"The morning you left the lab there were two captives that also escaped," Justin replied from Chris's phone.

Chris had set it on a holder by the center console and put it on speaker mode before he started driving. Justin had been relaying directions, but had gone silent.

Two escaped captives?

How had two managed to slip away? She couldn't even head down the hallway without running into a guard. Especially near the exits.

"Was it from the fire alarm I set off?" she asked.

"You were still in your lab when they ran," Chris replied. "Although your alarm may have given them some extra time."

"Why didn't you pick him up, too?" Tamsin asked.

"We would have," Chris replied as he stopped at a light. "But we couldn't. He ran in the opposite direction, and our current guest needed some help."

"Then you set off the alarm, and we picked you up," Justin added.

Tamsin felt her gut clench. If she had waited, would they have been able to save the other man?

"Not like we could have tracked him, either," Chris added.

"What do you mean?" Tamsin glanced over at him.

His eyes were on the road, but he looked at her and flashed her a smile. "We're good, but not that good. We have to have a way to find someone. You had a tracker."

"What about your current *guest*?" she asked.

"We were hot on his trail," Justin answered. "We knew where he went, and I was in wolf form tracking him. It wasn't too hard to find him."

"If we hadn't seen him go, and followed right away, we wouldn't have found him," Chris added.

Justin cheered, and announced, "They've lost him!"

"Why is this good? If they've lost him, how can we find him?" Tamsin asked, confused by the grin on Chris's face and excitement in Justin's tone.

"I know where he is," Justin chimed. "I've got him on video. He just passed the camera of an overly-paranoid used car dealer."

"Keep your eyes on him," Chris ordered.

"Oh, I will," Justin assured him.

"Why overly paranoid?" Tamsin asked as Chris moved down the streets. She'd thought this was a small town, but it was larger than she thought.

"He has a bunch of cameras. Most are on the cars, but he has two on the streets," Justin laughed under his breath. "Guess he thinks if someone steals one of his cars, he'll get a good shot of them driving away."

"What's he doing?" a female voice said over the phone.

"Is that Sierra?" Tamsin asked softly.

Chris nodded, a frown on his forehead. "What do you see, Sierra?"

"He's just... strolling down the sidewalk."

"Act like you belong," Chris answered. "Blend in, in plain sight. That's what he's doing. But that's good for us. How far from our current location?"

"ETA five minutes," Justin announced.

"What do we do?" Tamsin asked, the reality of the situation hitting her.

These three were *trained operatives.* She was just a scientist. Sure, she had a panther inside her, and some self-defense training, but she didn't know anything about covert work.

"We're going to intercept him," Chris replied calmly.

"What do you want *me* to do?"

He must have heard a note in her voice because he offered her a reassuring smile.

"I'm not sure," He looked at the road. "We need to assess the situation. If he's rational, we offer help. If not, we tranq him, and take him into custody."

Take him into custody.

He said it so casually. Like they were going to the store to pick up a gallon of milk.

"So, um, how do we do that?" she asked hesitantly, pretty sure she wasn't going to like the answer.

"I distract him, and you shoot him," Chris replied evenly, like it was no big deal.

"I... shoot him," she echoed slowly. "I've never shot anything in my life."

"It's easy," Chris reassured her. "Just point and pull the trigger."

"He's picked up his pace," Justin's voice was tight with tension. "Put a move on. He's headed to the trees. I'll lose him if he—*shit.*"

"What?'" Chris snapped as the engine roared and the van went faster.

"We just spotted a team of the Sons of Asena," Sierra answered.

"Those guards are on the street," Justin added. "They don't see him yet."

"That's why he picked up speed," Sierra said urgently. "He must have seen them."

"How many?" Chris's jaw was tense.

Tamsin's stomach clenched. Chris said all she had to do was point and pull the trigger. She knew aiming had to fit in there somewhere. He was counting on her, and she had no clue what to do. This fun adventure had quickly turned terrifying.

"Three," Justin said. "I don't see any others, but that doesn't mean anything."

"No," Tamsin added, glad she could provide something useful. "That's their normal team size. I always saw them in groups of three."

The three members of the Nightfair crew discussed what action to take, and Tamsin listened in. This was a world she never really understood. She marveled at how calm they were. They were talking about possibly *incapacitating someone* like it was an everyday occurrence. Chris was completely unphased.

She studied his profile and couldn't stop her slight smile. He was a good man to have at her back. She never really gave him a chance before. But things were looking good. Maybe they could make a go of it. In her mind, her panther purred its approval. It urged her not to wait. Take that step *now*. Show Chris they belonged together.

Her mind ground to a halt. Her panther had them all but mated. She wasn't ready for that. And maybe Chris wasn't, either. Sure, he'd flirted with her all the time. But that didn't mean he wanted to actually have a relationship. For all she knew, right now it was just a booty call. That would actually be for the best. She wasn't sure what type of future she had. Not unless she could get her serum to work. She resolved to just enjoy it while she could.

Her thoughts were brought back to the task at hand when Chris parked the van and turned the motor off. He jumped out of his seat and opened the door to the back of the van. It was a full partition that separated the front from the back, but the door was small, he had to turn sideways to slide through.

She took off her seat-belt and twisted in her seat to watch him.

"Connecting communications." He opened a cabinet next to the tech equipment.

She marveled at all the racks and shelves lining the van in addition to the tech. From the outside it looked like a normal work van, like a plumber drove. From the inside, it was cloak and dagger headquarters.

"What—" Tamsin began when Justin interrupted from Chris's phone.

"Copy that. We've got a set here and are putting ours on, too."

"Your what?" Tamsin asked.

"Can you grab my phone and come back here?" Chris asked with a quick glance in her direction.

Tamsin nodded and picked up the phone before she moved to the back of the van.

"What do you need me to do?" She held out his phone.

Chris took it with a smile and held up a small device that looked like a Bluetooth earpiece. "Put this on."

She took it and fit it into her ear, watching as Chris did the same.

"Test," Justin's voice came through her earpiece.

"I hear you!" Tamsin said, startled.

Chris grinned at her response, and replied, "Copy that."

He moved around her and closed the small door they'd used to get to the back.

"Most work vans like this have a partition. We needed a door, so we had it modified."

"Why even have the partition?" she asked. "And why a window?"

"When we're driving, the door usually stays closed so no one else can see what's going on," he replied. "But the driver is part of the team, so we open the window, and they know what's going on. And as for why, to keep the equipment hidden, in case anyone looks in the front when the van is parked."

Chris moved around her and went back to the cabinet. He grabbed something out of the cabinet that looked like a bunch of nylon straps. "Hold out your arms."

"What is that?" she asked, trying to figure out what he wanted to put on her.

"Holster. Goes over your shoulder," he replied, sliding it over her arm.

"Is that for the tranq gun?"

He moved around and secured the holster on her. She still wasn't certain about this.

Didn't you have to oh, know what you were doing, to use a gun?

She had a vision of playing one of those games at the fair. The ones where you pulled the trigger on the water gun and tried to hit the moving target, water going everywhere. Only, in her mind, suddenly little darts were all over. In trees, dirt, squirrels. Chris.

"Yes." Chris gave her an excited grin. "You're my back-up. This is only if I need you to knock him out while I distract him. Hopefully it won't come to that."

He looked like he was having *fun*. Sure, she'd been excited at first. But now, not so much. This was *way* out of her comfort zone. She'd never even shot a *real* gun.

"Hopefully," she echoed nervously.

"You'll be fine." He gave her a fast kiss on her mouth that startled her into a smile.

He took a hand gun out of the cabinet, quickly checking it.

Her smile faded as it all got really *real*.

He pushed a button on the stock and nodded. "This is the tranq gun," he said. "Here's the safety. It is currently on. Push this button and it is ready to fire. Don't point it at anything you aren't planning to shoot."

She almost smiled at that. "Right."

She carefully took the gun and studied the safety. She pointed it at the ground and pushed the safety button. It gave a soft *click*. She pushed it again, and it gave another *click*.

"Put your finger in here, hold it like this, and firmly pull the trigger," He put her hand in place and positioned her arms.

She nodded when he looked at her expectantly. "Got it."

"The subject is almost at the tree line," Justin announced. "You need to go. Now. Or you might lose him."

Chris took the gun out of her hand, quickly checked the safety, then slid it into the holster.

He opened the rear door of the van and jumped out, gesturing for her to follow. "On our way."

Tamsin quickly looked around after she followed him out of the van. They were parked right by a bunch of trees. In fact, the van was backed up to them so the doors had opened to the trees. She took a couple steps to look around the van and saw the small town on the other side of the street. They were in some sort of pull-off parking space. A vehicle drove down the street heading away from them. She didn't see any people. No guards, no someone who may have escaped from the lab, no random people either.

"Where is everyone?" she asked, shivering at how eerie it looked. If not for the few cars, she'd think they were in a deserted location. "I thought he was at the tree line?"

"Justin had us park about a block away from his location," Chris replied as he locked the van. "Come on."

He broke into a jog, and she scrambled to follow him. Chris fluidly moved through the trees, lightly jumping over jutting roots and dodging branches.

Justin gave a report of what was going on, and which street the guards were moving on. She had no idea if that meant they were near or not. She tuned it out, focusing on her running.

Tamsin stumbled as a hidden root caught her foot. She managed to regain her balance and not fall, but barely. She slowed a bit. It would do no good if she tripped and broke something. She ducked to avoid a thick branch and felt a shock of pain in her thigh as a lower one she didn't see hit her.

Chris slowed next to her. "You doing okay over there?"

She glanced at him as another branch smacked her shoulder.

She was not good at this.

"Yeah, I'm fine," she muttered.

"Look, maybe it would be better if you shifted," he said. "You could navigate better."

"No, I'm fine," she replied, her toe catching on another damn root. "I've got this."

He slowed to a stop, and she stopped to look at him. "You're having issues. I didn't think. Just shift."

"No," she snapped. "If I shift, I can't be your back-up."

"It'll be fine," he said. "You can back me up by finding him first. And not alerting everyone to your location."

She knew she was making a ton of noise. He didn't need to point it out. But she wasn't shifting. "I've got this," she ground out between clenched teeth.

He clenched his jaw and studied her. Finally, he nodded curtly and started running again. "Keep up."

She narrowed her eyes at the way he said it. She wasn't some child who was disobeying. She just wasn't going to shift. She ran after Chris, reminded of why it wouldn't work between them. He didn't understand.

But he didn't know, a little voice whispered in her mind. *And he wouldn't.*

There could be nothing between them until... she stopped that thought.

Her panther growled in the back of her mind, unhappy. But there was nothing it could do about it. It was as stuck as she was. She tried to keep her eyes on Chris as he ran ahead of her.

He was getting farther and farther away. She could still see him between the trees, though.

The leaves slid under her feet, making her footing uncertain.

If she was going to run like this in the trees, she needed to get some better shoes.

She didn't hear Chris slipping and sliding all over.

"He's just ahead," Chris announced.

She tripped, and a branch whapped her on the side of her head as she stumbled to a stop. The branch knocked the earpiece out, and she jerked to the side and fumbled as she grabbed for it. It bounced on her palm, and by sheer luck she managed to close her hand and hold onto it.

Grace of a cat, her ass. More like a drunken deer on a frozen pond.

But she'd never been graceful, so it was nothing new. She put the earpiece back in and started running again. She was intently watching for new obstacles she had to dodge, trying to keep the branches from catching in her hair, or hitting her in the arm.

Her panther was growling in alarm in the back of her mind. It took her a moment to realize what had upset it. Her heart froze for a second.

She'd only heard Chris in her earpiece.

Tamsin stopped running and looked around. Chris was nowhere in sight. She turned in a circle, looking for any sign of him, her heart pounding in her chest.

It wasn't the fear of getting lost that had her worried. She'd eventually find her way out, even if she had to climb a tree to do it. No, it was knowing the guards were out there somewhere. She didn't know if they had made it to the trees or not. Justin may have said, but she'd stopped listening. The guards may not even know she was missing. She had no intention of tipping them off.

"Chris, I don't see you," she did her best to keep her voice calm as fear made her hands grow cold. She didn't see any trace of his passage, either. Of course, he'd moved through the forest like he was one with it.

She took a deep breath, trying to find his scent trail, but she only picked up soil, sap, and the sharp smell plants gave when crushed. Mostly from the ones around her.

"Chris?" she called when she didn't get an answer.

The angry roar of a tiger ripped through the air to her right. It didn't sound close.

Was that Chris?

She turned in the direction it came from.

Chris might have shifted.

If he had, it probably meant he needed her help.

Before she could take a step, she heard a sharp snapping sound behind her. Like someone stepping on a small branch. She froze in her tracks.

The hairs on the back of her neck rose in alarm. Someone was right behind her.

And it wasn't Chris.

Chapter 16

Chris ran through the trees, letting his tiger take lead. He'd learned long ago that was the best way to avoid tripping over everything, including his own two feet.

Tamsin ran along behind him, stumbling like a drunk panda. He'd suggested she shift, but she refused, and he couldn't figure out why. She clearly wasn't comfortable running in the trees.

He saw a glint ahead through the trees, and his tiger snarled in triumph.

They'd found him.

"He's just ahead," he announced. More for Tamsin than Justin, although he needed to know, too. He wanted Tamsin to know the run was almost over.

He took a deep breath, but didn't pick up any new scents.

That was odd.

If what he saw had been the sign of someone, the scent should have carried to him.

"The three guards reached the tree line," Justin reported.

"Proximity?" Chris asked, focusing on the target ahead.

"Not in your trajectory. You'll be—"

"What?" Chris demanded, alarmed at Justin's sudden loss in communication. "Report. We'll be... what?"

"Another group of guards just arrived, and they're entering the tree line near you," Justin replied tensely. "They're close. Really close. Looks like they're on an intercept course."

"Copy that," Chris acknowledged, slowing down. "Ready for action?"

He glanced behind him when Tamsin didn't respond. His gut clenched when he didn't see her there.

He'd been running parallel to the road, the tree line wasn't far away. The guards would be here soon. His tiger didn't care. It had one thought on its mind.

Find Tamsin.

"Tamsin," he impatiently waited to hear her reply through the comm earpiece.

It remained silent.

"Justin, can you find Tamsin?" Chris bit out, fighting his tiger's panic.

All of the communication pieces had a small tracking chip in them. Maybe...

"All I know is she's within twenty-five yards of you," Justin replied.

He needed to find her. Now.

Chris grabbed his shirt and yanked it off while toeing off his shoes. His tiger pressed at his skin, anxious to be out. *I have to get the clothes off,* he reminded his primal side. If they shifted while dressed, the torn clothing could trap them. Then it would have to be ripped off, wasting even more time.

"Chris, you gotta keep it together," Justin said urgently. "She's okay, man. And she's close. Her tracker is close to you."

A low growl rumbled from his throat, that was the best response he could give. His tiger needed to find her. She'd been lost before, and he'd only just found her.

"Shit," Justin sounded worried, but Chris couldn't bring himself to care.

Chris managed to get his pants to his ankles before his tiger took over. His viewpoint changed and was lower to the ground. The colors became muted, but everything was sharper. He stepped out of his pants as the scents slammed into him. If he hadn't been prepared for it, he would have been overwhelmed.

But his tiger was in control, and it quickly sorted through all the scents, dismissing everything that was not relevant. *Tamsin.* That was all that mattered.

The musk of a wolf shifter caught his attention, and he roared in challenge.

Enemy.

He crouched with a low warning growl. *Danger.* He had to get rid of them. They were a threat to Tamsin.

Threats were not tolerated.

He silently stalked through the bushes in the direction of the scent. He was in hunt mode, and nothing would stop him from getting to his prey. The air shifted, and he picked up the scents of two wolf shifters close to his location. He suppressed an angry growl and tensed his muscles, prepared to attack.

Wolves fight in packs.

But they weren't in wolf form, the musk wasn't right. It would be easy for him to eliminate the shifters in their human forms. Their fragile skin would stand no chance against his claws and teeth.

Chris fought his tiger for control. When it realized he wanted to use strategy, it receded slightly. Anything to find Tamsin faster. It had waited too long to get her.

No more.

Killing them would be messy, and complicated. He needed to incapacitate them. Take out one, and you take out two or three as the others remove the fallen member to safety.

His tiger growled, not liking the idea of leaving an enemy alive to attack another day.

But these weren't really the enemy. They were mercenaries doing a job, just like Nightfair. His tiger reluctantly agreed and gave full control to Chris.

He'd never had his tiger fight him so hard before. He'd have to figure out why.

Later.

Right now, he had a pair of wolves to take out.

Chris silently moved through the thick foliage to get a better view of his adversaries. The two wolves stood several feet apart, facing away from each other.

Amateurs.

They must not be used to fighting when not everyone was in the same form. Of course, they were wolves. Maybe they only fought in large packs.

Whatever.

He'd use their positioning to his benefit.

Chris noiselessly approached the guard on the right. The wolf in human form scanned back and forth, staring intently into the bushes. He kept his gaze focused on the ground and didn't even bother to look up into the trees.

Stupid.

He had ears and a nose. He had to have known he was fighting a tiger. There was no way he could've missed Chris's roar. Everyone knew cats were the threat that not only attacked from the ground, but also dropped from above.

Perhaps the shifter they were hunting was a wolf, like them. It didn't matter.

He got close enough to the guard and gathered himself. With a powerful pounce, he flew through the air and rammed into the guard. As he connected, he slammed his heavy paw into the guard's head, careful to keep his claws sheathed. The guard didn't even grunt as he went down, knocked unconscious by the strong blow.

Chris didn't waste a second before he pivoted to leap on the other guard. There had been no way to silence the first guard's fall, and his partner was turning to see what the noise was.

The remaining guard's eyes widened in alarm and he raised his arms in a classic shooting stance, trying to point a gun at Chris. He didn't get the weapon in position before Chris plowed into him, knocking him into the tree behind him.

The man grunted as he connected with the tree, and his hands lost their grip, the gun tumbling through the air. Chris didn't give him a chance to get his bearings before he took him to the ground.

The guard wore thick combat pants and a tactical vest. Chris could easily tear them apart with his claws, but he didn't want to kill the guard. He wanted him out of commission.

Killing him wouldn't accomplish anything, and it might make the other mercenary company go on a vendetta mission against him, and possibly even Nightfair.

He moved to bash his paw into the guard's head when the man slammed his fist into Chris's ribs. Chris roared, startled. The hit didn't really hurt. The guard didn't have good leverage, and there had been no power behind it. The guard clearly wasn't going down without a fight.

Chris didn't have time to indulge him. He needed the man out, but he was squirming underneath him. If he hit the guard wrong, Chris could break his neck instead of knocking him out.

The guard twisted and slammed a rock into Chris's head. The sharp stab of pain distracted him, and the guard managed to pull himself to his feet. He looked at Chris for a heartbeat, then turned and ran.

Chris leapt after him. The man stumbled, and instead of catching him on the shoulders and knocking him down as he intended, Chris landed fully on the man's body.

He heard a sharp crack, and the man cried out in pain. Chris jumped off the guard's body and saw the man's leg was at an odd angle. He must have caught it in a root or something and wasn't able to get it freed before Chris landed on him.

The pressure of Chris's weight on his body must have broken his leg. The guard started to get up, but then his eyes rolled up and he passed out. Chris took a deep breath, but didn't smell any blood. *Good.* The bone hadn't broken through the skin.

Justin had said there were other guards in the trees. Chris let out another roar. If they were all wolves, they'd come to investigate and find their fallen companions.

Now to find Tamsin.

He pivoted and started in the direction where he last saw her, his claws digging into the ground, giving him better traction. He had only taken a step when he heard a soft pop and a *thwack* as something hit the tree next to him. He immediately recognized the sound. A glance to the side confirmed it.

A tranq dart quivered in the bark of the tree.

Chris jumped forward and spun to face the threat. A guard stood there with a tranq gun pointed directly at him. Chris had forgotten that Tamsin had said they traveled in threes. The man watched him coldly, his arms steady in a firing position.

There would be no surprising this one.

Chris tensed his body, ready to jump.

He heard a soft moan from the location of the first guard that he'd knocked out.

He was coming to.

Chris pulled up his lip in a silent snarl and took a step back.

Let me go, and I'll leave you alone, the action silently said.

The guard's eyes narrowed, and he primed the gun. All he had to do was pull the trigger, and it'd be lights out.

Chris was under no illusion that he was faster than a bullet. If it had been a human holding the gun, he might have been able to charge him before he fired. But it was another shifter with reflexes as fast as his.

They silently stared at each other, both waiting for the other to make the first move. Chris knew his time was running out. It was just a matter of time before the other guard fully woke and joined the first.

Plus, Tamsin was off somewhere, possibly lost and in trouble. Maybe even captured by another group of guards they didn't know about.

He needed to get to her.

That wouldn't happen if he was knocked out by a tranquilizer dart.

He had no choice.

There was a crashing noise in the trees to his right. Someone was headed this way, fast. The guard's eyes stayed locked on Chris. As much as he wanted to know who, or what, was tearing through the brush, he kept his attention fixed on the guard, waiting for his chance. All he needed was a second's distraction.

A faint whine split the air. *Sirens.*

The guard he'd knocked unconscious stumbled to the man watching Chris.

"Pad's over there." He tilted his head in the direction of the guard Chris had injured. "Looks like broken leg."

The guard narrowed his eyes at Chris. "Mobile?"

"Negative."

"Splint it, we'll call in for back-up."

The guard moved back into the trees, and Chris heard some sticks breaking as he made a splint.

"We seem to have a bit of a problem. I can't tranq you and haul your tiger ass out of here with a man down." He curled his lip in a sneer. "And I'm not leaving a prime test subject behind."

Chris snarled, his tiger waiting for the man to slip.

"But these tranq darts are unpredictable," the guard continued. "If I shoot you now, you might wake up before my back-up arrives."

Just his luck, he got an idiot who loved the sound of his own voice.

"Duke, you almost done?" Mr. Talky yelled to the other guard.

Chris wondered what his nickname was. It wasn't likely they were using real names right now.

"Yeah, Cathy," Duke replied. "Just about. He's stable. We can get him out of here."

Cathy? Wonder if that was for Chatty Cathy. Fits.

"What about the back-up?" Cathy didn't stop looking at Chris as he spoke.

Chris was going to have to risk it. The asshole wasn't going to give him an opening.

"Delayed. There's been some sort of incident."

The sound of the sirens grew louder.

Ginger and burnt sugar.

"Fuck it. I'll just shoot you twice and hope that it won't stop your heart and kill you."

Tamsin's scent was practically on top of him. Chris snapped his head to the right to see Tamsin stumble to a halt a few feet away. A man he didn't recognize stopped next to her.

Who was that?

He smelled like a panther shifter and was standing too close to her.

"Freeze," she ordered, pointing the tranq gun at Cathy.

"What do we have here?" Cathy's eyes darted between Chris and Tamsin.

Duke stepped up next to Cathy, an unsheathed knife in his hand by his side.

"You hear those sirens?" The stranger next to Tamsin smiled tightly. "Cops are coming. You wanna explain this situation to them?"

The two guards exchanged a look.

Cathy looked at Chris with an off-kilter smile. "Another time. We'll just get our man and be on our way." They slowly backed away, keeping the gun pointed on Chris.

When they reached their injured man, Cathy put his gun in its holster. Chris suppressed a wince at the inept way they hoisted Pad over Duke's shoulder.

Chris moved next to Tamsin, and the stranger took several steps away from her side. She slowly dropped her arms until they were pointed at the ground. He'd noticed her stance was off when she held the gun. He'd have to give her lessons on how to handle a weapon.

They were lucky Cathy hadn't noticed.

"Are they the reason you shifted?" Tamsin asked, her hand briefly touching his head.

His cat rolled in his mind, happy to have her touch him. Happy to have her safe and with him again.

The stranger moved to look after the retreating guards, and Chris again wondered who he was, and how Tamsin had found him in the forest.

Was he the escaped captive they were looking for?

And if he was, how did she manage to stumble across him? He didn't look injured at all, unlike the other captive they'd rescued. In fact, he looked almost artificially roughed up.

His scent was familiar, too. Chris inhaled deeply, but couldn't quite place it. He didn't know the man, he was certain of that. But still… the scent was familiar.

Very familiar.

Tamsin's ginger and burnt sugar, combined with the acrid burn of broken branches, filled his senses. He couldn't get a good read of the stranger.

He was being paranoid.

"Where are his clothes?" the man asked.

Tamsin glanced around and shook her head. "I don't know. He was wearing them when we got out of the van."

Unhappy with them talking over him, Chris brushed against Tamsin, then darted through the forest to retrieve his clothes. It wasn't that he was uncomfortable when naked. No, it was the sirens growing ever louder. He was pretty sure they were headed in their direction.

Humans didn't tend to react positively when they encountered a tiger. It was usually scream and shoot first, ask questions later. He didn't feel like getting shot at today. One gun pointed at him had been enough. Human law enforcement frowned upon naked people in public, too.

Best to just get dressed.

It didn't take him long to make it back to where he'd stripped, but he puzzled over the stranger's scent as he went.

Where did he know it from?

He reached his clothes and quickly dressed, relieved to find he hadn't torn them with his claws. His keys were even still in his pocket. *Good.* That meant they wouldn't have any issues getting back in the van.

His earpiece.

He studied the ground for the small black plastic piece, hoping he hadn't stepped on it and destroyed it. He shook his head to get rid of an irritating buzz.

"If Justin would just shut up, I'd find it faster," he muttered to himself.

He heard Justin's voice.

Chris wanted to smack himself upside the head. The only way he'd hear Justin's voice was through the earpiece. He tilted his head and followed the sound of the noise.

There it was.

It sat safely by the base of the tree, nestled in a pile of leaves. He grabbed it and slid it in his ear.

Justin's worried voice said, "Justin to Chris, Justin to Chris. Come in, Chris."

He kept repeating it, and his voice had a strained quality, like he had been saying those same words for a while.

Since Chris shifted.

"Justin to Chris—"

"I'm here," Chris interjected.

"About time," Justin cried. "What the hell happened? You both went dark on us, and I couldn't get eyes on anything."

"We both went dark?" Chris asked, jogging back to Tamsin. "Tamsin, too?"

"Yeah, we didn't realize it until you started growling," Justin still sounded a little tense. "I tried to reach her and got no response. What the fuck happened?"

What happened to her comm?

Chris didn't plan to tell Justin that his cat went crazy because he lost Tamsin again. So, he stuck to the other half of the truth.

"We encountered a group of guards," he stated and briefly reported the highlights of the conversation.

Justin gave a low whistle. "Well, we know for a fact they're abducting shifters. We just don't know why."

"Or if it's only here, or elsewhere, too," Chris concluded darkly.

"Regardless," Sierra broke in, "you need to get out of there. I'm monitoring the local law enforcement, and someone called the police."

Chris picked up the pace until he was close to where he'd left Tamsin, then he slowed. His tiger didn't trust the stranger with her, and he had to agree.

Who was he, and where did he come from?

Chris changed his trajectory so he arrived from a different spot than he'd left. He paused behind a large tree and studied them. The man was tall, but a bit shorter than Chris. His skin and hair were dark. He could be white with a heavy tan, or Hispanic.

His clothes looked a bit worn, but that could have been from the run in the trees and bush. He stood close to Tamsin.

Too close, Chris's tiger thought.

They were talking softly, and he could see both their profiles. Tamsin had a concerned look on her face as she watched the stranger.

"Ray, can you remember anything? Anything at all?" Tamsin asked, and the stranger shook his head, a slight frown on his face.

Ray? How did she know his name already? Chris also wanted to know what they were discussing, but the sirens were close. *Really close.* They needed to get out of there.

His tiger wanted to push them apart. Shove the stranger away. *He didn't belong here.*

There was something about the stranger, *Ray,* that bothered him.

He took in a deep breath to try to get himself under control and pulled in their combined scents. His eyes widened with shock

Ray's scent had traces of Tamsin's lab. He had been there. Recently.

"Oh, Ray," Tamsin said and suddenly she was in the stranger's arms. He embraced her and dropped his head to her shoulder.

Chris froze in place as his tiger roared in anger over the embrace. He had to fight his primal self's desire to tear them apart. They didn't belong together. They shouldn't be embracing.

The other male needed to be gone.

Under all of that, his tiger growled one word.

Mine.

Chapter 17

Tamsin saw the terror in Ray's eyes. "Oh, Ray." She stepped forward to touch him and ground him in the here and now.

His arms wrapped around her and pulled her into his body in a tight embrace. In the back of her mind her panther growled uneasily. It didn't like him this close. She froze for a second then put her arms around him. He clearly needed the touch of pride.

She was the only panther around and would smell of kin. Even though he wasn't in her pride, and she hadn't seen him in years. But she knew him from long ago. That was enough for their primal selves to accept. Although hers wasn't too happy with it. It still accepted the touch as a pride member needing help.

Tamsin drew in a deep breath and picked up Chris's scent. She turned her head and met his angry eyes. His jaw was clenched, and he looked like he was a breath away from attacking.

With relief, she pulled away from Ray and glanced around quickly, looking for the threat. Nothing else was around except the three of them. She didn't examine how she'd rather face the threat of attack than be in Ray's hold. Instead, she focused on Chris.

What had made him so angry?

"We've got to go," Chris's voice was a breath above a growl.

He quickly moved forward and his hand locked with hers. For all the anger in his face, his touch was gentle. But the hold was tight. He wasn't letting go. She squeezed his hand, letting him know she wasn't letting go either.

She didn't have time to examine her reactions. He started walking in the direction of the van, tugging her along behind him.

"Chris, what's going on?" Tamsin tugged on her hand to get him to slow down.

His hand tightened on hers, and Chris tilted his head slightly to the left, then glanced over at her.

"What happened to your comm?" Chris asked in a tight voice.

"My what?" Tamsin asked.

She decided to give up on getting her hand back, and instead, focus on what the heck was going on. The sirens were behind them and were no longer growing louder.

They must have stopped.

"Where are we going?" Ray asked from her left.

Chris had a dark look on his face when he glanced at Ray. "To the van. To get out of here."

"Why are we in such a rush?" Tamsin asked.

"Did you hear the sirens?" Chris's tone was a bit softer as he answered her.

"Yeah," Tamsin answered. "How could we miss them? They had great timing."

"Great timing. Right. Why did you call the police?" Chris asked with a look at Ray.

Ray had moved up next to them, keeping close except to dodge the many trees and bushes.

Ray looked at Chris with wide eyes, like he was surprised by the question. Something about it struck Tamsin as off. Her panther snarled and she got the feeling it thought he was lying. She tilted her head, unsuccessfully trying to figure out why her panther felt that way, and about what.

"I didn't," Ray replied with a shake of his head.

"You told them you did." Chris shot him a cold look.

What was wrong with him?

He was being downright rude and practically calling Ray a liar. They were shifters, and it was practically impossible to lie to a shifter. There had to be some misunderstanding.

"Chris—" Tamsin began, but Ray cut her off.

"Did I? You sure you heard right?" He dodged around a tree.

Chris replied in a flat tone, "You implied you did when you said the cops were coming. Why?"

He was moving quickly through the trees and bushes, but not so fast that she was having trouble keeping up. In fact, he seemed to be taking care to find routes she could easily navigate. It was at odds with his cold interrogation of Ray.

What was she missing?

"I heard the sirens," Ray answered. "I used it to my advantage. I figured if they were holding guns on people in the forest, they wouldn't want to meet with any cops. Plus, I never said *I* called the cops. Just that they were coming."

"Tamsin had a gun," Chris looked sharply at Ray.

Ray smiled at her. "Yeah, since when do you use guns?"

Chris's eyes widened in surprise for heartbeat, then an indifferent mask fell over his face. "You know him?"

"I do," she said, relieved to clear all of this up. "We knew each other long ago. Ray went to high school with me and was in my pride. "

"How'd you end up together in the forest?" Chris asked, still carefully leading her through the trees.

Ahead, the van's white paint beckoned like a beacon of safety. She was relieved they were almost out of the woods. She'd spent too much time in them lately.

Way too much time.

"He was running from those," she hesitated, not sure what she should name the mercenaries they'd been looking for. "Guards."

"Really? What a coincidence," Chris commented flatly.

"I call it good timing," Ray replied with a friendly smile. "If I hadn't run into Tamsin, I might've been caught."

"Why were you running from them?" Chris asked.

"Because they were chasing me?" Ray said with a grin, inviting Chris to join in on the joke.

Chris did not seem amused. "Why were they chasing you?"

He stopped at the edge of the tree line. The van was just ahead, but he didn't move into the open area.

Ray looked at Tamsin with a pleading expression. "Why do I get the feeling he doesn't trust me?"

"Because I don't trust you," Chris stepped forward so his body blocked Tamsin from Ray. "Who are you?"

She recognized it as a sign of protection. It struck her as a little odd, though. She was the one with the gun.

Maybe Chris was afraid she'd shoot him by mistake.

The thought made her panther huff in laughter in her mind. Most likely, he'd forgotten she had a gun and was just falling back into his training. Protection mode.

"I'm Ray," he answered with a wounded look.

"Where did you come from, Ray?" Chris drew out his name like he thought it was false.

"You wouldn't believe me if I told you," Ray replied calmly.

"Try me," Chris's voice was hard. "Tell me where you came from."

"Look, the cops are coming." Ray's brow furrowed with worry as he looked in the direction they'd left. "I don't trust them. Can you at least give me a lift out of here?"

Chris shook his head. "No, I don't think so."

Chris's legs were apart, and his back muscles were tense.

Tamsin realized he was ready to attack. She wasn't sure why Ray wasn't telling Chris what he'd told her, but they didn't have time for... whatever this was. Not if the police were on their way. She had no idea if the gun in the holster was legal, but she'd seen too many movies where police saw a gun and suddenly everyone was on the ground getting yelled at.

"He came from the lab," she blurted out.

"What was that?" Chris snapped.

She heard the same words from his earpiece. Justin must have yelled them.

Why was that such a surprise?

Wasn't that the reason they came charging off, to find someone who had escaped from the lab?

"Do we have time to talk about this?" She took a step to Chris's side, and he moved to keep her behind him.

Tamsin managed not to roll her eyes. Ray was not a threat.

She hoped.

Chris tilted his head a tiny bit to the side, and she got the impression he was listening to his earpiece. Justin must have been talking very softly, or she would have been able to hear him. She frowned and wished her earpiece hadn't stopped working.

"Let's go," Chris said curtly. He stared at Ray. "You too."

Chris turned and headed to the van. Tamsin happened to be looking at Ray just after Chris turned and saw him narrow his eyes, and his nostrils flared. A sneer crossed his face. It was only there for a moment, and if she hadn't been looking right at him, she would have missed it. Then his expression returned to being slightly worried.

Ray met her gaze and gave her a relieved smile. "Glad he's not leaving me behind."

Tamsin swallowed, not so sure about it. Ever since Ray snuck up behind her earlier, she'd had an odd feeling. She put it as just worried about the entire situation, but maybe that wasn't it.

She hurried to catch up to Chris who was only a few steps ahead. He paused and looked over his shoulder. He hesitated, then held out his hand for her to take.

Well, at least he wasn't simply grabbing her hand like a doll this time.

She grumbled at herself. That wasn't accurate, and she knew it. He'd taken her hand, true, but she held on.

And his hold had helped her navigate through the brush and trees.

There were tiny lines of tension around his eyes that seemed to ease when she slid her hand into his. A small smile curved his mouth, and it felt like a hug to her insides.

Then he glanced at Ray, and the smile disappeared.

"Let's go," Chris ordered.

They made it the few feet to the van without encountering the police. For some reason, she half expected them to come pouring out of the bushes screaming *Freeze*. Her imagination was clearly running away from her. She decided to blame it on television. She didn't get a lot of time to watch it, but when she did it was always investigation and crime shows.

Chris unlocked the back door to the van but didn't open them.

"What's wrong?" Tamsin asked when he simply stood there. "Aren't we leaving?"

She glanced around to see if he'd noticed some threat she missed. But it was quiet. Just the three of them. Even the road in front of the van was empty.

Chris looked at Ray. "Take three steps toward the front of the van and face the road."

"What?" Ray asked.

"You heard me," Chris replied and stared impassively at Ray, crossing his arms over his chest.

Chris clearly didn't plan to move a muscle until Ray walked to the front of the van as he'd ordered. She couldn't figure out what was so important about it.

Was this some kind of male dominance bullshit? If so, they didn't have time for that.

"Chris, I don't know why the police aren't here yet, but they'll head this way and find the van." Tamsin glanced around, worried about the cops arriving any minute now. "Don't we need to go?"

"We do," Chris agreed. "But not until I blindfold him."

Tamsin stared at Chris, certain he had to be joking. "Not funny."

"I'm not joking," Chris replied, his jaw tight.

This was a side of him she'd never seen.

Was this Chris in work mode?

The laughing, playful guy who normally teased her was gone. The one in front of her was a soldier you did not want to mess with. She found this serious side of him intriguing.

Very intriguing.

Ray took a step closer to her. "Tamsin, can't you—"

A low growl from Chris had him taking a hasty step back.

Okay, then.

If she didn't know better, she'd think Chris was warning Ray away from her.

"Can't you talk some sense into him? We need to get out of here. Not waste time arguing over stupid shit," Ray finished.

She glanced at Chris's hard expression and shook her head. "His toys, his rules. Just do what he said and we can go."

"But I have to be blindfolded? What do you have in there, something illegal?" Ray scoffed.

Why was he arguing?

Chris folded his hands behind his back and adjusted his stance so his legs were somewhat apart. She realized he was in a military rest position. *Damn, he's fine.* His shirt pulled tight over his chest, outlining his muscles. The hard line to his jaw made her catch her breath. She knew the fun, playful Chris, but this serious stranger was fascinating.

Ray's shoulders dropped when he looked at Chris and seemed to realize he meant it. Ray finally moved toward the front of the van and faced the road.

Tamsin almost felt sorry for him. She wouldn't want to be blindfolded, either.

Chris yanked open the door and jumped in the van. She moved to the door so she could see him and watch Ray, too.

"Why do you want to blindfold him?" she asked softly.

Chris moved to the door and crouched to reply in an equally quiet tone.

"I don't know who he is. He doesn't need to see what's in the van," he replied.

"You could just put him up front and close the door." She gestured to the compartment separator. "If the window's closed, he can't see in the back."

"True," Chris nodded, "but there's a few problems with that course of action. First, it separates me from my back-up. If that window is closed, you won't be able to hear what's going on up front."

A warm feeling ran through her at that.

He still considered her his backup.

"Unless we get me a different earpiece," she said, pulling the defective item off her ear and holding it out to him.

Chris took it off her hand, and his eyes lit with laughter. "Did you touch it?"

"Well, yeah," she said with a perplexed frown. "I had to, to get it on."

"No." He shook his head, and his thumb moved on the side of the device. "After you put it in."

"I didn't…" she began, and paused. *Did she touch it when the branch hit her?* "Maybe."

"It's off." He handed it back to her with a grin. "Here's your comm back."

That's what he meant by comm.

"Thanks." She decided to ignore his heart-stopping grin and put the earpiece back on. "Don't know how that happened."

"Your comm was off?" Justin exclaimed.

"Apparently," Chris replied, his eyes laughing with her. He covered his mouth.

"Don't you laugh," she warned.

"Well, at least we know why she went dark," Justin muttered, his voice thick. She had the impression he was fighting laughter, too.

Tamsin took a breath and decided to get things back on track.

"Okay," she said briskly. "So, I can stay in the back and you can keep him in the front, no blindfold needed."

"Not a good idea," Justin said over the comm.

"Why not?" she asked.

"We have to keep him with us right now," Chris replied.

213

"Are you going to take him back to the hotel?" She figured they'd drop Ray off a few blocks away, or something.

What did keeping him with them have to do with blindfolding him or not?

"That's the plan," Chris replied. "If he is an escaped captive from the lab, he needs to be debriefed. If he isn't, then I want to figure out what game he's playing."

"And we don't want him to know our current base of operations," Justin added.

Chris nodded and stood. "So, we need to blindfold him."

She felt like this was some crazy circular argument. Looked like Ray was going to get his eyes covered. She suppressed a shiver. The idea of not being able to see what was happening or where she was going made her stomach churn.

"Why didn't you blindfold me when you first brought me to the van?" she asked.

Chris gave her a laughing grin as he opened a different cupboard than the one her gun had been in. "I was there to rescue you. You don't blindfold the person you're saving."

She laughed at his logic. Then a thought struck her.

"Wait, we came here to rescue Ray, too."

The smile immediately fell from his face, and he grabbed a folded piece of cloth off a shelf. "That remains to be seen."

"We'll need to get another room," she muttered. "Yours only has one bed."

"Won't be an issue," Justin injected.

"Why not?" Tamsin asked. She wasn't going to share a room with Ray. Chris, on the other hand... she wouldn't mind a repeat of earlier. Her body grew wet just thinking about it.

"Current plan is to head out tonight," Chris answered. His eyes met hers, and he inhaled slightly. She saw heat flare to life in his gaze. "We need to get our guest to HQ. And now we have Ray, too. The sooner we get them in a secure location, the better."

The heat in his gaze told her he was thinking about getting alone with her, too. She couldn't stop her smile.

He returned the smile, then closed the cabinet. She started to take a step back and remembered she still had on the gun.

"Do you want to put away the gun?" she asked and reached to begin unhooking the holster.

Chris shook his head. "No, hold on to it."

He moved to the van door, and she stepped back.

"Why?"

He jumped out and stepped around the door, his gaze locked on Ray. In a low voice that only she could hear, he said, "We might need it."

His words sent a chill down her spine, and she shivered again. All thoughts of tangling in the sheets evaporated.

She hoped he wasn't right.

Chapter 18

Chris clenched his jaw, fighting for control.

His tiger did not want *Ray*, if that was his name, near Tamsin. It didn't want him in the van. And it most definitely didn't want him heading to the motel room with them.

"Tamsin," Justin called quietly over the comm.

"Yeah?" she replied as softly.

Chris turned on the radio. Alternative rock filled the van. He didn't want Ray hearing their discussion. The other man sat stiffly in the passenger seat, clearly unhappy about the blindfold.

At least he didn't cuff Ray.

Not that Chris hadn't considered it. But Tamsin was right. Ray may be a victim in all of this. Just because the man made his tiger's hackles stand up didn't mean he was lying.

Chris wished he believed that. There was just something *off* about Ray.

"You said you knew Ray, right?" Justin asked.

Although she hadn't had her comm on, Justin had heard her comments through Chris's.

"Went to high school together, yeah. Why?" she asked curiously.

She still kept her voice quiet, and Chris only heard her through his own earpiece. It was unlikely Ray could hear her.

"What's his full name?"

Chris didn't bother hiding his grin. Not like Ray could see him. If he'd had his head on straight, and not been in such a knot about Ray, he would have thought about that, too. If Justin had Ray's last name, he could dig up some information about him. Possibly even verify his story.

"Raymond Harris."

Chris's smile faded with her answer. Raymond Harris. Not a very unique name. Chris thought about how Justin would trace down those leads as Justin asked her a series of questions to narrow it down.

Chris reached the motel just as Justin finished his questions. He drove around the block in a different pattern than he'd used before. There were really only so many ways you could circle a building, but Chris tried to mix it up. It wasn't so much an attempt to give someone the slip as it was to make sure no one was following him.

He turned on the street past the motel and drove down another block. He'd been here two nights. If they were going to stay, he'd have to find a different motel. They weren't, though. The mission was to rescue Tamsin. Since she was sitting in the back of the van, safe and sound, the mission was complete. His tiger purred over that thought.

Tamsin was safe and sound.

But the mission would truly be a success once they returned to Oakdale. Not that he anticipated any trouble before then, but paranoia came with the job.

"We've sent all the information you gave us to Mac," Sierra announced.

"Why?" Tamsin asked.

"To find out what we can on him," Justin replied. "I could dig it up, but my connection is slow. His isn't. He'll be able to get the information much faster."

"Any word on when we're pulling out?" Chris asked in a normal tone.

With Ray sitting next to him, there was no way he could speak softly enough for the other man not to hear. So, he might as well act like he was just now talking to them. Maybe Ray would buy it, maybe not. It really didn't matter unless they were told to bring him back to HQ. It'd be better if he came willingly, but Chris had no reservations about tranquilizing him and bringing him along unconscious, either.

"Not yet," Sierra answered. "Our guest is resting fitfully, but I'm not worried about him crashing. If we need to head out, we'll be fine."

Chris pulled into the parking lot of the motel, sure he didn't have a tail. He parked near the room and looked over at Ray, his foot on the brake and the car still in gear. He could make the man stay blindfolded until he got in the room.

Would it matter? They were leaving soon anyway.

Truth be told, he didn't have to put the blindfold on him. What would Ray do, go tell the Sons of Asena where they were? The only way he could do that would be if he ran away and called them. If he disappeared, they'd be gone in a heartbeat. Besides, if he really had escaped from the lab, they were the last people he'd want to talk to.

When they had watched the man escape on the video, they hadn't been able to get a good shot of his face. Maybe that was what caused Chris's unease. *No.* It was something else. He just wished he could put his finger on it.

Something about Ray made his tiger snarl, and that was all he could get out of it.

Ray had no idea they were Nightfair. Of course, once they took him back to HQ in Oakdale, he'd figure it out. But by then, he'd be cleared to go, or Damien would have a plan to deal with him.

With a silent sigh, Chris put the van in park and turned off the engine. As much fun as it would be to keep Ray blindfolded, he knew he couldn't do that. Tamsin would probably object, or something.

Plus, it wouldn't matter if Ray saw the outside of a motel room or not.

"We're here," Chris announced. "You can take off your blindfold."

Ray immediately removed the piece of cloth tied around his head and blinked in the light. He stared at the row of motel room doors.

"This is it? This is your base of operations?" Ray asked.

Base of operations?

Chris racked his brain to determine if he'd said anything that would indicate they were an organized group.

Nope.

"Our base of operations?" Chris said with a raised brow. "Interesting phrase to use."

Ray's shoulders stiffened, but he gave Chris an easy smile. "I don't know what else to call it. I mean, you brought me to a motel."

"Where did you expect us to take you?" Chris asked, keeping his tone light.

"I don't know." Ray frowned. "You know, I didn't really think about it. But with all the blindfold stuff, the communication earpieces, and the secrecy about the van, I gotta say a motel was not on the list."

Chris heard Tamsin open the back door of the van, and he casually closed the window on the separation to the back. He didn't want Ray to see what was back there.

He opened his door. "You might as well get out. We're going to be here for a bit."

Chris got out and closed his door. He saw Ray give a curious glance to the door in the separation, but he got out of the van. *Good.* If the other man had gone for the door, Chris would have tranqued him and taken him back to HQ, no matter what.

Chris reached the door and saw the *Do not disturb* sign Tamsin had left was still there. He took a deep breath, but didn't pick up any stray scents on the door.

"Careful," Tamsin warned when he reached for the handle with the key card in hand.

Chris paused and glanced at her with one brow raised in question.

"One of my... pets is still loose," she explained with a small smile.

Right. The mouse.

He looked at the door handle then slid in the key card and opened it. He could hear the mice scurrying around in the cage. They froze when the door opened.

One of them was on a wheel, and it rolled up and back with the wheel as it stopped. Chris moved in, scanning the room for the missing mouse.

No sign of it.

"She's still here." Tamsin announced as she followed behind him.

"How do you know?" Chris asked.

Ray also came in the room and spoke at the same time, "Who's still here?"

"The food's gone," Tamsin replied, pointing to the box on the floor. "I put some pellets in there before we left, hoping to lure her out."

"Well, it worked," Chris replied. "She came out while we were gone. Too bad she didn't wait until we returned."

"But she's still here," Tamsin argued. "I wanted her to know there was food here, so she'd stay and not go hunting."

"Who's still here?" Ray asked again.

This time Tamsin glanced at him. The friendly smile she gave him made Chris want to growl. The warm smile Ray returned made him want to do more than just growl.

"My pets," Tamsin replied, pointing to the mouse cage.

"You have... mice... as pets?" Ray said slowly.

"Sure, why not? They are easy to clean up after and don't require a lot of care," she answered.

"Seriously, why are you in a motel with mice?" Ray frowned in confusion. "Tamsin, what's going on?"

She glanced over at Chris, her eyebrows up in a silent request for assistance.

If they were going to take Ray to HQ in Oakdale, Chris had better give him some info. But he wanted some first.

"Ray, you told Tamsin you escaped from... where?" Chris began.

Tamsin opened her mouth and he gave a small shake of his head. He wanted to hear what Ray had to say.

"I'm not really sure." Ray met Chris's gaze and oozed sincerity. "It was some sort of facility surrounded by woods. A lab facility. I managed to escape, but I know they're after me."

"Who's after you?" Chris asked.

"How did he know it was a lab facility?" Justin asked softly.

"Guards, soldiers," Ray said with a dark frown. "They moved like they had military training. Ordered us around. Forced us to go to different rooms."

"How did you get there?" Chris watched him carefully, looking for any tell-tale signs that he was lying.

"I don't know," Ray said with a heavy sigh. "I was taking a walk, and then I woke up on a hard cot."

"What happened?" Tamsin moved the box on the floor to the side of the room and dropped more mouse pellets in it.

"They brought me into a room," Ray said, a haunted look on his face. "It smelled of disinfectant. There was one chair. A guard returned with someone in lab coat. So, I guess I could have been in a hospital, but it didn't look like it.

"The guy in the lab coat carried a tray that had a syringe and an alcohol pad. He started to set the tray on a table, but the guard touched his arm and shook his head. I don't know why, but they left the room."

"What was in the syringe?" Tamsin asked as she sat on the corner of the bed.

"I don't know," Ray replied. "After they walked out, I tried the door handle and found it unlocked."

Ray paused and ran his hand over his face. Chris almost felt sorry for him. *Almost.*

"What did you do?" Chris crossed his arms and leaned against the wall.

"What anyone with any sense would do," Ray said with a wry smile. "I ran. I made it to a door that looked like it went outside and made a break for it."

"It makes sense," Justin commented. "Mac says to give him the cover. We should bring him in. If nothing else, offer him sanctuary."

Chris's tiger growled angrily in his mind. It had decided it didn't like Ray and wanted nothing to do with him. Chris clenched his jaw. Things were about to get worse. He knew what *bring him in* meant.

They only had one means of transportation. *The van.* Mac had taken the car back to Oakdale yesterday.

The van had two seats up front, and two bolted in the back. The two in back were fine for an op, but not a several hour drive. Plus, there were six of them. One was currently unconscious.

There was no way they'd all fit in the van comfortably. Which meant they'd have to rent a car. And he'd have to drive Ray and Tamsin home.

The only other option wasn't one he, or his tiger, would accept. Sierra had to travel with their unconscious guest. Someone had to be in the van with her. That would be either him, or Justin.

If it was him, then Justin would drive Ray and Tamsin.

Not going to happen.

Chris wouldn't feel comfortable with her out of his sight until they got back to home territory where it would be less likely that she'd get nabbed off the street.

"Chris." Tamsin looked at him curiously.

He knew she'd heard Justin's comment.

"We're friends of Tamsin's," Chris gave the cover story. "She was working at a lab in town and ran into some... trouble."

"What kind of trouble?" Ray gave Tamsin a worried look.

"Not quite the same type you did, but nothing good," Chris answered. "We came to take her home."

"You still live in Oakdale?" Ray asked.

Tamsin nodded. "Yeah, I do."

"I haven't been back in years," Ray said wistfully. "I should go back, see old friends."

Your wish is about to be answered.

"Look, if we just send you on your way, it's likely you'll get nabbed again," Chris said, doing his best to not sound as unhappy about this as he was. "Why don't you come with us? We'll get you safely to Oakdale, and then you can go... wherever."

Ray's eyes widened and a hopeful smile crossed his face. Chris couldn't stop the thought that it looked contrived. *False.* He shoved the thought back. He was a professional. Just because something about this man put his teeth on edge, didn't mean he couldn't push past it and help him out.

"That'd be… great." Ray blinked rapidly. "Just great."

Laying it on a bit thick, aren't you?

Chris glanced at Tamsin to see if she was buying into it. She had a soft smile on her face as she met his gaze. There was something in her smile. Almost a wry look.

"Shit, we have trouble," Justin warned.

Tamsin's smile fell and alarm took over her features. Ray looked at Chris with wide eyes, and Chris knew he'd heard Justin.

If Ray didn't think their comms were connected to anyone else, he was an idiot.

Chris stood up straight. "Report."

"I've been listening to the audio," Justin rushed the words.

Chris knew he meant the comms from the Sons of Asena via the earpiece their guest had given him.

"And?" Tamsin asked.

"I also connected my laptop to the video feed at the lab," Justin said, still speaking faster than usual. "Screen's too small to see all the feeds, so I've been switching between the cameras. Something happened. Don't know what, but they're boiling like a smashed beehive. Giving orders left and right. I think they may have figured out Tamsin's missing."

"I just updated Mac," Sierra injected. "He says we need to get out, *now.*"

"Copy that," Chris replied, calm falling over him like a blanket. His mind raced. They'd planned for a fast pull out, but not with three additional people, plus bags and mice. "Pack up. We'll be there to get you in ten."

Over the comm, Chris heard drawers opening as they packed up.

Tamsin met his gaze and gave a sharp nod. She jumped to her feet and started packing the things she'd gotten out for the mice.

Ray stood by the door, shifting from one foot to the other. "What can I do?"

"Stay out of my way," Chris growled. He didn't put things in the drawers in hotels. Everything was in his bag. He grabbed it and did a quick check in the bathroom. He hadn't left anything.

They quickly had everything gathered up, and Chris loaded the bags in the back of the van.

He went back into the room to find Tamsin on the floor, her jean-covered ass in the air. His body immediately came alert and his hard-on pressed against his jeans. All the blood left his head and went to his wayward member. It took him a moment to figure out what she was doing.

And that Ray was missing.

"What—" he started when Ray stepped out from the bathroom.

"No sign of a mouse in the bathroom," Ray reported.

"She's here, we just have to find her," Tamsin muttered, her head still under the bed.

Chris moved to the end of the bed to stand between her and Ray. He didn't want the other man drooling over her sweet ass.

Mine.

"Tamsin, what's so special about this mouse?" Chris forced himself to focus on the task at hand and not how much he wanted to get her alone again.

"Just get another one in Oakdale," Ray added.

Chris snarled and glared at Ray. His tiger was in his eyes and the other man swallowed when he met his gaze. "What was that?"

Ray took a step back and shook his head. "Nothing."

She sat up and met his gaze. Her eyes shone as they looked at him and her smile warmed his heart. "I can't leave this one, Chris. We need to find her."

He resolved to find out what she'd been testing on these mice. *Later.* If she had smuggled them out of the lab, they had to be more than simple pets. If they were that important to her, he'd find the damn thing.

He got on the floor and looked under the bed. She moved to the head of the bed, and Ray got on the floor on the other side.

The clock ticked in the back of his mind as the three of them crawled around the hotel room. Against his better judgment, he took a shallow breath near the carpet. His nostrils flared and he coughed.

He knew better.

Floors *never* smelled good.

This one was a motel and had the scent of an old, dust-spewing vacuum. *The thing must spit out more dust than it sucked in.* He did pick up the scent of the mouse, but it was everywhere.

He slowly moved around the bed, trying to track the mouse. His path took him to the far side of the bed, closer to where Ray was looking, but that didn't stop him. He saw Ray go behind the partition by the closet.

Where are you, troublesome rodent?

"Any sign of her?" Tamsin asked.

Her voice was muffled, and he dropped down to see her fully under the bed, squirming her way around as she sniffed for the mouse. *Tenacious.* He loved her spunk.

"Her scent is everywhere, I can't pick up a specific trail," Chris replied, frustrated.

He was just about to suggest they call in Justin to sniff out the creature in his wolf form when he saw Ray make a snatching motion out of the corner of his eye.

Chris snapped his head around and saw Ray had the mouse in his hand. The man's claws sprang out of his fingers.

"What are you doing?" Chris snarled.

Ray's head jerked up, and his eyes widened in surprise as they met Chris's. His gaze darted around like he was looking for a hiding place. Then he smiled. "I think I found him!"

Tamsin squirmed out from under the bed and cheered when she saw the small creature in Ray's hands. Hands that no longer had claws extended.

"Her," she said as she carefully took the mouse from his hands and put her in the cage with the others, softly cooing at them.

They may have been lab mice, but she clearly cared for them, too.

Chris had the feeling she'd have been deeply upset if something had happened to it. More upset than just the loss of a research animal.

He looked at Ray, and the other man met his gaze. Chris forced himself to give a friendly smile, which Ray returned. The man's shoulders relaxed as he thought Chris bought his ruse.

But Chris had seen the claws. He had a feeling the man had planned on killing the mouse.

Why?

Was it to hurt Tamsin, or her research?

Chris didn't buy Ray's story, although he couldn't identify what had tipped him off. He didn't believe the man's story of innocent victim. He may have been at the lab, but Chris wasn't so sure Ray hadn't volunteered, or wasn't more involved. Everything that had happened had been too pat.

Ray knew more than he was letting on. His actions with the mouse said that.

Chris just had to figure out what Ray thought killing the mouse would accomplish. What his plans were. If the man was a plant, then Chris needed to get him to Nightfair to find out what he was up to.

He'd let the man think he bought his story. But he'd keep his eye on him and make sure he didn't hurt Tamsin.

She walked past him, and her scent washed over him, erasing his anger and calming his tiger. Suddenly, he was even more anxious to get back home. They'd danced around each other for years.

He realized he was done dancing. He didn't want to play around anymore pretending he didn't want to be with her. He wanted the tenacious, frustrating, smart, amazing woman. Her eyes met his and widened slightly at whatever she saw on his face.

Mine. His primal self thought. Chris's human self agreed. *Mine.*

She picked up her mouse cage and moved toward the door, glancing at him uncertainly.

Now he just had to convince her.

Chapter 19

"Tammy!"

Tamsin jerked at the cry, and her heart jumped. She immediately knew who it was. Not only did she recognize the voice, but there was only one person who ever called her *Tammy.*

She was only surprised Anjanae hadn't shown up sooner. She'd texted her as soon as they'd arrived in Oakdale an hour ago. Of course, the text was from Chris's phone, so maybe she'd ignored it.

Tamsin jumped up from the computer chair and had taken a step toward the lab door at the Nightfair headquarters when her twin appeared. A tension she hadn't even realized was there left her body in a rush, leaving her feeling almost light-headed.

"Gigi," she whispered, blinking back tears. She hadn't realized how much she'd missed seeing her until now.

Anjanae's curls bounced wildly around her head as she raced into the room and plowed into Tamsin. Her sister's arms clutched her tightly, and her breath was choppy as she buried her head in Tamsin's shoulder.

"Shhh," Tamsin said, a knot in her throat as she felt her sister's tears soak her shirt.

Then Anjanae shoved back, grabbed Tamsin by her shoulders, and gave her a hard shake.

"What the hell happened?" Anjanae yelled, her eyes flashing with anger as Tamsin's head jerked back and forth.

"Hey," Chris growled from the far side of the room, "Take it easy!"

Tamsin grabbed her sister's shoulders and held tight.

"Anjanae," she snapped, her tone making her sister stop.

Anjanae growled low but held still. Tamsin held up a hand in a staying motion to halt Chris's advance across the room. She loved that he was trying to protect her, but this was her sister. He had brothers and should understand.

"It's okay, Chris, I've got this," she told him.

He stopped his advance, but his brows drew down with lingering anger at her sister's action.

"You can just stay out of this." Anjanae glared fiercely in his direction.

Tamsin gave a small shake of her head when Chris glared and opened his mouth to answer. She knew her sister's temper. She'd dealt with it her entire life. It was better if she took the brunt of it, she knew how to defuse it quickly.

Anjanae had always been like that. Fierce. Quick to take offense and jump in to fight. Her panther lived very close to her skin and was always ready to break out. Unlike Tamsin's. But her sweet sister was also equally quick to forgive.

"Gigi," Tamsin said firmly. She continued once Anjanae stopped glaring at Chris and looked at her. "I'm sorry I worried you. I left a note so you'd know I was okay. I had no idea you'd think I was in trouble."

"What else was I to think?" Anjanae said with a wounded look as she released Tamsin. "You didn't answer my calls, return my e-mails, or anything. You just disappeared."

Tamsin swallowed thickly and dropped her arms. She hated to hurt her sister. "I know, Gigi. And I'm really sorry."

"I only find out you're okay because I get a message from Damien yesterday. Then he said they weren't even bringing you home right away." Anjanae took two agitated steps away, then turned back. "What happened, Tammy? And why didn't you call me?"

She gave Anjanae a brief explanation, leaving out the part about the creepy guards. She didn't need her sister charging off to teach them a lesson. She was safe now. That's all that mattered.

"And once I was out, I couldn't call you. We were afraid they'd trace my phone," Tamsin added. "Chris's people are putting a blocker in my phone right now."

The machine in the corner beeped, letting her know that the test results were ready. Tamsin looked at it, hope warring with fear.

"Your project?" Anjanae asked with a half-grin, her anger gone like it'd never been.

Tamsin nodded and looked back at the machine. This could answer *everything*. Or it could put her back at square one.

"What is it?" Anjanae said, accurately reading Tamsin's apprehensive expression.

"An injured shifter escaped the lab," Tamsin said. She stopped as she realized they didn't even know his name yet. He hadn't regained consciousness long enough to tell them, and had no identification on him. "I think they may have injected him with my serum."

All they knew was he escaped the lab building where she'd been naively working. Thinking they supported her research. She'd had no clue they planned to exploit it.

Chris moved next to her and gently touched her back. His warm hand helped chase some of the chill away. Anjanae's eyes widened at the touch, but she didn't say anything.

"Why do you think that?" he asked.

She quickly filled them in on what she overheard the guards saying about test subjects. "I'm pretty sure they stole some samples and were experimenting with them."

"And? So, what if they did?" Anjanae questioned.

"He was hurt badly," Tamsin explained. "Chris's team rescued him and brought him back here."

When they loaded up the injured shifter into the van, Tamsin had been prepared for him to be in bad shape since he wasn't waking up. But she had been far off from the reality of it.

She'd been shocked when she saw him. His face and body were bruised and swollen, and he had deep cuts that Sierra had stitched up. Someone had clearly given him a severe beating. If he hadn't been a shifter, it might have killed him.

"That's great," Anjanae said with a sharp look at Chris. "Way to go, hero. But why does that matter?"

Chris didn't react to her sister's comment, just watched Tamsin, waiting for her to continue.

Tamsin suppressed a sigh. Her sister had always been impatient.

"My serum has never been tested on anyone injured. I have no idea what it's going to do. Chris got a sample of his blood for me." She gave him a grateful smile. "This test will tell me if it was given to him."

"Then what?" Chris asked.

"I run another test." Tamsin pictured the steps in her mind. "There's the possibility he hasn't woken up because the serum is boosting his healing."

"How would it do that?" Chris asked.

She grinned at him, used to these types of questions. "You want the technical answer, or a general one?"

He laughed. "General. I don't know anything about chemistry. A technical one would go right over my head."

"The short answer is it's a type of gene therapy that targets that which makes us shifters. Including our faster healing abilities."

"You think your serum may be healing him?" Chris asked.

"No." Tamsin shook her head. "It doesn't work like that. But in someone severely injured, it may boost our healing ability. Encourage it to go into overtime."

That wasn't what her serum was designed to do, but it might be a side effect.

If he had her serum in his blood, it would confirm they were stealing her serum, but also permit her to see how it might react in a living shifter. So far, she'd only been able to examine it with a drop of her blood. And her blood didn't have the right components, so it didn't tell her much.

Of course, with how severe his injuries were, the answers would likely be skewed, too.

Tamsin took a deep breath as she took a step toward the computer. It was hooked to the diagnostic equipment, and the report was just a file away. Her mouth was dry, and her hands were icy.

The lab equipment at the Nightfair headquarters was everything she could ask for. Everything she needed. Her answers were right in front of her. All she had to do was look. Yet, she hesitated.

"You okay?" Chris asked when she stopped moving.

She turned and met his concerned gaze. Her panther purred in her mind, glad he was there with her, even if he didn't know how important this was. She swallowed hard, wanting to believe she saw more than just desire in his eyes.

She wanted to take those few steps and burrow in his arms. For years he'd teased and flirted. She'd thought he was just playing. But now, she thought she saw something more. After all this time...

No. Not until she knew.

"Just nervous," she told him.

The mice squeaked from their cage in the corner, and one ran on the wheel, making a *whirling* noise.

"Why do you have *mice* in the lab, Tamsin?" Anjanae took a step away from the cage.

"It's a long story," she replied. She glanced at Chris. "You sure no one will mind them?"

Chris studied the mice. "Well, they *are* noisy."

A surprised laugh burst out of her. "That's not what I mean. Will the scientist who works in this lab mind?"

"What did Damien say?" Chris gave her a teasing grin.

"What makes you think I asked him?" Tamsin replied with a raised brow.

Chris's grin turned into a rakish smile. "You didn't?"

That smile made her want to kiss him. But she knew what would happen if she did that. She'd get the distraction she wanted, but her results wouldn't get checked. Plus, she wasn't sure she wanted to make out with him while her sister was in the room.

"Fine," she said with a huff, fighting her own smile. "He just shook his head. What does that mean?"

When she'd asked, the head of Nightfair had studied her with his dark eyes sparkling with mirth and shook his head, his thick braids brushing his back. She couldn't figure out if that meant the scientist wouldn't care, or what, and it was driving her crazy.

"That sounds about like him," Anjanae said with a huff.

Tamsin shot her a look. *Was there something going on between her sister and Damien?*

Anjanae looked at her with an innocent expression, her brows up.

"We don't have a dedicated scientist who works here," Chris said, narrowing his eyes in thought. "Some of the team members have backgrounds in chemistry and biology and will use the lab when they need to. But no one's assigned to it or claims it."

"That explains it." She nodded, a bit relieved. At least she wouldn't be stepping on anyone's toes.

She was stalling.

"Explains what?" Chris asked, his head tilted.

She walked to the counter next to her mice and picked up a cast-iron frying pan.

"This." She held it up so he could see.

Chris burst out laughing.

"What the hell?" Anjanae said.

"A frying pan?" Chris said once he got himself under control. "What's that doing here?"

"I have no idea." Tamsin grinned as she put it back where she found it.

"Tamsin," Anjanae sighed. "You're stalling."

She nodded. Her sister knew her too well.

She'd put it off long enough. She needed to see what her results revealed.

Tamsin sat at the computer and pulled up the file. She scanned the data, the lines and numbers telling a clear story. She wasn't sure if she should be elated, or desolate. There was no mistaking what she saw.

"Well," Chris said impatiently.

"No question," she answered. "He's been given my serum."

She pulled up another report and looked at the results.

"That's odd," she mumbled.

"What's odd?" Damien's deep voice asked.

"Glad you could join the party," Anjanae said sarcastically.

Tamsin gave her sister a glare for being so rude, but Anjanae's attention was locked on Damien. Tamsin looked over to see the head of the Nightfair Company standing at the door to the lab. He met her gaze and held up her phone.

She got up to get it, trying to figure out how to answer him in non-technical terms.

"I've not seen this response before," she answered. "It's like the blood and the serum are combining and working together. The serum is boosting his body's healing abilities."

"What happens when he's all healed?" Damien asked.

"I don't know. My serum is a prototype. Not meant for use yet. It isn't perfected. The serum may use up all of its energy repairing him."

"If it doesn't?" Damien asked.

She thought about the timid mice who had been her test subjects. The serum had made them bold. She'd never tried it on an already bold mouse. Her mind raced as she thought about how it might impact its behavior.

"I'm not sure," she replied. "He may get hyper-aggressive…"

She trailed off as the two men exchanged a glance.

"What?" she asked.

"Hyper-aggressive?" Damien asked.

Tamsin nodded, looking between them, trying to figure out what they knew that she didn't.

"As in, he might attack others?" Chris leaned forward and studied her intently.

"He could, I guess." The way they kept looking at each other made her stomach churn.

They definitely knew something they weren't sharing.

"Would you say," Damien stilled, like a predator catching a scent, "his behavior might resemble a shifter in the throes of blood-lust?"

She frowned, a cold knot in her stomach. The Nightfair crew hung out at her sister's bar. She often helped out in the evenings and heard a thing or two. The pieces fell into place in her mind. She shook her head in denial.

"No," she whispered. "It can't be. I haven't tested it on anyone other than my lab mice."

But she had been working on the serum before she went to the lab. It hadn't been in a really secure location, and someone could have taken a sample without her knowing. Unlikely, but possible.

"Well, someone has," Damien replied darkly. His eyes then lit with excitement and he asked, "Do you have a way to reverse the effects?"

She felt like she was in a frozen block. Everything was so cold. "No. I never thought it would be necessary."

Damien briefly closed his eyes, and a resigned look crossed his features. "Do you know what the effects of multiple doses are?"

"In the experiments I ran," she answered slowly, thinking it out, "after the doses wore off, the test subject returned to normal. Subsequent doses brought increased aggression."

Damien gave a sharp nod and disappeared out the door.

"Way to say goodbye," Anjanae called after him.

"My serum is causing the rogue issue, isn't it?" Tamsin asked Chris.

He nodded and crossed the room to stand in front of her, worry furrowing his brow. "I think it might be."

"Tammy," Anjanae said softly. "What did you do?"

What had she done?

"I made a mistake, Gigi," she told her sister. "But I'll fix it."

Somehow.

Chris gently pulled her in his arms. Tamsin held on to him, trying to ground herself as her world spun apart. She'd heard the Nightfair crew talk about loners getting targeted and drugged. She just hadn't put the rogue attacks together with the drugging.

Or that the drug used might be her serum. She'd been too busy working on her project. Her *cure* that was turning out to be a *disease*.

And now she had to find an antidote. *Fast.*

She inhaled deeply, pulling in Chris's calming scent. She felt lost. Like Alice in Wonderland, not knowing the rules.

What was she going to do?

Her panther paced unhappily in the back of her mind, as agitated as she was. This was not how things were supposed to work out. She was supposed to find a way to fix herself and others like her.

Not make something that turned people into insane killers.

What she needed was a test and a control. But where was she supposed to find two shifters who would meet her qualifications? Without telling them anything about the project. Sure, she could find them. But it would take time. Time she didn't have.

Chris gently rubbed her back. The touch was light, soothing. But slowly it started to become something else.

A calm in the storm. Someone to rely on.

She inhaled his scent, and her panther purred in the back of her mind.

She would find a way to fix this. Then she would claim him.

He was hers.

Chapter 20

Chris's tiger rolled around in his mind, happy to have his mate with him. Everything was right. *Perfect.*

Suddenly, from the other side of the room, Anjanae let out a high-pitched squeal and yelled, "*Shit!*"

Breaking the perfect moment.

Tamsin pulled out of his arms, and he expected to see a distressed expression on her beautiful face. He was surprised to see she looked… *hopeful.*

Maybe the moment wasn't broken, after all.

She glanced at her sister, eyebrow raised curiously.

"What's wrong, Gigi?"

"We might have a little problem," Anjanae said quickly, her eyes darting around.

"What kind of problem?" Chris asked with a sinking feeling at her tone.

She was really close to the mouse cage. She didn't… she wouldn't…

"Uh." Anjanae chewed nervously on her lip. "I might have, you know, done a thing."

The mouse cage seemed to be missing an occupant.

"Where's the fourth mouse?" he asked.

"Gigi, please tell me you didn't open the cage," Tamsin said, alarmed.

"Okay," Anjanae said, looking around the floor at her feet.

"Okay, what, Anjanae?" Tamsin asked in a firm voice.

"Okay, I won't tell you," Anjanae replied.

Chris scanned the floor, looking for the wayward rodent, but didn't see any sign of it. There were shelves along the wall, plus the large machines. Plenty of places for a small creature to hide.

Tamsin hurried to her sister and looked in the cage. "Subject Alpha is missing."

"You named your mouse Subject Alpha?" Chris said with a half-smile. "What are the others? Theme Bravo, Issue Charlie, and Thread Delta?"

Tamsin looked at him and rolled her eyes. "Sure, make fun of it. And it isn't *Alpha* like the military use for *A*. It's Alpha as in first. And they are all *subject*. You know... test subjects?'

"How do you know Alpha is missing?" Anjanae asked, looking at the remaining mice. "They all look the same to me."

"No, they don't," Tamsin argued. "Look, Bravo has a pink ear. Charlie has that white spot, and Delta is solid brown."

"You really named them Alpha, Bravo, Charlie and Delta?" Chris couldn't stop himself from asking with a chuckle.

"Well, sure," Tamsin shrugged. "I had to name them something, and I heard you say those words for letters enough, it made sense."

He walked over to her and gave her a fast kiss on the lips. He wanted to do more, but her sister was there watching. Like some kind of a chaperone.

Tamsin gave him a bemused smile when he pulled away. "What was that for?"

"You, just being you," he replied.

Her eyes were warm, and her bemused smile became a pleased one.

Anjanae made a gagging noise, and they both looked at her.

"That was so sweet I think I'm going to be sick," Anjanae announced.

Chris was contemplating more ways to *make her sick* when he saw the mouse cautiously running along the wall. It was headed to one of the big machines in the corner.

He held out his hand in caution, focused on the rodent.

"I'll go to the door, in case she tries to get out this way," Tamsin said softly.

"I'll head over to this side then, I guess," Anjanae replied.

Chris quietly walked toward the mouse. The creature stopped, its nose twitching as it smelled the air.

He had an idea.

"Tamsin, wave your hands around, spread the scent around the room," he ordered.

Out of the corner of his eye, he saw her moving around, her arms flailing as she tried to spread her scent in the air without moving from her location. He caught a glimpse of Anjanae doing the same thing. *Identical.*

They were both the same distance from the mouse, and it stayed where it was, uncertain where to go. It stood on its back feet, nose and whiskers moving rapidly. Then it dropped down on all four feet, and Chris pounced.

He managed to scoop up the mouse before it took a step, and Tamsin cheered.

"Nice going," Anjanae said dryly.

"Wouldn't have been necessary if you'd left it alone," Chris commented calmly.

"Aren't you just an ass?" Anjanae asked cheerfully.

He ignored her and put the mouse in the cage, then glanced between the two women. He shook his head.

"You know, I always thought twins were similar. But you two aren't at all," he observed.

"What do you mean by that?" Anjanae snapped. "We are so similar."

Tamsin grinned. "He's right."

"Wait, what?" Anjanae did a double-take and looked at Tamsin. "What do you mean?"

"Well, look at it like this. You're outgoing, friendly. People like you. I'd rather be in my lab," Tamsin answered.

"You're friendly," Chris protested, not happy with how she compared herself negatively to her sister.

Tamsin gave him a grateful smile. "That's not what I meant. Gigi is the outgoing one. I'm calm. She gets riled, I don't."

"I do not," Anjanae protested hotly.

"We may look like each other on the outside, but on the inside, we're..." Tamsin trailed off, and her eyes grew wide. Her face lit up with excitement.

"You're what?" Chris prompted when she didn't finish.

"We're exactly what I need," Tamsin replied, rushing to the supply closet in the lab.

"For what?" Chris asked.

Anjanae leaned against the counter with a resigned sigh. "She'll get around to it eventually. No use rushing her."

Tamsin came racing out of the closet, a small plastic basket in her hand.

"This should work," she muttered. "Why didn't I think of it before?"

"Think of what before?" Chris tried to get her to answer, but she didn't seem to hear him.

"Blood, I need blood. Yours, too, Chris," Tamsin demanded as she approached her sister. "This might just work."

Chris watched her draw blood from her sister, label the container, then move onto him. He wasn't going to get an answer until she was done, so he decided to simply cooperate and wait. Once she had three small vials of blood, neatly labeled, Tamsin moved to one of her machines.

"What's she doing?" Chris asked Anjanae, since Tamsin seemed lost in her world.

Anjanae shrugged. "I don't know, but I gotta head to the Ice House. Tammy, I'll see you later."

Tamsin waved her hand vaguely in the air.

"I needed a test and control," she said. "I didn't think of it before, but it's perfect."

"What's perfect?" Chris asked, feeling like a broken record.

He felt his phone vibrate before he could ask anything else. He pulled it out to see a text from Damien.

Need to see you. My office.

"Everything okay?" Tamsin asked, glancing at him.

He grinned, glad she wasn't totally lost in her research.

"Yeah, Damien just needs to see me. You okay if I—"

"Go," she ordered. "This'll take me a while."

He hesitated, wanting to give her a kiss, but she was focused on her research. He turned and left the room, letting the door close quietly behind him.

Chris made his way to Damien's office and knocked lightly on the door.

"Come in," Damien replied.

Chris opened the door and saw Damien sitting at his desk, Eli in the guest chair across from him.

The honey badger slouched in the chair and looked irritated. Of course, Eli always looked slightly irritated. Unless his mate was around.

"Where's Ginny?" Chris asked him.

"Doing some surveillance in the comm room," Eli replied. "She lost the bet."

He had a satisfied look in his eye, and there was an air about him that just dared Chris to ask about it. He knew better, though. If he asked Eli, who knew what kind of crazy story the honey badger would come up with.

"I didn't get a chance to debrief you," Damien explained. "I asked Eli to be here since this seems like it might have to do with the loaner situation. And he needs to know what's going on."

"Mac fill you in on the other stuff?" Chris asked.

"He did, and he's digging into some additional information for me."

"Okay," Chris ordered his thoughts. "I'll start from right after he left."

Chris succinctly told Damien and Eli everything that had happened. When he mentioned the captives they saw in the video from the night, Eli's eyes grew wide. Damien just nodded like it was nothing new.

He got to the part about rescuing Ray, and Eli let out a low growl.

"Something wrong?" Chris asked him.

"I don't like him," Eli snarled.

"You don't like anyone," Damien commented.

"I like Ginny," Eli replied with a grin.

Chris laughed, both at the expression on Eli's face and the tone of his voice. Eli liked to play the nasty honey badger to the hilt. He acted like he hated everyone. The crew knew it was an act, though. He was one of them.

"I'd hope so," Chris said. "She's your mate after all."

"I'm not a moron," Eli proclaimed. "You idiots may not have realized what an amazing woman you had in front of you. But I wasn't gonna let her get away."

"Back to the topic at hand," Damien ordered.

Chris finished his debriefing, and Damien asked a number of follow-up questions. Eli chimed in here and there, as well. By the time Damien had wrung every drop of information from him and dismissed them, more than an hour had passed.

Chris's stomach rumbled, and he realized Tamsin might be hungry too.

He and Eli left the office and ran into Ray. The panther stumbled back like he'd been caught somewhere he wasn't supposed to be.

Or maybe he was trying to listen in.

"Where's your escort?" Eli snarled.

"My escort?" Ray asked, looking around like he'd misplaced a piece of paper. "I don't know, he was here a moment ago."

Eli's upper lip curled, but he didn't say a word.

Ray's face blanched, and he took a hasty step backwards. "I think I'm going to go back where I last saw him. He is probably in the head or something."

Ray turned and quickly headed in the opposite direction. He looked back over his shoulder once, then disappeared around the corner.

"Did you have to scare him?" Chris asked Eli.

"All I did was snarl at him." Eli gave Chris an innocent look. "Not my fault if he's afraid of honey badgers."

Chris laughed and shook his head. "We're giving him sanctuary. Can you at least try to play nice?"

"No." Eli replied, a pondering frown on his face and laughter in his eyes. "I can't."

"I just asked you to try." Chris tried not to laugh.

The humor faded from Eli's face, and he looked at Chris.

"He's always lying," Eli grumbled.

"What do you mean?" Chris glanced in the direction Ray had gone. "Shifters can smell a lie. I've never smelled it on him."

"You haven't been paying enough attention," Eli responded with a raised brow.

"But shifters can't lie to each other," Chris argued, feeling like he was missing something.

"Can't they?" Eli turned to walk away.

Chris watched him go with a sinking feeling.

He hadn't liked Ray from the moment he met him. He'd put it down to jealousy at seeing Tamsin try to comfort him, but now he wondered.

Had he picked up something without realizing it?

Honey badgers had a reputation for not caring. Chris knew better. Eli just didn't put up with any shit. If he distrusted Ray that much, and he'd only just met him, then there was something going on.

Ray was in Nightfair HQ, but that didn't worry Chris. Everyone here could take care of themselves. They made paranoia a way of life. There was no way Ray'd sneak up on any of the crew members.

Except Tamsin wasn't one of the crew.

Chapter 21

A change in air currents alerted Tamsin someone was in the lab with her.

Her wary glance at the lab door quickly changed to a surprised grin.

Chris stood there with an air of anticipation, a large insulated bag hanging from his arm, and a look of mischief on his face.

"What's with the look?" he asked with a raised brow.

They'd arrived at the Nightfair HQ yesterday, and she'd been working on the counter to her serum. She kept getting interrupted by various members of the Nightfair crew. First, someone had a question about her serum and its effects. Next was a progress check on her counter. Followed by an update on the shifter in the infirmary, which really was just an excuse to be nosy and check out the lab.

She'd rapidly gone from amused to irritated. The lab wasn't anything new.

"Your crew members keep poking their noses in to *check on me*," she groused. "What's with all the interest?"

Chris's eyes lit up and he laughed.

"You're a novelty," he explained.

"How so?" she demanded.

"Here you are, in our headquarters, using our under-utilized equipment. They know you from the Ice House, but not in your professional capacity. For many of them, they didn't even realize you're a chemist."

"What did they think I was?" She tilted her head curiously.

"I'm not sure," he told her. "They only saw you in Anjanae's bar. They didn't spend the time talking to you like I have."

"Did they think I'm a waitress?" she asked. "And they're checking on me to make sure I'm not a fraud?"

The idea amused her, and her panther huffed with laughter in her mind. The way some of them cautiously examined everything about the lab, she could tell they had no idea what any of the equipment was, or how to use it.

She could be making rock candy, and they wouldn't know the difference between that and a serious experiment. She'd briefly considered making some rock crystals to give them something to check on. Her experiments weren't flashy, and she had nothing for them to observe. Her cat found the idea of the mercenaries coming in to watch rock crystals form amusing.

Of course, if she did that, they'd simply be in here more often. Not that she minded, but every time that door opened, she was distracted. She needed to focus or she'd never get answers.

Some members of the crew seemed more knowledgeable about the lab, and she figured they were the ones with the scientific backgrounds Chris had mentioned. When she asked if they needed to use the lab, they'd held up their hands and shook their heads, happy to let her have at it.

Chris grinned. "No, I'm pretty sure they knew you weren't a server, and in any case, no one thinks you're not a scientist. It's more a case that you are familiar, yet new, and now in our territory. That makes you a novelty."

"You never have guest experts at HQ?" she asked skeptically.

He shook his head. "You have the privilege of being the first. Most times Damien just recruits whatever experts he needs. Then finds ways to entice them to stay on the team long-term."

She thought about Damien's recent visit and his interest in making sure she had all that she needed. The lab was decked out with high-end equipment, too.

Was that his plan for her, too?

Sneaky bear. Her cat approved.

She shoved that idea away. She had no idea what her future entailed. The top priority was finding a counter for her serum. Everything else could wait.

Chris grinned at her and practically vibrated with eagerness.

"Your assignment done?" she asked.

He nodded. "Sorry about bailing on you last night. There were some loose ends that had to be wrapped up from an earlier situation. I didn't plan to leave you alone your first night at HQ."

She waved her hand and smiled. "It's fine. You had an emergency. And the spare rooms here aren't too bad. Not as comfortable as my home, but they work."

"It won't be for long," he assured her. "Damien's going through the proper channels to shut down that lab and figure out what the Sons of Asena are up to. As soon as the danger is neutralized, you can return to your home."

"I know," she reassured him.

He'd left after they'd shared dinner with some of the other members of the crew in the break room. Ray had been there, and she had been about to return to the lab when Damien had stepped in. He didn't go into details, but had ordered Chris and three others to *suit up.*

She figured that had meant to get the comm gear and head out. Chris had given her a fast kiss and promised to get back as soon as he could. That left her alone with Ray, Eric, and Nora. Eric was serving as Ray's escort, which she read as guard. She was glad someone kept an eye on him. There was something about him that put her panther on edge.

She tried to remember he was a victim in all of this, but he didn't make it easy. He didn't have any respect for her personal space and seemed to make it his mission to crowd her whenever possible. She'd take a step away, and he would move in close again. At first, she thought he was looking for comfort from a pride member, but there were other cats at Nightfair HQ and he didn't act that way around them.

They may have been in the same pride years ago, but it had been so long ago there was no longer any tie. Other than a shared history, there was no connection. If he was looking for comfort, any cat would do. Yet, he didn't crowd Caleb or Leslie.

His attitude also set her on edge. She could tell by the way the others reacted that they felt the same way. Ray alternated between condescending and fawning. Not only to her, but to everyone. He seemed to be an expert on everything and would argue about it even after he was proven wrong.

Would the real Ray please stand up?

Tamsin made it a point to stay away from him. Plus, her cat continually growled in his presence. It had decided that it didn't like him. *At all.*

Before she could beat a hasty retreat, the two men left and Nora stayed at the table with her. She'd wondered if Nora was acting as her escort when she had accompanied Tamsin to the lab.

Tamsin had asked her point blank, and Nora's astonished expression quickly reassured her. The wolf had been waiting to check out the lab and see what Tamsin was doing. It turned out she had been patiently waiting for her turn. Tamsin liked the wolf and had been happy for her company.

Chris still hadn't returned when she finally dragged herself to her assigned room. It had an old-fashioned lock, and she'd been glad to find the room locked when she got there. No one had messed with her things. Not that she figured any of the Nightfair Crew would, but she didn't trust Ray.

When Damien had shown her to the room earlier in the day, he'd casually mentioned that Ray's assigned room was on the other side of the building. No one would be in the rooms near her. There had been a knowing look in his eye that made her think he was trying to give her and Chris privacy.

Unfortunately, she'd been more exhausted than she realized and had passed out. Chris didn't return until after breakfast, either. He'd hunted her down and let her know he was fine. Then he'd crashed in one of the spare rooms for hours.

She studied him, looking for signs of stress.

He looked well-rested. Relaxed. Happy.

She couldn't stay put any longer and walked over to him, her panther wanting to touch him.

He immediately pulled her in his arms, holding her tightly. "I missed you," he said warmly into her hair.

She laughed. "You saw me a few hours ago."

He pulled back and gave her a wounded look. "That was *hours* ago."

"You're hungry, aren't you?" she teased. "You only seem to show up when it's meal time."

His eyes danced with laughter and he frowned at her. "How can you say that? I also show up at snack time, too."

Tamsin stuck her tongue out at him in mock reproach.

"Promises, promises," he sighed.

Her hand brushed the large insulated bag he brought. "What's this?"

He grinned, his eyes lighting up. "You've been staring at your computer all day. I thought maybe we could take a little break."

She glanced back at the screen, the tension headache that had been forming at the base of her skull receding. She'd been staring at the data for hours, trying to make sense of it.

A break did sound good. She pulled off her lab coat and put it on the peg near the door.

"What do you have planned?" She took a deep breath to figure out what was in the bag.

All she picked up was the mouth-watering sunshine and browned butter that meant Chris. *Figured.*

He waved his finger back and forth. "Nu-huh. It's a surprise."

"Really?" She tugged playfully on the bag's zipper.

He nodded and snagged her hand to entwine his fingers with hers. "Come on."

"Where are we going?" She followed him out her lab door and down the stairs.

"You'll see," he answered cheerfully.

Her heart sped up with anticipation.

"Are we going to the break room?" she asked.

"Nope." He headed through the building.

"Where are you taking me?" She had never been this way.

"You'll have to wait and see." He opened a door and the late-day sunshine hit the floor.

She had no idea HQ had a back door. It made sense, but she hadn't thought about it.

"Are we going on a picnic?" She'd never been on a real honest-to-God picnic before. The idea was exciting, and sweet.

"Maybe," he replied as he headed to the woods behind HQ.

A thrill ran through her.

"What's back here?" She took a deep breath, but only picked up the distinct smell of pine and aspen trees.

Squirrels scolded them from the branches, and the breeze gently brushed her cheek. The wind was so light it didn't mess with her braided hair at all.

Chris headed deeper into the forest. He moved like he had a specific destination in mind.

"I found this place," he casually told her, "by accident. It's a bit off the beaten path, and secluded. But not too far from HQ."

"How'd you find it?" she asked, intrigued.

"I was wandering around in my tiger form," he replied.

"Is it safe?" They had to be careful to keep humans from seeing them in their shifted form. Most of the safe places they could roam were pack or pride lands.

"There aren't any hiking trails around here," he answered. "So, people don't tend to come here. Mostly just us shifters."

He wasn't following any path that she could see, but before she could ask how close they were, a cleared area appeared in front of them. She looked around. The trees and bushes were thick all around, except for the opening Chris had used. If someone approached it from any other direction, they wouldn't find the break in the foliage.

Chris set the bag down and unzipped it. On top was a blanket that he spread on the ground. No scents came from the bag, yet Tamsin's stomach rumbled. Whatever was in there had to be cold entrees.

What was it?

He moved the bag to the edge of the blanket and knelt next to it. He gave her a knowing look and pulled out several covered dishes. She recognized the logo on them. They were from a nearby Japanese restaurant.

"Come here." He patted the blanket.

Tamsin dropped down on the ground next to him, watching as he uncovered his surprises.

He pulled the lid off the first plastic container, and her mouth dropped when she saw her favorite sushi rolls.

"Is that—" she trailed off when he opened another container full of more rolls.

"A salmon sushi roll? Sure is." His tone was smug as he handed her a pair of chopsticks.

"That's my favorite." She used the chopsticks to lift a roll and slide it into her mouth.

Tamsin couldn't stop her moan as the flavors exploded on her tongue.

When she looked at Chris, his eyes were dark and a seductive smile curved his lips.

"Not the reaction I anticipated." He scooped up another roll and held it to her mouth. "But I'll take it."

She opened her lips and took his gift, slowly chewing it while watching him. She thought about stripping him and riding him in this secluded corner of the woods. She felt herself grow slick and hot. He swallowed and his nostrils flared as he took in her scent.

"If you keep looking at me like that," he muttered, "we won't finish our meal."

A smile curved her mouth, and she dropped her gaze to the food.

"That would be a shame." She narrowed her eyes in thought, a different hunger riding her.

The dishes were all on the edge of the blanket. He'd only uncovered two so far. The salmon rolls and what looked like Philly rolls. She took the lids to each and set them back on top of the containers, resting her chopsticks on the side.

"I thought you were hungry." He watched her with hooded eyes.

"I am." Tamsin pulled her shirt off and tossed it to the side.

Chris sucked in a deep breath, his eyes devouring her. He placed his chopsticks next to hers and reached for her. His hands left trails of heat where they touched her.

The breeze brushed her skin as he removed her bra and laid her down on the blanket. She didn't feel cold, though, as he stripped the rest of her clothes off her body.

She watched him as he rapidly shed his own clothes, then laid on the blanket next to her. His erection proudly jutted out, a drop of pre-cum already glinting on the tip. He clearly wanted her as much as she wanted him.

He ran his hands over her body, followed by his mouth. He licked, nipped and sucked. Fire burned through her veins. He reached between her legs, his fingers easily finding her slick opening.

"You're soaked," he groaned as he rubbed her clit.

She pushed on his shoulder, impatient. His startled eyes met hers.

"I don't want to wait," she told him. "On your back. Now."

With a knowing smile, he laid down. His cock stood up proudly, and she didn't waste any time. She straddled him, and he smoothly slid inside her.

They moaned in unison at the sensation.

She arched her back and took a deep breath. His hand closed over her breast, playing with the peak. His other hand moved between them to rub her bud.

Tamsin was hot and wet, and her body was aching. She leaned forward and put her hands on his shoulders. She lifted her hips, pulling herself up, then dropping down. Riding him. Slowly.

It was delicious torture, and she loved it. He filled her like they were meant to be joined. Like they were made for each other. She moved up and down, sliding on his shaft.

He groaned as she moved, and his hand moved to the other breast, playing with the peak until it was a hard nub. He continued to rub her clit with his other hand, hitting it just right and sending shocks of pleasure through her.

She started to feel the pressure build, but he wasn't hot enough. She moved faster and saw his breath catch. His hand on her breast stilled and his nostrils flared.

He moaned and rubbed harder on her clit, sending her over unexpectedly. She cried out her release, and her body throbbed around his cock.

Chris grabbed her hips, moving her body over his, pumping his hips beneath her. The pleasure was too much. She felt herself explode again. He shouted out as he came with her. He pumped his hips a few more times, then stilled.

Tamsin collapsed against his chest, her breath choppy.

Chris's warm hand was on her ass, and the other gently rubbed her back. Her cat purred in her mind.

"Wow," he muttered.

She laughed. "Yeah."

He dropped a light kiss on her head. "I didn't plan on that."

Tamsin grinned. "I didn't either, but I'm not unhappy about it."

"I was pretty damn happy a few seconds ago," he replied.

She felt a light vibration from his chest. "Are you purring?"

"Yeah," he sounded sheepish. "Can't help myself."

She moved to his side, worried she was crushing him, but she didn't want to stop touching him. "I like it," she admitted.

Her stomach rumbled, and he chuckled. "Let's feed your other hunger."

Reluctantly, she sat up. He grabbed his shirt and handed it to her. She gratefully pulled it over her head.

Chris pulled two plates from the bag and opened the rest of the containers. Her heart melted as she realized they were all her favorites.

"How did you know?" she asked.

"Know what?" He picked a roll from each dish and put it on a plate, then handed it to her.

"That these are my favorites," she replied.

He grinned. "I pay attention."

"But we've never eaten sushi together," she argued.

"No," he agreed. "But we've had plenty of discussion about food."

She thought about all those evenings at the Ice House. They'd never gone out on dates. Not formal events where they ate at fancy restaurants, went to movies, or took walks in the parks.

What they had done was talk. Hours upon end as they bickered and argued at the Ice House. She knew more about Chris than practically anyone else.

They ate in comfortable silence, and her cat purred in her mind. She'd never had anyone do something like this for her before. She ate her last piece of sushi and picked up a piece of pickled ginger.

"So where do we go from here?" he asked, breaking into her thoughts.

"Back to HQ," she teased.

His gaze was serious, and the smile fell from her face.

"I don't want to go back to the way it was," he told her. "I want to give this thing between us a chance."

Her heart jumped into her throat. She wanted nothing more. But she couldn't make any promises.

Not yet.

"What do you mean?" she asked as her panther fought against her. It wanted to take what he was offering without hesitation.

"We've been pretending there's nothing here," he answered seriously. "These past few days have proved otherwise. I want to stop playing. I want to see where this leads."

She sucked in a sharp breath. This wasn't just a booty call. This was more.

Her panther pushed her to accept. She wanted nothing more. But she was broken. Until she fixed herself, she couldn't make any promises.

She opened her mouth, not sure what she was going to say.

He looked at her, his heart in his eyes as her own heart pounded in her chest.

There was only one thing she could say.

"Okay."

His eyes lit with joy, and he pulled her into his arms. His mouth covered hers in a kiss.

She had no choice. She had to make sure her serum worked.

Chapter 22

Tamsin glanced at the clock on the wall. It was about time for Chris to check on her again.

Part of her loved how he wanted to make sure she was okay. But another part wanted him to let her focus on her work.

She had to get this done.

She stared at the data on the computer. Her shoulders were tight with stress, and she was tired.

So tired.

Creating a counter to her serum was just as challenging as creating it had been in the first place. But before, lives weren't on the line. She may have changed the notes for her formula that she left back at the lab, but she had no idea how much of her serum was stolen. How much of it was out there somewhere. Just waiting for them to use on an unsuspecting victim.

There was also the possibility that they could take what they still had and make more. They didn't need the actual formula. Like making bread starter. All it took was a small part of the original.

She stretched, arching her back. She'd been working on this nonstop. The only breaks she'd taken were ones to catch a little sleep here and there. She could see the worry in Chris's eye when he checked on her. But he didn't understand. This was her responsibility. She had to fix this. And she had to fix herself if she wanted any kind of future with him. And she did want it. Very much.

She heard the click of the door behind her, and her shoulders tensed. Each time Chris had come in, he'd gotten more insistent that she take a break. She didn't have time for breaks.

"I don't need a break." She turned around in her chair to face the door.

Tamsin stopped speaking when she saw Ray standing there.

"Okay." He gave what he probably thought was a charming grin. "Then I won't make you take one."

Her panther snarled in the back of her mind. The smile was slick, practiced. Smarmy. It made her skin crawl.

"Can I help you?" she asked coldly. "I'm in the middle of something."

"Oh yes," he looked around the lab curiously. "I've heard you were doing some... project. What is it?"

He looked at her with his eyebrows raised in interest, but something about it seemed *off*.

Why was he so eager?

They'd returned to Oakdale several days ago. Ray had not made any move to leave the Nightfair HQ. He wandered around the headquarters, poking his nose into everyone's business. Although Tamsin had her head buried in her work, she'd heard the Nightfair crew commenting as she passed them on her way to get food.

Chris had even said something a couple times. Ray had everyone on edge. She wasn't sure why they didn't ask him to leave. Or why he didn't simply go.

He was a captive. Maybe he's afraid to leave.

She tried to be understanding, but it was hard when he made her cat growl with irritation in her mind.

Ray moved forward and leaned down to look at her screen, invading her personal space. Her cat snarled silently.

"What are you doing?" she snapped, jerking back so he wasn't almost touching her.

He gave her a wide-eyed innocent look and replied, "Just looking at the data."

"Really? Do you even know what you're looking at?" she asked, still annoyed by his audacity of moving into her space like that.

Sure, they knew each other long ago, but other than that offer of comfort when they found him, she hadn't touched him since. Hadn't invited him to touch her, either. Yet, here he was, all up in her space. If he were any closer, he'd be sitting in her lap.

"Sure, I do." His eyes scanned the screen blankly.

"Is that right?" She smiled sweetly.

He didn't smell like he was lying, but she had a feeling he was. You couldn't lie to another shifter, but you could deflect. She would know. She'd had years of deflection experience.

"It's very clear." He met her gaze. "I've had some experience in a chem lab, you know."

"So, what do you make of this?" She pointed to the graph on her screen.

"Oh, that... what does it tell you?" he replied.

"I thought you said it was very clear." She crossed her arms.

"It is, I just didn't want to make you feel inferior," he said with a huff.

Of course, he didn't.

"Very considerate of you," she commented.

"So, is this your serum?" He casually gestured to the data on the screen.

Her cat went on alert. His tone was casual, but his body was tense.

"My serum?" she replied, keeping her tone light. "What are you talking about?"

He laughed, but it had a false ring to it. "You know, that project you were working on back at the lab. That place I barely escaped."

She'd never mentioned her serum. It was doubtful any of the Nightfair crew had, either. But Ray always seemed to be lurking around. Perhaps he'd heard something. But why did it even matter to him?

What was he after?

"How do you know about my project?" She turned narrowed eyes on him.

"Oh, well, when I was *back there*." He looked to the side, like he was trying to avoid a bad memory. "I heard things."

"What kind of things?" She focused all her attention on him.

"The guards… they talked. They said how they had something that made shifters go nuts. Become the perfect soldiers. Just point 'em in the right direction, and they'd tear through anything."

Her hands grew cold. "That's what they said, huh?"

If her serum was given to a normal shifter, it *could* cause that reaction. Exactly what Damien had said earlier.

"I got to thinking." His tone was thoughtful. "Why would someone create something that made a shifter go nuts? Was it deliberate, an unintended side-effect, or did someone find a better use for it?"

Make a shifter go nuts.

That's what Damien and Chris had said. The drug made shifters go nuts and slash and kill. Her heart clenched.

She did that.

"It wasn't ready," she said softly.

He continued, showing no sign of hearing her. "I've heard rumors. Defective shifters. Ones who couldn't shift. Broken. Freaks"

Defective shifters. Defective.

Each word felt like a punch to the gut that robbed her breath.

True. They were all true.

"What good is someone like that?" His voice was soft. Insidious. "What shifter would knowingly mate with them? They might pass the defective genes to their cubs."

He walked around, casually looking at the machines around the room. The mice froze in their cage when he paused to look at them.

"And if such a female *did* find a mate, what pride in their right mind would accept them? Maybe they'd even challenge him, try to take him out for mating with someone who can't even shift. Who wants that in their pride?"

He shook his head as if it would be *such* a shame. The asshole.

All her life she'd kept her secret. Afraid of this very thing. What if her pride rejected her? She never thought she'd mate. But now... would they kill Chris just to make sure they didn't have children?

"What if there was someone who was like that? What would they do to fix themselves? To become normal? Would they do *anything*? Even create a weapon?"

She jerked back and protested, "It wasn't meant to be a weapon..."

He smiled coldly. "It sounds like that's what it was to me. Make a shifter the perfect killing machine. No pain. No fear. Just a need for destruction."

Her body grew cold, and her heart pounded in her ears. He made it seem like that was the purpose of her serum. It wasn't.

All she wanted to do was fix herself. Make herself normal.

"I heard the rumors in high school. That you never shifted. Ever. But your sister did. Were you trying to fix yourself, Tamsin?" he asked softly.

"I—"

"You could, you know. Be normal. Have a life. Mate," he whispered. "With the right resources, the right backing, you could correct your problem. No one cares about broken shifters. But they do care about weapons. I know people. People who would be interested in this. *Very interested*. What's your formula, Tamsin? Let me help."

His words hit so close to home. But she snapped out of it when he mentioned weapons and asked about her formula. She didn't know who he'd talked to, but there was no way she'd let him in on her research. Her serum wasn't meant to be a weapon.

Give this asshole her research? Not likely.

He stood a few feet away from her, his eyes locked on her. There was something menacing about it. Her heart raced with fear.

"Thanks, but I don't need any help," she replied. "What I need is to not be distracted."

"Okay," he said, standing and giving her an insincere smile again. "I'll just stand over here and watch you work."

That felt even more like a threat. She swallowed what felt like a lump of cotton.

"Really, Ray," Tamsin said. "I work better by myself. Go away."

She made her tone as dismissive as possible.

"I can stand in for Amy." He raised in inquiry. "Give you an extra hand."

How did he know about Amy?

She hadn't mentioned her assistant at all, other than in a private meeting with Damien. She was positive Ray hadn't been anywhere near her at the time.

"Amy, what do you know about her?"

He must have seen her fear in her expression because his eyes narrowed and a flash of satisfaction crossed his face. If she hadn't been watching him so carefully, she would have missed it.

"Oh, I'm sure I heard you had an assistant somewhere." He waved his hand dismissively. "Anna, Amy, something like that."

"Where did you hear that?" she asked, her panther growling in the back of her mind. She wanted nothing more than to take a swipe at him.

"Oh, I don't know," he said with that false smile again.

The door opened, and Sierra stepped in. Her attention locked on Ray.

"What are you doing here? I thought you had to use the head." She scowled in irritation.

His eyes narrowed angrily for a second, then that fawning smile appeared again.

"I did," he said. "But I caught Tamsin's scent in the hallway and followed it here. Tamsin and I are old friends. I just wanted to stop in and say hey. Catch up."

"You've rejected our offer of five different safe houses," Sierra said through clenched teeth. "Until we can find a place that will work for you, it is imperative that you follow our rules. You *must* stay with your escort."

"I know." He ducked his head in a gesture that was probably supposed to look remorseful, but it fell far off the mark. "I feel so safe *here.* No one will come after me at the Nightfair HQ."

Sierra heaved a huge sigh, like this was not the first time they'd had this discussion. "And Damien told you this is not a permanent location where we can house you. Come on, you can help with KP duty."

Sierra turned to the door, and Tamsin saw Ray's jaw clench before he smiled again and turned to follow her.

"I'm all thumbs when it comes to food," he whined. "Why don't I just—"

"You can make yourself useful, or leave," Sierra snapped as they stepped out the door.

Leave. Please leave.

Tamsin frowned as the door closed behind them. That entire conversation felt like one giant threat. She went over it in her mind, but couldn't pinpoint anything specific he'd said that she could use as proof, other than his comment that he *knew people*.

Her instincts were screaming in alarm. If Ray didn't want to help out, why didn't he just accept a place at one of the safe houses? And how did he know about Amy?

She took out her phone and pulled up Amy in her contacts. She should be safely with her family by now. Tamsin decided to send her a text to make sure she was okay.

How's vacation?

She hit *send.* There was no instant reply. She stared at her phone, like that could make a reply magically pop up.

"It's probably nothing," she said to the mice in their cage. "Someone may have mentioned Amy in passing, and he picked it up."

The mice had resumed their normal activities after Ray stopped looking at them. They didn't halt their activities anymore when she spoke to them, and now was no different.

"Thanks for the reassurance," she muttered, and turned back to her computer, uneasy. She set her phone next to the monitor and pulled up the results.

Before she could look at the data, the door opened behind her again and Tamsin's shoulders stiffened in fear.

"Ray—" she began, then stopped as she realized what her nose was telling her.

"Sorry to disappoint, but I'm not Ray," Chris announced.

She turned around to see him with a disgruntled frown on his face.

"He was just here," she explained.

"So, he can interrupt your work, but I can't?" Chris asked.

"Wait, what?" Tamsin said, not expecting that.

"Look, I'm just trying to help. You won't take breaks and are drowning yourself in your work," his worried eyes studied her.

"I have to find the answer. I'm so close. I can't stop now," she said, still off-kilter from Ray's visit.

Chris didn't understand.

"Taking a break for an hour to go for a run won't matter," he said. "You'll feel better after."

She shook her head. "I can't leave now. I just ran another test, and these results—"

"Your panther is probably going crazy," he interrupted. "You haven't shifted in days. Just come for a run. We'll climb some trees, stalk a rabbit or two. After, we can have dinner with my family. I want you to meet them."

You haven't shifted in days. He had no idea how right he was.

She hadn't shifted in days. Months. Years. Ever.

The thought sent a stab of pain through her as her panther clawed to get out, but couldn't. Never would. Not unless she could find some answers.

Her stomach churned, and she felt like she was going to throw up. Chris wanted someone to run with. Someone whose cat could play with his. Climb trees together. Hunt together.

Someone like her sister. Not someone defective.

Not someone like her.

And he wanted her to meet his family. From there it would be his pride. And somehow, they'd figure out she was broken, just as Ray had.

Would they attack Chris, hurt him, *kill him*? Because of her?

"I can't leave, can't quit. Not until I have the solution."

"A few hours won't make a difference." His brow furrowed with frustration.

What if she couldn't find a solution?

She couldn't put his life in danger like that. Wouldn't risk him getting hurt because of her. Her panther snarled in her mind, pain shooting through her at what she had to do.

"Why did you even make it in the first place?" he asked curiously, unaware of what was going on in her mind. "What were you trying to do?"

She blinked and realized she'd never told him.

"To jump-start an unassertive shifter," she said tightly, waiting for him to put the pieces together. A shifter that couldn't shift was practically unheard of.

"What's an unassertive shifter? Like… a submissive wolf?"

Her stomach churned. She'd have to tell him. She couldn't dance around it anymore.

"No. It isn't like that at all," she said softly. "Some shifters are passive. Their primal self is dormant."

"Dormant, I've never heard of that." He crossed his arms.

"Most haven't. The primal side is there. They just can't bring it out." She couldn't bring herself to blurt it out. She could barely make herself think it.

His brow furrowed as he thought about what she said. "How would you not be able to bring out your other self?"

She felt like she was going to throw up. She'd have to say it. Out loud. "Shift. They can't shift, okay."

He jerked back and looked at her like she wasn't speaking English. "How could they not shift? The ability to change and shift is what makes a person a shifter and not a human."

She flinched.

"No, it doesn't," she replied angrily. "They just can't change shape. They still have their other half."

"What stupid shit was Ray feeding you?" Chris shot an angry look at the door.

"He didn't tell me anything," she snapped. "I know this for a fact. Some shifters just can't shift."

"I've never heard of this." He took a few steps away, then turned back. "Where are you getting this information? I think you were played. Someone tricked you, and with your big heart you decided you'd try to find a fix."

Someone tricked her?

"I'm not an idiot, Chris. No one tricked me." Her voice was low and controlled, even though she wanted to scream at him.

It had never occurred to her that he wouldn't believe some people couldn't shift. Sure, it wasn't common. She didn't know of anyone else who couldn't shift. But she was living proof it could happen. Tamsin refused to believe she was the only one.

She couldn't be. There had to be others out there like her. Others her research would help, too.

"Somewhere, someone sold you a bill of goods," he growled. "Show me one person, just one, who can't shift."

"Me, okay? I can't shift!" The words tore out of her in a scream. She'd never said them before. Only her sister, parents, and pride Alpha knew, and it had been her parents who told their Alpha.

The look of shocked horror on her Alpha's face when they'd told him had said it all.

A similar look was on Chris's face right now. He froze and stared at her. His eyes shifted, and his tiger looked out at her for a heartbeat.

He took a deep breath and his shoulders relaxed. "You had me going for a minute there," he chuckled.

"I'm not kidding," she said softly.

"But, your scent… you're a panther." His brow wrinkled in confusion, and he took a step away from her.

"Were you not listening to a word I said?" she bit out. "I told you I'm a shifter. I have a panther inside me. I can even grow claws. But that's it. I can't change form. I can't grow fur and run in the trees with you. I can't hunt with you."

"I don't… but you…" he trailed off, staring at her with wide, shocked eyes.

"I created my serum to fix myself," she admitted. "No one talks about those who can't shift. It's like we don't exist. We're a shameful secret."

"Your serum doesn't work," he argued. "It makes shifters go crazy."

"But I'm close to a breakthrough." She gestured at her computer. "I know it. If I can…"

"How long have you been working on this?" He glanced around the room at the equipment. "Making this serum of yours?"

She tilted her head, thrown off by the question. "I don't know. Forever? It's all I've ever done. I got my chemistry degree so I could work in labs and work on it on the side."

"And you don't have a working solution. Because there isn't one." His tone was gentle. "Maybe you should just give it up. Stop driving yourself crazy. Accept you can't shift."

His words were like a slap. Her panther clawed inside her. It wanted out. It had always wanted out. Sometimes it felt like her skin didn't fit, and she knew it was the panther inside her.

"I can feel it inside me. Fierce, primal. Feral," she said softly. "It wants to roar, to fight. To run."

"You don't need to worry about that," he said. "I can protect you. Keep you safe. I can fight for you."

If she couldn't find a way to free her primal self, then there was no future for them. She wouldn't put his life at risk when others found out. He had no idea what he was saying.

She couldn't take what he was offering. He would have no kind of life. And they would never have cubs. She wouldn't take a chance on giving this curse to her children.

But maybe he was right. Maybe she should just give it up. She felt like crying at that thought.

"I think you should go," she said softly, wanting to be alone with her misery.

"What?" he took a step toward her.

"Go. Get out of my lab. I don't want you around here."

"But—" He held his hand out.

She clenched her jaw and stood. "Leave. Now. I don't want to see you anymore."

"No, Tamsin." He moved toward her, his eyes dark and unhappy.

"If you have any respect for me, you'll get the hell out of my lab and stay away from me," she snarled at him. "It's too painful to look at you right now."

"You know I respect you," he said, standing his ground. "But I'm not going to leave you alone—"

"What, because now that you know I can't shift, you think you know better?"

"Wait, no—" he protested.

"I may be *defective,* but I'm still a scientist. I still have a job to do. And you're in my way," she angrily bit out the words. "Don't you have something better to do than bother me?"

His eyes flared and he clenched his jaw. "You're not defective, but you are clearly upset—"

"Oh, you think? Way to go, trained investigator. What other observation do you have to share? Or are you ready to leave and let me get back to my work?"

She knew she was lashing out, but couldn't seem to stop herself. A part of her wanted him to hurt as much as she did right now.

Pain flashed in his eyes, but she didn't feel pleased with her success. It only hurt worse.

She saw anger flare in his eyes as he took a slow, deep breath.

"Fine. I'll leave you to do your *job*." He stalked to the door and opened it with controlled movements.

It slowly shut behind him, and she stopped herself from calling him back. Her heart felt like it was breaking apart.

It was for the best. He should be with someone who could shift. Someone who could give him children that would shift.

The thought sent a shaft of pain through her heart. She sank down in her chair.

What had she done?

Chapter 23

The door to Tamsin's lab shut behind him silently, but it felt like he'd slammed it closed.

It took everything he had to walk calmly. Chris wanted to tear things apart with fang and claw. His tiger snarled and raged in his mind.

A red film of anger was over his vision, but he forced himself to act collected. If anyone knew how furious he was right now, they'd probably lock him up for everyone's safety. He needed to go somewhere to blow off some of the steam.

He'd seen Tamsin angry before, but this cold rage was something new. She'd shut him down without giving him a chance to talk to her. His tiger raged inside him, and his mind raced.

He messed up.

He realized how much he messed up as soon as he told her to stop driving herself crazy. But then she shut down on him. He then proceeded to continue on and stick his other foot in his mouth by telling her he could protect her. He clearly saw that mistake in her expression.

His mother always said you couldn't go wrong if you kept your mouth shut. Too bad he didn't remember that sage advice in time.

He more than messed up. He fucked up. Big time.

When she'd called herself *defective,* he lost his temper. He had no clue how to fix this. But he knew the perfect place to blow off some steam and get his head on straight. Maybe then he could think and figure out a way to make things right.

Chris opened the door to the Nightfair garage. He grabbed a set of keys off the hanger and headed to the bikes.

A fast Ducati was just what he needed. Followed by a no-holds-barred bar brawl.

He slid on a helmet and started up the bike. A part of him knew he was asking for trouble. Only one member of the Nightfair crew ever went alone to the bar he had in mind. In fact, as far as he knew, only one of the crew went to this bar, period.

It didn't take him long to reach his destination. Luckily, there weren't any police out to catch his blatant disregard of the speed limit. He studied the worn-down exterior. The bar had seen better days. It needed painting, at least.

The parking lot was riddled with potholes. It was only late afternoon, yet it was already full of vehicles.

Good. The more, the merrier.

Although he was brimming with anger and pain, his brain hadn't shut down completely. He found a concealed place to park the bike near the dumpster.

This was a shifter bar, and the bike had the Nightfair logo on it. The folks who visited here were typically on the lower rungs of society. The types of shifters most likely to give their Alphas the finger and cause Nightfair to intervene. They'd recognize the logo, and it might cause them to shy away. He didn't want to scare anyone off.

He hoped folks were already drinking. Even if they weren't, it shouldn't take much to throw this place into a frenzy. Not based on its reputation.

Chris didn't normally go looking for fights. Not that he ran away when they found him, either. He just wasn't in the habit of seeking them out. But today, a brawl was just what he needed. He bared his teeth in a feral grin and opened the door, looking forward to his fight therapy.

He was immediately hit with the scent of stale beer. He'd been expecting that. Most shifter bars made it a point to keep themselves on the cleaner side, given the enhanced senses of their patrons.

Not this one, though. Its reputation implied it liked to keep things *earthy*. He cautiously inhaled and was relieved that stale beer seemed as earthy as this one got.

Multiple pairs of eyes assessed him as he stepped inside. He saw eyes shift as wolves, bears, and other cats looked at him. The bears went back to their beer, not interested. *Don't start nothing, won't be nothing* was typically their motto. But if a fight broke out, they'd cheerfully join in.

The cats had different reactions. One lifted his lip in a slight warning snarl. His companion at the table flared his nostrils, but looked back at his drink. Neither would be a real challenge. They weren't really interested. The other cats had similar reactions.

Chris continued his scan of the bar, looking for the ones most likely to be ready to brawl.

A trio of wolves sat in the corner. They slouched like they didn't have a care in the world, yet their attention was fixed on him. One's eyes grew wide, and he did a double-take. He leaned into his companion and whispered something in his ear.

The other wolf's eyes snapped to him, and he snarled and flipped off Chris.

Perfect. He'd accept that invitation.

Three wolves against one tiger were decent odds. The usual rules in a bar fight were *no shifting*, not even partial. It would be his tiger brawn against the three slimmer wolves. An even match.

Chris made his way through the room in their direction, his attention fixed on his destination. He'd come to get a fight, and it looked like they'd give it to him. One of the wolves cracked his knuckles, and another tilted his head side to side, loosening his neck. The third stretched his arms, a look of eager anticipation on his face.

The wolf who'd flipped him off got to his feet, his chair making a loud scrape on the floor. He rolled his shoulders, took a final swig of his drink, and stepped to the side of the table. His arms hung loose at his sides as he waited for Chris to reach him.

"Where do you think you're going?" Someone growled next to him.

Chris stopped, his spine stiffening.

He knew that voice.

He turned his head and met Eli's laughing blue eyes in a stoic face.

How did he miss him?

There were two additional people at the table. One he recognized as Eli's younger brother, Milo. The other was a dark-skinned wolf Chris had never met. The wolf had a resigned expression on his face and looked put-upon.

"I'm heading over to that table." Chris tilted his head in the direction of the three wolves. "And I'm going to make some conversation."

"Looks like you're going to get your ass beat," Eli said, clearly amused.

Chris clenched his jaw. "Don't worry about me. I can hold my own."

"I can't believe I'm saying this," the wolf with Eli grumbled. "But do you see that table in the back to the left?"

Chris glanced over and saw four men at the table, drinking. "Yeah."

"They're all the same pack. One group. You go back there and start something, you'll have seven sets of fists pounding your face," he said.

"I'd have to bail your ass out, and Ginny made me promise no fights today. She gets all upset when I come home scraped up," Eli groused. "Plus, my brother is visiting. I'm trying to set a good example."

Milo snorted. "Since when?"

"Yeah," the wolf said. "Who the fuck are you, and where the hell is Eli?"

Eli flipped them both off. "Shut up, Tyrone."

"Sit down and join us," Milo said in the same tone he probably used to instruct one of his wayward students to behave. "So, my brother can show me how to be *civilized.*"

Chris's anger at himself ebbed with the interaction. He knew Eli would eagerly join in the fray. But he didn't want to be responsible for him to break his promise to his mate.

Mate. The word made Chris flinch.

"Tyrone, hold my beer." Eli held his drink in Tyrone's direction while he glared at Milo.

"Nope, ain't gonna do it," Tyrone replied.

Eli glared at him. "Why the fuck not?"

"Ginny'll be pissed if I let you fight your brother, that's why not. And I like coming over for dinner. If she's pissed, I might not get an invite." Tyrone took a swig from his glass. "Plus, it ain't gonna be my fault if you break your promise."

Milo grinned and raised one eyebrow when Chris met his gaze.

The three were carefully watching him, and he had a feeling they weren't going to let him go play with the wolves. Reluctantly, Chris pulled out a chair.

"Why are you here, and not with your *mate*?" Chris suppressed a wince at how he bit out the last word.

Mate. What a crock of shit. When you found your mate, it was supposed to be perfect. Not a shit fest like he'd made.

Eli's brow rose. "What stuck that stick up your ass?"

"I don't know what you're talking about," Chris snarled.

Eli silently stared at him before he answered.

"Ginny's on a surveillance gig with her team, so I have a boys' night out." Eli tapped his drink.

The wolf who'd flipped off Chris approached their table, cracking his knuckles. Eli dropped his chair to all four feet and scooted it back, making a scraping sound on the floor. The noise drew the wolf's attention.

The other shifter met Eli's hard gaze, and his face paled. His eyes darted around, panicked. He looked over his shoulders and saw his two wing-men backing up slowly, apologetic looks on their faces.

"Didn't realize he was a friend of yours," one said.

"Sorry, man," the second stammered. "Next round's on us."

The first swallowed hard and quickly pivoted on his foot to head back the way he came.

"I'm gonna have to find another place to hang out," Eli muttered. "Everyone around here's lost their balls."

"You probably should've thought about that before you took on that wolf pack last time," Tyrone scolded.

Eli grinned. "Place needed some ventilation."

"Shoving him through the wall might have been overkill." Tyrone looked at the wall on the far side of the bar.

Chris followed his gaze and realized there was a patch that looked newer than the rest.

"You shoved someone through a wall?" Milo asked before Chris could.

"Well, someone had already been thrown into it," Eli explained, tilting his chair to balance on the back two legs.

"Someone *you* threw." Tyrone shook his head. "Why did they even let you back?"

"I fixed it, didn't I?" Eli asked innocently.

A waitress plunked a beer down on the table in front of Chris, and he glanced up in surprise.

"I heard 'em," she said in a bored tone as she placed drinks in front of each of the others.

"So, what happened to bring you slumming here looking for a fight?" Eli took a long drink of his beer.

Chris picked up his own and sniffed it before taking a cautious sip. He coughed after he took a drink of the bitter swill.

"What the hell is this?"

"House brew." Eli took another drink of his. "It'll put hair on your chest if it doesn't kill you first."

Chris put his glass on the table and gave it a wary glance.

"Don't worry, it probably won't kill you." Eli laughed.

Chris really wasn't in the mood to be social. He wanted to slam his fists into faces. But Eli's knowing glance stopped him from saying anything. And he knew better than to pick a fight with the honey badger. Eli lived up to his reputation.

The honey badger considered him a friend, but that didn't mean he wouldn't hand Chris his ass. Eli fought *dirty.*

"Maybe I'm just looking for a fight." Chris leaned back in his chair.

"Bullshit." Eli raised his brow in challenge. "What'd you do?"

"What makes you think I did anything?" Chris objected.

"I recognize that look," Eli replied in a knowing tone. "You fucked up."

"Okay," Chris admitted. "I may have said some... things that pissed her off. But did she talk about it? *No.* She shoved me out. *What the hell?*"

He picked up his drink and took a large swallow, coughing after it went down.

"What'd you say?" Eli gave him an admonishing look.

Chris gave a recount of the conversation, leaving out the parts about Tamsin not being able to shift. He didn't care if she could shift or not. She was his *mate*. When he finished, anger raced through him again. He was a stupid ass, but she'd overreacted. He was sure of it.

Maybe it wasn't too late to go fight the wolves.

He glanced to the back and frowned when he saw the tables where the wolves had been were empty. Both of them.

Tyrone let out a low whistle, and Milo shook his head.

"I don't have a mate," Milo said, "and even I know better than to say something like that."

"But it wasn't just that," Chris argued, replaying the conversation again in his mind. "There was something else..."

"Of course, there was something else." Eli waved his hand at Chris. "You."

"What? What do you mean?" Chris asked.

Eli was supposed to be his friend. On his side. He was expected to agree with Chris. Not say that *he* was the problem.

Eli heaved a big sigh and exchanged a look with Tyrone.

"I was wrong," Tyrone said.

Eli nodded with a grin and took a drink from his beer.

Chris looked between them, confused. When he glanced at Milo, the other man looked as lost as he was.

"What were you wrong about?" Chris asked when Tyrone simply sat there with a disappointed look on his face.

"When Eli was being an absolute moron about Ginny, I told him he was the biggest idiot I'd ever seen." Tyrone took a sip from his beer and smacked his lips in pleasure. "I was wrong. You're clearly the biggest idiot. I should start charging."

"How am I the biggest idiot? And charging for what?" Chris looked between Eli and Tyrone, hoping one of them would clear this up.

"For my mating advice, obviously," Tyrone said. "I seem to be the mate guru around here."

Milo had just taken a drink of his beer and started choking as he laughed.

"You got a problem?" Tyrone glared.

Milo shook his head, fighting his grin.

"So what are your words of wisdom?" Chris impatiently asked.

"She was upset, tired, frustrated," Tyrone said. "*I* got that from what you said."

"Right, that's why I wanted her to take a break," Chris defended himself.

Tyrone heaved a sigh and glared at Chris. "Let me finish."

When the wolf kept silent, Chris nodded. "Go ahead."

Tyrone glared suspiciously at him, then continued, "Instead of telling her you understand, you push her and push her until she snaps."

"And like a fucking idiot, you walk away when she tells you to," Eli added.

"What was I supposed to do?" Chris blurted.

Eli gave him a sorrowful look and shook his head. "Hopeless. You're hopeless."

"So were you," Tyrone grinned.

289

"Yeah, but I was smart enough to know I was a fucking idiot and went crawling back and admitted it," Eli said smugly. "I thought this whole fated mate business was bullshit. Never been so wrong in my life."

Chris stared at Eli without really seeing him. He knew Tamsin was his mate. He *knew* it. The idea had been on his mind without it really hitting him. Until now.

She was his mate.

She was the only one for him. He thought about their conversation once more, and what had really upset her.

Was it because she couldn't shift?

He didn't care. She could be human and not shift. It wouldn't matter. He loved her as she was.

He loved her. It wasn't just that she was his mate. She was the most amazing woman he'd ever met. He loved her spunk, her dedication. Her tenacity. He loved Tamsin.

"So how do I fix this?" he muttered.

"You blindfold her, tie her up, and throw her in your trunk. Drive her someplace secluded, then let her out and run like hell," Eli instructed. "'Cause she'll be pissed as all get out."

"That doesn't sound like a good way to get her to forgive him," Milo commented.

"No, but I'd laugh my ass off when he told us how she kicked his ass for doing it," Eli grinned.

"How about something helpful," Chris said dryly.

"You could shift to cat form and chase her around," Eli replied. "Worked for me and Ginny."

"As I recall, when she told the story, she wasn't too amused," Chris said. "Try again."

"Roadkill," Eli replied. "Bring her roadkill."

Tyrone, Milo, and Chris exchanged a glance.

"You are not helping," Tyrone admonished.

Eli leaned forward and put his chair back on four feet. "Really, bring her roadkill. And make sure I'm there when you do."

"Why?" Chris asked, wondering at the honey badger's reasoning, although he knew better than to ask.

"It'll be hilarious," Eli laughed.

"Beg," Tyrone said with an admonishing look at Eli. "Tell her you're sorry."

Chris nodded, that's what he needed to do. And maybe... tell her it didn't matter to him if she couldn't shift. He loved her the way she was.

He started to tell the three men he was going to head out when Milo's eyes grew wide. His gaze was fixed on something behind Chris.

An angry roar reverberated through the room, immediately followed by the sound of splintering wood.

A body flew through the room and crashed into their table, knocking it askew and sending their glasses flying.

The unknown shifter sprang to his feet, his elbow slamming into Eli's jaw.

The honey badger's eyes shifted, and he growled.

All around them, shifters were jumping to their feet with growls. Fists started to fly.

"Fuck," Eli said as he got to his feet. "Looks like I'm going to break my promise to Ginny, and you're going to get that fight you wanted after all."

Chapter 24

Tamsin stared at the door and fought her panther's desire to go after him. She felt like her heart had been torn out of her chest, and it had been her own hands that had done it.

She gripped the chair, the cushion crushing under her hold.

It was for the best.

A sharp beeping cut through the fog in Tamsin's brain.

She tried to ignore the noise, but it was like a small hammer pounding in her mind. She blinked dully at the machine. Her tests were done. She had a job to do. She could at least see what the results were.

She turned to the computer and pulled up the data, expecting to see the same thing she'd seen before. And the time before that. And the one before that.

Each test had been slightly different. Change one thing, do it again. Change one more…

She blinked at what she saw, her heart pounding with excitement.

"Is that right?" she whispered.

If the information was correct, she may have found the counter to her serum.

But she had to be sure. She made new samples and put them in the machine to run the test again. It would take a while for the analysis to complete, but she didn't want to leave the lab. She had to be sure.

She wondered where Chris had gone to, and she thought about trying to track him down.

No.

She couldn't do it. She had to set him free. If she let him know how much he meant to her, he'd stay around. And be miserable. He wanted a mate who could run with him in cat form. A mate who would give him normal cubs. That mate wasn't her.

She focused on making sure everything was cleaned. From there she moved to refill the mouse food, even though she'd done it that morning. She cleaned their cage and gave them fresh water. They didn't seem to know, or care, as they continued about their mouse business.

Out of tasks to do, Tamsin looked at the timer. Her shoulders slumped when she realized very little time had passed. She paced around the lab and kept looking at the timer.

"Has the stupid thing stopped?" she muttered as she stared at the display.

The seconds ticked down, but not fast enough. Her stomach growled, and she looked at the clock. It was late afternoon.

When did she last eat?

Her stomach growled again.

Breakfast.

Her last meal had been breakfast, with Chris. The thought sent a stab of pain through her. The wounded look on his face as he left hit her again. She closed her eyes and bit down on her lower lip.

No, she had to be strong.

Besides, if this test came back positive, and she had the counter, she'd leave the lab and probably never see him again. Just because she had a counter, didn't mean it would cure her. She had to accept she'd never shift.

Shoving him away was for the best. She had to keep her distance. Stay away from him.

Except at her sister's bar.

She shoved that thought aside. She'd deal with it when the time came. For now, she might as well get something to eat while she waited. She set the timer on her phone so she'd know when the last test would be finished.

The Nightfair HQ had a small break room with a kitchen just down the hall. There was always food on hand. She made her way there, thinking she'd hunt up something from the fridge. Besides, this time of day, the room would probably be empty. She could eat in peace, then disappear back into her lab.

Tamsin opened the door to the break room, her mind on Chris, and pulled up short. There was a woman sitting alone at a table, a velvet evening bag on the table next to her. She was older and pleasantly plump, but she wore it well. In front of her was a bowl, and the unmistakable scent of a Caesar salad hit Tamsin.

Her mouth watered, but she didn't want to be rude and intrude. Plus she wasn't really in the mood for company. The woman seemed focused on her food and likely wanted to be left alone, too.

Tamsin started to step out when the woman glanced up. Her shrewd eyes studied Tamsin for a heartbeat, then she smiled at her.

"Don't just stand there hovering. Come in." The woman waved her in.

Tamsin hesitated and the woman waved again, gesturing for her to join her.

"I haven't seen you around here before." The woman stood and moved to the fridge.

She was small, barely five feet tall. Just a bit shorter than Tamsin. Her graying brown hair was pulled back in a ponytail. When she glanced at Tamsin with a raised brow, she noticed the woman's tanned face was lined from sun and age. She had on worn jeans with a flannel shirt that looked new, its sleeves rolled up.

"I guess you could say I'm kind of new." Tamsin watched the woman pull a large green plastic bowl out of the fridge.

The woman pulled back the top, and Tamsin saw it was full of Caesar salad.

"I saw your expression when you looked at my salad," the woman said with a sly smile. "So, I'll just dish you up some, shall I?"

"That'd be great, thank you." Tamsin moved to stand next to the woman, wondering who she was.

She couldn't stop herself from inhaling and pulling in the woman's scent. Her eyes widened in surprise.

She was a wolf shifter.

There were several wolf shifters on the Nightfair crew. That wasn't what surprised her. She'd thought she was human. Most shifters were pretty lean, their animal's need to run tended to burn a lot of calories. Before now, Amy was the only shifter she'd met who'd carried a few extra pounds.

To hide her surprise, she opened the cupboard in front of her to get a plate for the salad. It was full of glasses. She closed it and tried the next one. It was full of mugs.

Of course, it was.

She glared at the next cupboard and opened it. All she saw was bowls.

It figured.

She didn't want to dig through all the cupboards hunting for plates, so she got a bowl out instead. Maybe that was why the other woman was eating out of a bowl, too. "I'm Tamsin."

"Nice to meet you, Tamsin." Without hesitation, the woman opened the second drawer to her left and grabbed a big spoon out of it, clearly familiar with the kitchen. "You can call me Calvin."

Calvin dug out a giant scoop of salad and plopped it in the bowl. She assessed Tamsin with narrowed eyes and added a half scoop more.

"You look hungry." Calvin held the bowl out to her.

"Thank you." Tamsin took the bowl and moved to the table. When she reached it, she realized she'd forgotten to get a fork. With an internal sigh, she turned and studied the kitchen cabinets, trying to decide which one to start with.

Calvin put the lid back on the bowl and stuck it in the fridge. She opened a drawer and grabbed something out of it, closed it, and grabbed a paper towel off the roll. She headed to the table and handed Tamsin a fork and the paper towel.

"Sit, eat," Calvin ordered as she slid into her chair.

Tamsin's stomach rumbled again as she sat across from Calvin. She speared her fork into the salad and took a bite. Flavors burst on her tongue, and she closed her eyes in sheer enjoyment. She couldn't stop a small sound of satisfaction.

She liked Cesar salad, but she'd never had one this good. It even had chunks of chicken in it.

They ate in silence for a few minutes, and Tamsin focused on her food. Not her project. Not the still unconscious shifter in the infirmary. Not Chris.

Most definitely not Chris.

Not how his blue eyes lit up in laughter. Not how he moved in front of her to protect her. Not how he touched her. Held her.

"You're not one of the Nightfair crew, are you?" Calvin asked bluntly.

Tamsin coughed, not expecting the sudden question, especially since her mind had been locked on one specific member of the Nightfair crew. "What makes you ask that?"

"Haven't seen you around here before." Calvin scraped her salad bowl, pulling up some of the last few bites.

There was something about the older woman that inspired Tamsin to trust her. She couldn't put her finger on it. Perhaps it was her no-nonsense attitude.

"I'm here on a special project," Tamsin replied, spearing the last piece of chicken in her bowl.

"Pretty good, isn't it?" Calvin glanced at the almost-empty salad bowl with a grin.

"This is *really* good," Tamsin said after she swallowed another bite.

"Right? My daughter made it. Says I need to eat healthier. Worries about my weight," Calvin snorted and shoveled in a bite of her salad.

"Who's your daughter?" Tamsin studied Calvin, looking to find some features she recognized.

"Cameron," Calvin proclaimed proudly, like the name should mean something to Tamsin.

Tamsin scraped the last bite out of her bowl and looked down to hide her expression. She thought she'd met all of the Nightfair crew over the years, but the name *Cameron* didn't ring a bell.

When she looked up, Calvin had an expectant look on her face, and Tamsin knew she'd have to say something.

"I'm sorry," Tamsin finally admitted. "I don't know her."

Calvin laughed, "Good on you. Honest. Best way to be."

"Is she one of the Nightfair Crew?" she asked hesitantly.

"Hell no. That girl wouldn't know how to sneak up on someone to save her life. She can barely even hit her target at twenty yards," Calvin groused.

Hit her target?

Tamsin tried not to ask, but her curiosity wouldn't let her. "Hit her target?"

"Yeah, with her stupid-ass tacky blue Ruger nine-mil with speckles," Calvin huffed.

"A what?" Tamsin asked, completely lost.

What was a Ruger nine-mil with speckles?

"Right!" Calvin said triumphantly, waving her fork around in the air to prove her point. "I couldn't believe it when she came home with it either. I told her to get a pink one. But no, she had to go get that stupid looking thing instead."

Calvin looked at her expectantly, and Tamsin gave her a weak smile.

"Who wouldn't want... I'm sorry, Calvin, I have no idea what you're talking about."

Calvin picked up the blue velvet evening bag next to her and opened it up. She reverently pulled out a small handgun.

A pink handgun.

Tamsin's mouth dropped open in surprise.

"I had no idea they came in pink," she blurted out.

Calvin gave her a triumphant smile. "A beaut, isn't it?"

Shifters didn't usually mess with guns, the tranquilizer guns being the exception.

"It's a..." Tamsin hesitated, her eyes locked on the weapon in the other woman's hand. "Why do you have a gun?"

Calvin snorted. "Why use teeth and claws when a bullet is more efficient?"

Tamsin had a feeling the woman had said that more than once.

"Seriously?" Tamsin asked.

"Of course, I'm serious," Calvin snapped. "Why would I joke about something like that?"

"Well, most shifters seem to feel that when you come with natural weapons in your shifted form, why worry about any others," Tamsin said slowly.

"Ha, idiots," Calvin scoffed and gently set the gun on top of the velvet bag with a proud pat. "That's a stupid reason not to have a gun."

"Why do you have a gun?" Tamsin asked as she studied the weapon. It looked similar to the tranquilizer gun from earlier in that it was gun-shaped. But Calvin's looked more menacing, somehow. Despite the fact it was pink. Or maybe *because* it was pink.

"For fang and tooth to be effective, you have to get close, in touching distance." Calvin leaned in as she spoke, her eyes locked on Tamsin's. "If I'm going to fight someone, I'm going to stay as far away as possible and take them out of the picture before they can touch me."

"Like twenty yards away?" Tamsin asked, trying to make a joke of it.

Calvin gave a bark of laughter.

"Girl, do you know how far twenty yards really is?" She didn't wait for Tamsin to reply. "It's about 4 average-sized cars parked nose to tail. My eyesight isn't as good as it used to be. I wait until they're ten yards or less. That way I can look 'em in the eye, and they know I mean business."

"Don't you worry they'll shift and attack?"

"Fine, let 'em. I'll wait until they're tangled in their clothes and shoot. If they take the time to strip, well, I've got 'em then, don't I? This little pretty levels the playing field." Calvin picked up her empty bowl and held out her hand for Tamsin's.

Tamsin gave Calvin her bowl and felt like she was missing something.

"What do you mean, *levels the playing field*? You're a shifter, how does that level it? Wouldn't it give you an advantage?" She picked up the napkins and took them to the trash.

"If I could shift, sure, but I can't, so I take every advantage I can." Calvin put the dishes in the washer and closed the door with a flourish.

Tamsin felt like she'd been hit with a bat. Her world went sideways. There was no way she heard Calvin correctly.

She'd never met anyone else who admitted they couldn't shift. It was a dirty secret, and Calvin simply said it like the fact was completely unimportant. She'd showed more emotion when she presented her gun.

How could this be?

The woman moved around calmly, acting like her announcement was no big deal. Tamsin had to have misheard. That was the only thing that made sense.

"What was that?" she whispered, leaning against the counter.

"What was what?" Calvin looked around the room, then back at Tamsin with raised brows.

"You can't... shift?" Tamsin asked carefully, closely watching the other woman.

"Nope. Not at all. Can feel my beast. Hear it. Even grow some hellacious claws. But I've never been furry," Calvin replied factually, like she was discussing something commonplace. Normal.

Tamsin always knew there had to be others out there like her. Not that she'd ever met them. Of course, no one ever admitted they couldn't shift. It wasn't like she could go up to someone and ask, either. They'd stare at her in horror for suggesting it, scoff like Chris had, or possibly attack.

To even suggest someone couldn't shift was an insult. Yet this plump wolf simply announced it. Was Tamsin wrong? Could there be more shifters than she thought who were trapped like she was?

"I've never met anyone else who couldn't shift." Tamsin's mouth was dry. She went her entire life not admitting she couldn't shift, and now she'd told two people in the course of a few hours. One an almost-total stranger.

One who had children.

"Well, now you have," Calvin replied cheerfully.

"Do you... does your... I mean..."

"Spit it out, girl." Calvin pulled out her chair and sat.

"Your children, do they shift?" she blurted out.

"Have three," Calvin answered proudly. "And all three go furry just like their daddy."

"Did you worry?" Tamsin whispered as she slid into the chair next to Calvin.

"Every damn day," Calvin responded with a wry smile. "They were always causing trouble, getting into things. Hurting themselves."

"No, I mean, did you worry that they wouldn't shift? Did your mate worry?"

A look of comprehension crossed Calvin's face, and she glared at Tamsin.

"Did you tell him you couldn't shift and he brought up this baby nonsense?" she snapped.

"What, no..."

"'Cause that's a fat lot of bullshit. Your kids are your kids, if they can shift or not. If he's afraid your babies won't shift, then he isn't worth dick," Calvin snarled.

"It isn't him," Tamsin said quickly. "It's me."

Calvin's head jerked up and she blinked at her in surprise. "Well, fuck."

Tamsin waited for the other woman to continue, but Calvin calmly picked up her pink gun and slid it back in the purse.

"Calvin?" Tamsin prompted.

Calvin heaved a sigh and met her gaze.

"Please tell me you weren't a moron like I was," she said with another sigh.

"I'm not following."

"I can see it in your face. You were." Calvin's voice was resigned. "I saw it in your face when you walked in. Something was bothering you. I was going to leave you alone, but *no*, you have to remind me of my daughter.

"So, I invite you to sit down, eat some salad, and expect you'll start bitching about a man. I'll give you some sage advice, and send you on your way. Easy."

Calvin covered one of Tamsin's hands on the table with her own. "But now, I see it. Not so easy."

"Not so easy," Tamsin echoed, hearing the pain in Calvin's voice.

"Let me guess, you were afraid, right?" Calvin's eyes were full of sympathy. "Afraid the others would attack him if they ever figured it out. Afraid your kids wouldn't shift. Afraid he'd start to resent you after a while. Am I right?"

Tamsin's throat was closed with emotion, all she could do was nod.

Calvin's hand tightened on hers, then she said, "You are a fucking moron."

The words were spoken in such a gentle tone, it took Tamsin a moment for them to sink in.

She tried to pull her hand away, but Calvin held on tight.

"What?" Tamsin asked.

"You heard me." Calvin's voice was hard. "You are a fucking moron. I know this because I was too."

"But you're mated. You have three kids." Tamsin studied the other woman's face.

"Three beautiful kids. Couldn't be prouder," Calvin agreed. "And I wouldn't trade them for the world. I wouldn't love them any less if they didn't shift. And their father felt the same way."

Felt.

"Felt?" Tamsin said. "What do you mean? Did he change his mind?"

A look of sorrow crossed Calvin's face. "No, he didn't. No man worth his salt would. But he's no longer with us."

She looked so sad, Tamsin couldn't bring herself to ask what happened.

"But you understand my fears, right?" Tamsin asked instead.

"Oh, I understand them all right," Calvin snapped. "And I put my mate and me through misery for years. Wasted years. For what? *Nothing*. Not a damn thing. I don't give a rat's ass what those asshole pack members think. And you shouldn't either."

"But I'm afraid they'll attack him for mating with me. I can't put his life in danger," Tamsin argued.

"Life is danger, girl. I could get hit by a car. Have a tree fall on me. Get sucked up by aliens," Calvin bit out.

Tamsin jolted at the last example. "Aliens?"

Calvin grinned. "Just making sure you're paying attention. My point is we don't have control over a lot of things. Why court trouble? If you found your mate, grab him with both hands and hold on. Don't let your fear shove him away."

"But—"

"No buts. I miss my mate every day. But I don't regret any of the time we had together. I am who I am because of what life threw at me. I don't care that he went furry and I didn't." Calvin released Tamsin's hand and leaned back in her chair. "What I do regret is the time I wasted shoving him away. Don't have those type of regrets."

A buzzing came from the side of Calvin's blue bag. She dug out her phone and glanced at the screen.

"Always checking up on me," she said warmly. "Cam knew I'd be here. Sent enough salad for a small army. Even bought me this new flannel shirt. Said my old one was getting too ratty. I'd just got it good and worn in."

She stabbed out a reply with her fingers, a mischievous grin on her face.

"Why are you here, anyway?" Tamsin's head spun with everything Calvin had said, and she latched onto the comment for an anchor point.

Calvin met her gaze and smiled impishly. "Not too long ago, a honey badger and a bear brought a mess of kids into my territory. Next thing I knew, nosy Nightfair folks were up in my business. Now I'm in theirs."

"Eli and Ginny?" Tamsin asked. She'd heard something about Eli and children. She'd recently met his younger brother, Milo, when they came to her sister's bar. She thought she heard he worked with kids.

Something told her there was more to the story.

"Who else!" Calvin laughed. "My daughter's on her way to pick me up. I gotta go. I hope to see you around."

"Me too," Tamsin replied. She really liked the gruff wolf.

Calvin headed toward the door but paused before she stepped out.

She looked at Tamsin. "You can let circumstances define you and feel sorry for yourself. Or you can make the decision change to what you can and move forward. It's all up to you."

With those words, Calvin disappeared.

Tamsin thought about what Calvin said.

She needed to find Chris.

She stood up, determined to hunt him down, when the alarm on her phone went off. She pulled it out and blinked at it.

The test was done.

Suddenly, the results weren't so important. But it might help the man still in the infirmary. He woke up off and on, but wasn't in good shape. No one was really sure why. If it was her serum, this counter could help. Perhaps her serum was putting too much stress on his system.

Determined to get it done so she could go find her mate, Tamsin hurried back to her lab. Rushing to the computer, she logged in.

Her eyes grew wide as she read the results. It was the same as before. She pulled the samples out of the machine. Her hands grew cold as she stared at them.

"I've done it," she said.

She wanted to dance, shout, scream. She wanted to share it with Chris.

Tamsin took a syringe and drew out a dose. She opened the mouse cage and carefully extracted subject

Alpha. She cooed to the mouse and with practiced speed injected it with the serum. She put it back in the cage and watched it closely. If it was going to have an adverse reaction, it would happen very quickly.

The mouse ran up a tube and around, then got on the exercise wheel. It jumped off, and moved to the feed dish, munching on the food. All perfectly normal mouse behavior.

She waited a bit longer. They'd always reacted quickly to injections. Adverse reactions were almost immediate. Hope rose as subject Alpha continued to act normal.

Tamsin went back to the samples and filled a new syringe with enough for an adult shifter.

A small shift in the air currents raised the hairs on the back of her neck. The mice froze in their cage. Even the machines seem to stop humming. Tamsin turned to face the door and found Ray standing there, a sneer on his face.

His eyes dropped to the syringe in her hand.

"Going somewhere?" he asked coldly.

"Where's your escort?" she snapped, stepping back until she ran into the counter.

"You don't need to worry about them. They won't bother us. Let's talk about your *experiment*, shall we?"

Chapter 25

A chill ran up her body as Tamsin met Ray's gaze.

His eyes were flat, lifeless. *Mercenary.*

"We have nothing to talk about," she said sharply. She didn't have the energy to deal with this asshole. She needed to get the counter to the infirmary, and then find Chris. She didn't have the time, nor the desire, to humor whatever delusions Ray was dealing with.

Her mate was waiting for her, even if he didn't know it yet.

"Oh, we have a lot to talk about," he sauntered into the room and looked around with proprietary air. As if this was *his* lab.

Her panther snarled in the back of her brain. *How dare he? Who did he think he was?*

"Really?" She raised one brow, doubtfully. "What do you think we have to discuss?"

"What you're going to do with that little syringe in your hand," he sneered and smiled coldly. "That's worth a lot of money to my people."

"Your people? Who are *your* people?" Tamsin set the syringe on the counter.

She glanced around casually, looking for some sort of weapon. Right about now, she wished she had a little velvet bag with a pretty pink gun in it.

Not that she knew how to shoot.

"Did you really think I was a *captive* in that lab?" he sneered.

A cold knot formed in her stomach. "You weren't?"

He shook his head, a superior smile on his face. "Of course not. I'm not an idiot."

"Could've fooled me." Tamsin's eyes flicked to the door.

Ray looked a bit unhinged. She needed to get out.

He stood between her and freedom. She didn't think she'd be able to make it to the door before he grabbed her.

She wasn't defenseless. Even if she couldn't shift into her panther.

The thought gave her a measure of calm.

Ray snarled at her, "You have no idea. I'm not going to waste time trying to explain it to you. You wouldn't understand."

"I think you're lying." Tamsin raised her chin in challenge.

She needed to distract him. Make him forget what he was here for. Then maybe she could slip out.

"What do you know?" he snarled.

"I think you have delusions of grandeur." Her eyes raked him with contempt. "Somehow, you escaped the lab. But you couldn't handle the idea that someone caught you, so you made up this grand story that you weren't captive there at all. Let me guess, you volunteered?"

He laughed harshly, "Oh, I volunteered all right. But not like you think."

"Oh, really?" She crossed her arms. "Then why don't you tell me about it?"

His eyes narrowed in consideration, then he slowly nodded. "Why not? Not like you're going to tell anyone about it."

His words sent a chill down her spine. "And why is that?"

"I tried to tell you before, your serum is worth money. A lot of money." His eyes lit with greed. "I wasn't a captive at that lab. I'm an elite member of the team. We saw the videos. We saw that *Nightfair* stooge. It didn't take much to put one and one together. Where he was— your lab. We figured for some reason they were there to get you."

Something about this didn't quite make sense.

"So, what made you think they would rescue you if you pretended to *escape* from the lab?"

"It was a calculated risk." He slowly paced around, looking at the various machines. "We had a… subject that wasn't doing so good. Didn't think he was going to make it. We didn't want to dispose of the body, so we let him go. We let him *think* he escaped."

She thought about the condition of the man in the infirmary. To say he wasn't doing so good was an understatement. The air of satisfaction with which Ray spoke about it made her stomach churn.

"What did you do to him?"

"We gave him a," he smiled cruelly, "concentrated dose of your serum. Put him in a room with a couple others and sat back and enjoyed the show. What a show it was."

That explained why he was in such bad shape. Not only the injuries, but also why he wasn't waking. "You overdosed him deliberately?"

"How do you know what something is going to do until you try it? You're a scientist. You understand experiments." His eyes flicked over to the mouse cage. "And necessary casualties."

"I've never deliberately hurt them," she ground out. She was always very careful with the doses she gave her mice. The goal wasn't to increase the doses until they went crazy, but to find the tipping point when they became brave instead of timid. She had done minor modifications, carefully noting all behavior changes.

None of it was necessary anymore, anyway. She was done. She had a counter to her serum. If Chris was the man she thought he was, then he wouldn't care if she shifted or not. Calvin was right.

Ray threw his head back and laughed. "You're so naïve."

"Not so much." she stared at him in disgust. "I see you for the asshole you are."

His smile faded, and he glared at her. "*Stupid bitch*. I'm done wasting time on you. You have two choices. Give me the syringe, or come work with us."

"Not going to happen," she said flatly.

A cold calm came over Tamsin. She was afraid, but this asshole wasn't going to win. He wasn't going to get her. He wasn't going to get her serum. He wasn't going to get *anything*.

"I was hoping you'd say that," he said with a baring of his teeth. "Option number two it is."

She didn't reply and assumed a defensive stance.

He snarled and took a step forward, his eyes flicked to the counter behind her. "Give me the syringe."

"No." Tamsin sprang forward, keeping her body low.

She had been training in a variety of martial arts techniques since she was a child. If she couldn't shift, her parents still wanted her to be able to defend herself. Her favorite had been Jiu Jitsu, even though it was more about grappling.

Right now, she wanted him down. In sheer mass, he had the advantage. She had to use her size to her advantage.

She aimed for his shins, and he jumped back, startled, but not fast enough. She connected and pulled his feet out from under him.

Tamsin rolled away as he fell, and got back to her feet. He didn't stay down but immediately popped back up.

She realized with dread that the only shifter opponent she'd ever had was her sister. The rest were human. Many were larger than her. Heavier than her.

Slower than her.

She might be able to pin him, but then she'd be stuck holding him until she grew too tired to do so or someone came to check on her.

The only one who would do that was Chris.

And she chased him off.

Plus, Ray might just shift. There was no way she could hold him if he did that.

Ray snarled and charged her. She dodged out of the way, kicking him in the back of the knee, causing him to stumble.

He roared and turned to face her. His face was contorted with rage. He held his arms wide open, and he rushed her again.

She slid out of his way but wasn't fast enough. His hand latched onto her shoulder, and he pulled her into his grip. Years of training took over, and Tamsin twisted, grabbed his shirt, and managed to throw him over her shoulder.

His hand latched onto her lab coat. She slid out of it, leaving it in his grasp.

She danced back and watched him warily. He charged her again, and she ducked down, surprising him. She moved around and ended up on the other side of the room.

Her back was to the door.

She could escape.

It would be easy. Turn the knob, and out she'd go.

She didn't trust the expression on his face. It was almost as if he dared her to try it.

"Go ahead." His eyes were wild, and he didn't look remotely sane. "*Run.*"

A horrid thought occurred to her.

"Ray." She forced herself to keep her voice calm. "Did you use my serum?"

His smile was more a bearing of teeth than anything else. He was in front of her counter.

Where she left the syringe.

He reached behind him and charged her all in one motion. She couldn't tell if he picked up the syringe or not.

She waited until the last moment to slide out of his way.

His hand latched onto her wrist, and they spun around until he twisted her arm behind her. She tensed to make a counter move and felt a pinch in her upper arm. She froze for a heartbeat.

No.

She glanced at him and watched as he pulled the syringe from her arm then released her with a triumphant smile.

"What have you done?" she whispered, her eyes wide with shock.

"I don't have to do anything about you now," he growled. "You'll go crazy and the patsy Nightfair crew will kill you for me. All I have to do is wait, and then open the door and point you in the right direction."

It had been the counter in the syringe, not the serum.

She had no idea what it would do to her, but going on a crazy killing spree was the least likely result. It might actually work as a sedative and knock her out.

But she didn't want him to know that. She'd play along.

"No." She shook her head like something was starting to affect her.

She took a step back, and he stepped forward eagerly. His watched her with excitement as she pretended to be impacted.

Tamsin took another step back, her hands scrambling on the counter behind her.

There.

Ray followed her forward, keeping close enough that he could grab her.

Perfect.

She turned around and put her hands on the counter. Gripping it like she wasn't stable.

"You're about to lose control, and I'm going to love every minute of it," he growled.

Oh, she wasn't the one who was going to lose control.

Her hand closed on cold metal and she gripped it tight. With a deep breath, she swung around, her hand locked on the frying pan handle.

His eyes grew wide at her unexpected move, and he tried to dodge out of the way.

Too late.

The frying pan collided with the side of his head, and his face jerked to the side.

He turned in a complete circle and stumbled a few steps as the door burst open.

"Tamsin!" Chris lurched to a halt, his eyes wide.

Ray went down like a felled tree.

Chris's eyes locked onto hers. "Are you okay?"

She dropped the pan, and it loudly banged the floor. She didn't care. She rushed forward, beyond happy to see him. Not because he could save her. No, she saved herself.

He came back.

He met her halfway, opened his arms and engulfed her, holding her tight.

"I am now," she whispered into his shirt.

She breathed in his scent, her panther purring in her mind.

He smelled like sunshine and browned butter and more.

She pulled back. "Why do you smell like beer and blood?"

He didn't smile at her question. His blue eyes were serious as they searched hers.

"I'm sorry," he said in a low voice.

Her body froze. "For what?"

He took a deep breath and dropped his forehead to touch hers.

"For being an idiot. For trying to tell you how to do your research. For assuming you need me to protect you." He pulled back and looked at the unconscious Ray on the floor. "I was clearly wrong on that one."

"Chris, I'm sorry I shoved you away." She cupped his face with her hand.

A ghost of a smile curved his lips. "If you want to keep doing your research on your *cure,* I'll support you. But don't do it because you think I need my mate to shift. I don't. I just need you to be happy."

"You'll never run with me on four feet," she whispered. "Never climb trees or hunt."

He shrugged. "So? I love you the way you are. I don't need that. I'll curl up with you at night. I'll cook dinner with you. We'll fight and have insane make-up sex. Argue and bicker and play. That's all I want."

She saw the sincerity in his eyes, and her heart felt like it was going to burst.

"What if our cubs can't shift?" Even though Calvin's could, that didn't mean hers would.

"We'll love them just the same," he answered. "They'll be yours and mine. That's what matters."

Her heart full to overflowing, she pushed up on her toes and touched her lips to his. She opened her lips and he swept in, their mouths dueling. Heat sparked through her body, and she felt herself grow wet. A low growl reverberated through Chris's chest, and his hand moved down to cup her ass.

The door to her lab slammed open, hitting the wall.

They jumped apart to find Damien standing in the door, a fierce look on his face.

His eyes took in the scene.

"A frying pan?" Damien slowly grinned.

"Right?" she replied. "Who knew?"

* * *

Chris barely contained his impatience as Damien stepped into the lab, followed by Eli and two other members of the Nightfair crew.

He wanted to be alone with his mate, finish what that kiss had started. He could smell her arousal and knew she felt the same way.

A small, sane part of him was glad Damien had entered when he did. If they hadn't been interrupted, there was a strong possibility they would have had sex in the lab. Not that he was opposed to it, but Ray needed to be secured first.

Chris had gotten carried away with that kiss and just having her in his arms again; he'd forgotten about the piece of shit on the floor.

"We found Eric tied up and unconscious in a closet," Damien said darkly. "He must have knocked out his escort and come to get you. I'm glad you're okay."

Eli moved to Ray and nudged him with his foot. "He's gonna have a hell of a headache when he wakes up."

Damien took charge, and soon had Ray bundled up and off in custody. As Chris listened to Tamsin fill him in on what Ray had said, he couldn't stop himself from wrapping his arms around her.

He wanted Ray to wake up so he could hand him his ass. And then do it again. His tiger raged in his mind that he hadn't been there to protect her.

Not that she needed it.

Pride filled him that she'd defended herself.

With nothing more than a frying pan.

There was a slight tension in her voice as she spoke, and he had a feeling there was something else. He'd have to figure out what it was. Later. When they were alone.

All the other crew members had filed out of the room with Ray. It was just them and Damien.

"He was trouble," Damien said. "I just didn't realize how much."

"Is it possible he got any compromising information?" Chris asked.

"No," Damien answered. "Why do you think he had an escort? He may have slipped them a couple times, but not long enough to find anything out of value."

"What are you going to do about him?" Tamsin asked with a shiver.

Chris gave her a squeeze, and she relaxed in his arms.

"Interrogate him," Damien told her. "Tomorrow I have a confab with the other enforcement groups and we'll decide what to do about the Sons of Asena."

"You really think they were behind it all?" Chris asked the head of Nightfair.

Damien shook his head. "I don't know. But we'll find out."

"Oh," Tamsin said, "I almost forgot. It's ready."

"What's ready?" Damien asked.

"The counter serum," she pulled away and Chris reluctantly released her from his arms.

He watched her ass as she walked across the room, and his dick grew hard. He wanted to be alone. *Now.*

He was so focused on her body that he didn't see what she did, only that she turned around and had a capped syringe in her hand.

"Here," she handed it to Damien. "Have the doctor give this to the shifter in the infirmary. Ray said they gave him an overdose. This should help."

"Will he wake up?" Damien asked.

"It may take more than one treatment," Tamsin said. "But I want to be cautious. Give this to him, then we'll reevaluate in twenty-four hours. See how he responds. But I expect it'll do the trick."

Damien nodded and turned to leave. "I'll tell the doctor. Why don't you two head out? Go home. There's no reason to stay here. We won't find out any information until Ray wakes up."

Tamsin's gaze met Chris's, and he saw his desire reflected in her eyes.

Go home.

He hadn't had a chance to take her to his home. His territory. He had planned to, then everything blew up.

Now there was nothing stopping them, and his tiger wanted nothing more. The trip to his condo was a haze. He was focused on getting them there safely and couldn't remember what vehicle they used, or who drove.

As soon as the door closed behind them, her mouth was on his. Fire roared through his veins. Clothes tore, and then her bare skin was under his hands. Her fingers traced trails of heat along his body. Her nails dug into his back in delicious abandon. Chris kissed his way down

319

her jaw, nipping and sucking and biting as he backed her against the door.

He knew he should take her to the bed. Or the couch. Somewhere other than the front door. But he couldn't get himself to move.

He could smell her arousal, and it made him even harder. He wanted to be buried deep inside her. Join with her.

His mate.

"Chris," she moaned as he nipped the tips of her breasts and then sucked hard.

He slid his hand into her wet heat. She was soaking. Practically dripping. His dick throbbed with the need to be inside her.

He rubbed her nub, and her little moans were all the encouragement he needed. She pumped her hips into his hand, and he rubbed harder. Her hand gripped his erection, and he almost came right then.

He locked down iron control and rubbed her hard. Her cries grew louder, and then she arched her back. He slammed his fingers inside her and felt her body throbbing.

Chris pulled his dick from her hand, lifted her up, and impaled her on his shaft. She was swollen and slick and tight. Her body still throbbed from her orgasm as it tried to wring him dry. She wrapped her legs around him, and her arms gripped his shoulders.

He waited until she stopped pulsing, then he started thrusting. He pulled out and slammed in hard. She cried out in pleasure.

It felt so good he couldn't stop himself from doing it again. He was balls deep, and it had never felt so good. But he couldn't hold still. He was too close.

He pulled out and thrust back in, increasing the pace. The pleasure built, and he could feel the pressure at the base of his cock. He knew he was going to come, but he wanted to take her with him. He reached between them and found her swollen clit. Her juices coated his finger as he rubbed her.

"Yes," she cried.

He slammed into her as he felt her body clench around him. He roared as his body released. He came inside her as she pulsed around him. When he finished, he held her against the door.

She dropped a light kiss on his shoulder, and he shivered. He pulled back and looked in her eyes.

"I love you," he told her. "My mate."

A brilliant smile lit her face. "Mate. I never thought I'd be anyone's mate."

His tiger looked through his eyes, and he saw her panther look back at him.

"I love you, too," she whispered.

He felt himself start to grow hard again. Her eyes widened as she felt it too.

Time to take this to the bedroom.

This time, he wanted to take his time with her. Worship her like she deserved. Show her with his mouth and hands and body that she was his.

Forever.

Epilogue

Tamsin stepped into the Nightfair headquarters, excitement buzzing through her. She couldn't wait to see Chris.

He'd been gone for the past week on some stake-out and was due back sometime today. He'd managed to slip away a few times, but only for short periods. Just enough time for them to have amazing sex when he should have been resting.

But when he came home, they couldn't keep their hands off each other. It felt like they were making up for all the time they lost over the years when they'd been bickering and fighting. Looking back, it had been a courtship of sorts, yet neither had realized it.

"Tamsin," Damien called as she passed his office.

She turned and went back. "What's up?"

"How's the new equipment you requested?" He glanced up from his computer with a raised brow.

"The lab was already beyond what I needed," she answered. "You didn't need to order more."

"I want our chemist to have everything she needs," he explained with a grin.

When he offered her a position at HQ, she'd been certain it had been just for form. But he didn't let up until she finally accepted. It turned out they had a lot of need for someone with her skills. And like Chris had said, Damien simply recruited what they needed.

"It's great," she said. "I've got all I need and plenty to do."

In fact, she was now actively hunting for an assistant. That thought reminded her.

"Any word on the search for Amy?"

Damien shook his head. "We got all we could out of Ray. He knew she'd been taken, but not much else."

"So, he *was* part of that other mercenary group? The ones those guards worked for?" She still couldn't believe it.

Damien nodded. "Yeah, Sons of Asena, but a new recruit. As far as we can tell, that was some sort of splinter sect. But we're hunting them down. And we're following all leads on the shifters they abducted. We'll find her."

"What about anyone back at that lab? The place where Ray was?"

"Deserted," Damien sighed. "Justin still had a feed going after we pulled out. When we looked at the recording, we realized that shortly after you returned to Oakdale, they abandoned the facility. Pulled everyone and everything out that was related to the Sons of Asena."

"What about the other research groups, and..." *Faith.*

"All gone. No trace left."

"There was an animal care specialist there," Tamsin told him. "Faith. Can you see if you can find her, too?"

She'd tried to reach Faith, but when she'd looked for the contact in her phone, it hadn't been there. Faith had been concerned about her battery being low. Maybe it had died before she could save it. Tamsin had been in such a hurry, she hadn't checked. Now she regretted it.

Damien nodded and jotted it down. "I'll have our team search for leads. Can you tell me anything about her?"

Tamsin gave a quick description and added, "She loves animals. She'll fight for them. That might be a lead."

"Got it," Damien nodded. "Let me know if you need anything else."

Tamsin recognized a dismissal when she heard it and headed up to her lab. That was the only damper on her spirits. She worried about her former assistant and Faith. She'd never received any replies to her texts or calls to Amy.

Looking back, she should have said something to Damien after Ray mentioned Amy, but it had slipped her mind.

She made it to the top of the stairs, and a wave of dizziness made her freeze. When it passed, Tamsin grinned. It had started after Chris left, and she hadn't mentioned it when he called. She didn't want him to worry. When he had come home for those brief visits, well, they had other things on their minds.

But now, she couldn't wait to share her news. And she would when he got home sometime today.

She opened her lab door, and the mice squeaked in greeting. Well, maybe they were just squeaking, but she always took it as a greeting. Tamsin fed them, then looked at the results of the test she'd run overnight.

She was lost in the data when she felt a slight change in the air. The hair on her neck stood up, and the scent of sunshine and browned butter reached her.

Chris's arms wrapped around her, and he nuzzled her neck. "Hey beautiful, I'm home."

She turned in his arms, and his mouth covered hers. She pulled back before she could get lost in the kiss and forget everything.

"What?" he said with a slight frown.

"I have news." She bit her lip in excitement.

He inhaled, and his eyes grew wide. They lit with joy, and he kissed her again.

She kissed him back, the immediate heat he ignited in her flowing through her veins. He moved and slid his leg between hers, putting pressure on her crotch. It felt so good, she moaned.

The sound jolted her out of her fog, and she pulled back.

"Chris, wait, I have news," she said again.

"I know," he replied, kissing her along her jaw. "I can tell."

Something in his tone told her he thought he knew what her news was.

"What do you know?" she asked.

His grin was blinding. "I can tell by the change in your scent. This is… unexpected, but wonderful."

"It is?" she frowned.

How could he tell by her scent?

He nodded and gave her a fast kiss on her lips.

"My family's going to be so excited." He gave her a tight hug. "By the way, Mom said she wanted us over for dinner as soon I got back, so we should probably do that. We can tell them in person."

"Tell them, what, in person?" They definitely didn't have the same news.

"That you're pregnant," he said with raised brows. "Isn't that what you meant?"

Her jaw dropped, and she looked at him with astonishment. She'd thought the dizziness was because the injection Ray had given her had worked. It was supposed to be a counter, but somehow *it* was the cure. That morning she'd actually shifted into her panther form.

Looking into Chris's eyes, she decided she'd show him later. Right now, he was so excited about becoming a father, she didn't think any other news would matter.

After all, he loved her just the way she was.

* * *

Chris hadn't expected, hadn't planned, on getting Tamsin pregnant. They hadn't done anything to prevent it, but hadn't been trying either.

Of course, they had crazy monkey sex all the time. He could barely keep his hands off her. He hadn't noticed her change in scent before now, but it was crystal clear.

He couldn't wait to tell his family. They'd be overjoyed. They hadn't met Tamsin yet, but were eager to do so.

They'd had dinner planned a couple times, but something always came up, and it got postponed. He wasn't worried. Chris knew they were going to love her.

He nuzzled her neck, drawing in her altered scent, and his dick grew hard. He glanced around her lab.

"You know, we haven't broken in your lab yet," he said.

"What?" She looked at him, then shook her head. "No. People come in all the time. We are *not* having sex in my lab. Besides, the other shifters would know. They could smell it."

He knew she was right, but he wanted to claim her. He took a deep breath to try to shove it back, but her scent washed over him again.

"If I can't touch you like I want, I'd better go down and check in," he said regretfully.

"You haven't checked in yet?" she said with a wide-eyed laugh.

He shook his head. "Nope, came up to see you first."

"I'll come down with you," she announced. "Damien was waiting for these results, anyway."

He linked his hand with hers, his tiger purring in his mind. He never thought he'd be this happy.

With his mate by his side, they made their way down the stairs. They'd just reached the landing when they saw several members of the Nightfair crew standing in a semi-circle. Eli and Milo were on the side near them. Milo was on vacation for another week.

Chris moved near the honey badgers. If something was going on, they would help protect Tamsin. She'd demonstrated she could protect herself, but his tiger was in over-protective mode. He pushed his mate behind him and stepped forward cautiously. They were talking in low tones, their voices excited.

"Everyone calm down." Damien's voice cut through the commotion.

Everyone stopped talking and stared at him.

"I'm looking for Chris O'Neal," a woman proclaimed into the silence.

He pushed through the group to see what was going on. He could feel Tamsin right behind him.

A dark-skinned woman stood surrounded by the Nightfair crew. Her shoulders were back, and she boldly met Damien's gaze. She had on some type of hat that hid her hair.

"What do you want with Chris?" Damien asked.

Chris knew Damien had seen him push forward. Yet the bear deliberately avoided looking at him. In fact, everyone kept their attention locked on the young lady.

"That's between Chris and me," she replied haughtily.

"I don't think so," Damien argued. "You came here. You can start with telling us who you are."

She studied his face, and then looked at the sea of faces around her. She drew in a deep breath, and her eyes grew wide. Her head swiveled and locked onto Eli and Milo. Then she snapped her attention back to Damien.

"Fine. My name's Ryn," she said shortly.

Damien inclined his head. "Ryn, what brings you to the Nightfair Company headquarters?"

Her jaw clenched, then she smiled. "Because you need to help me."

"We do?" Damien said flatly. "And why do we need to do that?"

"Because your reputation is on the line. I know where Amy is, and you're going to help me get her."

Tamsin pushed forward causing his tiger to snarl in protective protest. He pushed it back and made room for her.

"How do you know Amy?" Tamsin demanded.

Ryn studied her, and her shoulders relaxed. "You're Tamsin, right? You look just like Faith described."

"You know Faith?" Damien injected.

"Is she okay?" Tamsin asked.

Ryn nodded. "Faith and Amy are my friends. Faith's fine. But Amy's in trouble, and word on the street is you caused it."

"Tell us where she is, and we'll rescue her," Damien ordered.

Ryn shook her head. "It doesn't work like that. These people won't trust you. But they trust me. I just need a partner, one person, to go with me."

Her gaze scanned the room and landed on Eli and Milo. She pointed at Milo.

"Him. You'll send him."

"They can't. I'm not a member of Nightfair," Milo said, his shoulders stiff.

Damien moved closer to Milo and quipped, "You are now."

A note from Julye Evans

Thank you so much for reading Chris's and Tamsin's story! If you enjoyed it, please take a moment to leave a review at your favorite online retailer. I'd really appreciate it!

The next book, <u>Honey Badgered</u>, is coming soon!

Find out the latest information about up-coming books and new releases:

Like me on Facebook:
www.facebook.com/JulyeEvansAuthor

Follow me on Twitter: https://twitter.com/JulyeEvans

Get <u>Tiger's Heart</u> as a free gift when you sign up for my newsletter: https://Julye-Evans.com/newsletter

Like to review books? Join my Advance Reader Team: https://goo.gl/forms/5hkG1FCtT2M2yN9Z2

Visit my website: https://Julye-Evans.com

Other Books

Tiger's Heart, Nightfair Shifters #1

Stalkers and secrets can kill ...
As a tiger shifter, Eileen Donnovan is used to handling her own problems. When a powerful member of her pack starts stalking her, she has nowhere to turn. If she tells anyone about his attention, her family will be in danger.

Jace Peters never imagined doing a favor for Caleb Donnovan, his best friend, would turn into a life-altering event. When he meets Caleb's sister, Eileen, she immediately intrigues—and attracts—him.

Something's going on with her, and if he doesn't solve that mystery soon, more than just this tiger's heart could be at stake.

He must protect her at all costs. Trust is hard to build, but keeping secrets could destroy them both.

Jace is a Nightfair mercenary, and they always take care of business.

Tiger's Heart is a newsletter gift, or you can purchase it from your favorite on-line retailer.

Visit the website at: https://Julye-Evans.com/books to find available retailers.

To get this book for free, sign up for Julye's newsletter at: https://Julye-Evans.com/newsletter

Wolf's Secret, Nightfair Shifters #2

Handsome, heroic, mysterious … and bossy.

That's all Danni Braden knows about the man who saves her.

With murderous gunmen on her trail, she has to run, hide, or figure out who they are before they kill her.

As a shapeshifter mercenary, Mac Williams is used to dangerous situations.

Gunmen? Chaos? Just another Tuesday. However, he never expected to fall for the feisty damsel he just rescued.

 Nightfair mercenaries do not take kindly to threats against those under their protection, especially potential mates.

The men after Danni have no idea of the beast they've awoken within Mac.

Mac is a Nightfair mercenary, and they always take care of business.

Bear's Perfect Match, Nighfair Shifters #3

She follows the rules... he breaks them.

When someone starts attacking loner shifters, Nightfair mercenary and bear shifter Ginny Coleman goes undercover to investigate.

She has to pretend to be the mate of a sexy, stubborn honey badger shifter who doesn't seem to care about anything.

If she can't find a way to work with him, her mission will fail… and failure is not an option.

Eli Thomas is a loner with no ties and he likes it that way.

When an old debt is called in, he has no choice to but work with the infuriating dark-skinned bear shifter beauty.

Compromise isn't in his vocabulary, and he's not looking for a mate, even if she does invade his dreams and make his heart race.

She isn't sure what's harder – pretending to be a loving mate to the world's most annoying honey badger, or fighting her attraction to him. Either way, innocent lives are on the line and Nightfair mercenaries don't quit until the job is finished.

Author Bio

An avid reader and storyteller all her life, Julye finally sat down and started writing those tales running through her mind. She grew up reading ElfQuest and fell in love with wolves. That was her first introduction to a shape shifter and the idea never left her. Now she writes stories that allow her to combine that fantasy with happily ever after.